A Maryl's Mysteries Novel

A GHOSTLY AFFAIR

Madeline Nixon

Also by

Feathers

Robins

Last Christmas I Love-Spelled Us Apart

Like A Love Song Books

Emergency Lullabies

Not Actually

Stories In

Heart's Lock, Love's Key

Ignited By Hope

Mistletoe Moments

A Note From the Author

Dear reader,

Welcome to my first foray into mystery. Though I've been reading and writing mysteries my entire life, this is the first to see the light of day. *A Ghostly Affair* was inspired by a very real legend at Dalhousie University. If you look it up, Penelope's story dates back somewhere around the early to mid-1900s. There is no outright proof of anyone by her name going to or attached to the school, and yet, a woman in a blue dress is still sometimes spotted around Shirreff Hall. For the purposes of this book, her timeline was adjusted. As far as these characters know, she died and has been seen on the fourth floor of Old Eddy since 2001.

This book is darker than my romances (though still quirky!) and on par with my ghost stories. These pages deal with things like death, grief, infidelity, sexual harassment, pregnancy, and power imbalances, along with other paranormal concepts. If these are not things you're capable of dealing with in the moment, come back to the book later. Otherwise, I welcome you to Maryl's first mystery.

- Madeline

Cover Design by Dana Isaly

Interior Design by Madeline Nixon

Edited by Shelly Zev

ISBN-13 (print): 978-1-0673973-2-6

ISBN-13 (ebook): 978-1-0673973-3-3

Thank you, Dad, for instilling a lifelong love
of ghosts and Halifax in me.

This book would not exist otherwise.

Chapter One

MY BRAIN WORKS AT warp speed through curse word upon curse word, never permanently landing on any thought I can grasp. No course of action, just...

Shit.

Light filters in through the blinds of mine and Lottie's dorm. I haven't slept. I keep picturing Lottie pacing back and forth in the space between our beds, in prime Lottie Arthur Freakout mode. I waited for the moment she finished pacing and had her ah-ha moment, as per usual, but it never came. So I brushed it off, pretending it was nothing, and coaxed her off the ledge enough for her to go back to sleep at 3 a.m.

But I'm still here, stuck in a doom cycle because I had sex with our Creative Writing TA, Lewis Pickering.

And it's not like I *knew*. It's the start of winter semester, classes haven't started yet, and I was only just added to the course after months on the waitlist. I had no way of knowing. If it wasn't for Lottie's stalker skills, I would have been blissfully ignorant until Tuesday. She'll make the perfect journalist with everything she's able to so seamlessly dig up. With a name and a description or location, she's able to magically figure out who anyone is. She's been pawing through archives and scouring the internet for years in search of her birth parents. All this practise is at least good for something, I guess. But all of that still doesn't change appearances. An act like this unfortunately screams *I Fucked You To Ace This Class*. And while that's kind of a him problem for sleeping with a student, it's also a me problem for...Well, I don't know. But it's not on purpose.

Nestled underneath the ugly grey comforter that twins the one my mom has on my bed back home, I feel the least secure I ever have here in Halifax. Is this the worst mistake I've made so far at Dalhousie? Or was it that time I went to the wrong lecture, didn't realize until halfway through, then stayed the whole two hours because it was too awkward to leave? Or was it when I stumbled on that guy with the super cool kraken tattoo snaking down his leg sobbing upstairs, made enough noise for him to hear me, then slunk away? Or maybe it was that night I kissed Riley from the swim team even though I keep a strict no swim team policy.

My eyes slide toward Lottie's fluorescent pink, old school alarm clock and squint. I can just make out the time without my glasses, which I may or may not have forgotten in my TA's bedroom. It is, in fact, early. I've spent the night looking at all of Lewis's social media profiles, including his blog. Before tonight, I'd only seen him around campus. He's got the whole scholarly vibe going on, briefcase and dark rimmed glasses, well-groomed brown hair, scruffy beard. I thought he took himself a little too seriously, but he's cute. Very cute. So I excused it. And that's probably all anyone needs to know about my red flag history with men.

He happened to be at the beginning of the year swim party tonight and I happened to be bold enough to approach him. We didn't waste time. He took me back to his place, we had a little fun, he fell asleep. So I left a note and slipped out. Maybe not the most tactful way to leave, but what does he expect of a one-night stand?

During my obsessive, mentally swear-laced internet search, I've learned a thing or two. He's a master's student here, studying philosophy, assisting Professor Denver Keyes in his introductory creative writing course. He's interested in history, languages, and ultimately enriching the lives of those around him. Yes, he made a post where he literally said the thing about enriching. I inwardly groaned when I read it. He named his cat Mephistopheles, waxed poetic in an Instagram caption when his girlfriend broke up with him over Christmas break, and made multiple blog posts about how you shouldn't be able to form opinions on society unless you've read philosophical literature. There was more, but my eyes glazed over and I kind of wanted to throw up. So I put my phone down and stared at the ceiling until light reflected against the full length mirror Lottie framed with fake flowers.

I throw my covers to the floor and stand. I didn't change from my casual jeans and a nice top party outfit, which makes me feel sick now. I glance at Lottie, still sleeping, curled into a ball, blonde hair a mess of waves around her. I sigh and grab my phone.

Maryl

Getting food! You'll probably still be asleep when I get back. Didn't want you to freak out tho.

I send the text and watch as Lottie's phone lights up. I grab my coat from the foot of my bed, shrug into it, and fish through my swim bag until I find my wallet. It fits snuggly in my coat pocket, right next to the extra pair of glasses I snatch off my bedside table, in case I need to do the distance thing. Our door creaks, but I have solid sneaking skills from years of climbing through my third floor, Montréal hometown bedroom window. I tiptoe through and enter the still, silent hallway. Nearly 8 a.m. on the first Sunday of the school year, no one is around.

I know where I'm going. The route is easy. Just enter the twisting, almost always empty, stairwell and climb until I hit the fourth floor of Old Eddy in Shirreff Hall. Then, turn right, walk to the end of the hallway, and stop at one lone window. This is *my* spot. And I only say it's mine because apart from the one time with the tattoo guy, I've never seen anyone hanging out here. Lottie says the girls find it creepy. Something about someone dying here years ago. But, hey, it's an okay place to die, I guess, should I have to choose.

I lean against the window and breathe. The cool air wafting off it chills my face. It's fresh and clean and everything I need in this moment. The cold air stills my whirling thoughts. I close my eyes.

Breathe.

"Oh, you really shouldn't have done that."

I startle and turn to the source of the voice behind me, but no one is there.

Chapter Two

I STUDY THE FOURTH floor of Old Eddy. It's hardly spacious, a dead end at the end of a hallway. If you wanted to hide, you'd have to turn into a dorm room or jump out a window. And four floors up, with concrete down below, no one in their right mind would do that.

Real person or not, though, it's not like I haven't had that thought. I should *not* have done this. I had no way of knowing that Lewis Pickering was my TA, yet I still feel stupid. I put on a brave face for Lottie and pretended like I was fine with my mistake, but it *was* a mistake, and I'm not okay with the implications or consequences of my actions.

"Seriously," the same woman speaks.

I turn and set my eyes on the owner of the voice. A young woman, slightly older than me, stares back, her eyes wide, green saucers.

"What?" I ask. "What did I do?"

I know the answer, obviously, but I've never seen this girl before in my life. Somehow she knows me enough to place judgement. She must live here. Shirreff Hall has four wings to it. Lottie and I live in Newcombe, the only section of the residence that is still just for women. There must be a ton of people I don't know here. Maybe she heard me talking to Lottie through the door...

"You've been talking to yourself," she says. She looks at me strangely, a question forming in those seafoam eyes, a crease between her eyebrows. She opens her mouth and speaks slower. "That's how I know about your TA."

"I was?"

She nods.

"I don't normally talk to myself. Actually, I don't remember ever talking to myself."

She shrugs and smirks as though she's holding back a laugh. "I don't know what to tell you. Either I'm a mind reader or you were talking to yourself. Which one would you like to believe?"

I open my mouth to respond, but realize how ridiculous this conversation is and laugh instead. She smiles and hesitantly steps closer. Up close, her eyes are just as bright. I'd never seen eyes quite like this until I met Lottie. This girl is short, likely no more than 5'2". She looks as though she's in good shape, an hourglass for a waist and a chest even I can appreciate (and maybe even be a little jealous of, since a swimmer's body doesn't leave room for much boobage). She's a little too fancy for this early in the morning, though. And way too summery. A light blue sundress, with frills where the dress ends at her knees, clings to her body. The tangerine scarf around her neck is only for decoration, definitely not to give any warmth.

"Aren't you cold?" I ask.

"We're inside," she deadpans. "Aren't you hot?"

I actually am hot. "I was just stopping by before I go outside and become a block of ice. I like the view up here."

Her expression sours. She stares out the window like she would love nothing more than to jump out and leave this hallway forever. Waves of anger radiate off her and seep into my skin. But before I have a chance to ask what's going on, she speaks, "It *is* a nice view."

She swallows and tugs at the scarf wrapped around her neck. When she turns back to me, her expression has changed. The light is back in her eyes and her smile appears genuine. But my skin prickles in goosebumps, as if something is wrong. I want to ask again, but once more, she beats me to it. "I'm Penelope, but I go by Penny. What's your name?"

"Maryl," I reply.

Penny nods. "Like Streep."

"Kind of," I say. It's what I always say. "Just not the same spelling."

"Oh, that's interesting. Why'd your parents pick the name but not go with the popular spelling?"

I shrug. "I don't know. They named my brother Stephen so it's not, like, a thing for weird names. I guess they liked this one."

"Oh, I like it too," she says quickly, waving a hand to make sure I'm not offended. "I think names are interesting. There's a lot that goes into naming someone. There's usually more of a process behind it than picking a name out of a hat."

"But that would be a pretty cool story to tell your kid."

"Only cool if they don't hate it." She smiles once more.

I purse my lips and watch Penny pace down the hall. Is our conversation over? She looks like she's building up to something, but I don't know what. She flips her long blonde waves off her shoulders and sets her gaze on me, an unfamiliar intensity behind her eyes.

"What?" I finally ask.

Penny walks toward me in three large steps, invading my personal space and bringing a blast of cool air with her. She grabs hold of my hands and chills run through my body. I almost snatch my hands away, but I've never felt like anything is as important as what she needs to tell me. Her sad eyes meet mine and I look away. I need some sort of barrier between us.

"Look," she says and my eyes snap back to hers. "I haven't told anyone this in a long time, but you need to hear this because what you did was stupid and you cannot continue it."

"You mean..."

"I mean sleeping with your professor." I open my mouth to correct her, but she gets there first. Again. "Your TA. Maryl, it's the same thing. You have no idea what sort of position you're putting yourself in if you continue this. If you have an affair, you're going to get burned."

"Well, it's not really an affair if the person's single and—"

"Maryl, listen to me. The semantics don't matter. I have been in your situation and it does not matter if the person is married or in a relationship or completely unentangled. Do not continue this. Don't mention it ever again. If he brings it up, tell him that's it. Don't go back to him. He is not worth your education or life. Okay?"

She drops my hands and starts to walk away.

"Wait," I say. She pauses, and her shoulders square. "What happened to you? You're still here, you're still getting an education. What was so bad that you needed to warn me like that?"

Penny nods and smirks. She worries her bottom lip between her teeth until she responds. "You're right. I am still here."

And with that, she leaves me in the empty hallway. I turn back to the window, watching the windblown swirls of fallen snow across naked trees and metal benches. Hard as I try, I can't get Penny out of my head. Her warning—if I can call it a warning—affects me more than it should. She didn't tell me anything I hadn't already worried over but something seems off. She was too intense, too sad, too cold.

A door opens further down the hall, snapping me from my reverie.

"Maryl?" Lottie calls. "I thought I'd find you here." She shivers as she steps toward me. "This place always gives me the creeps. I have no idea why you like it so much."

I shake my head, feeling similarly now. "Let's go get some food."

Chapter Three

"So, HAVE YOU DECIDED what you're going to do about the LP situation?" Lottie asks.

I squint at my cornflakes, working out LP, feeling like we're in grade seven again with codenames for boys we like. Of course, like the codenames as a preteen, LP is unbelievably easy to figure out. I snort and eat my cereal.

"It doesn't matter."

"Of course it does! You see him tomorrow!" she says. She pulls her hair back into a ponytail, meaning business. "You have to figure this out. Your horoscope says that you have to address your situation head-on."

"Can you stop reading my horoscope, please?"

"I know you think they're full of crap, but I read them for everyone I love. Yours isn't wrong."

"So you're telling me that every Pisces has a situation that they need to deal with today? Every single person born in March?"

"Mid-February to mid-March. You say you don't care and yet you know your sign."

"Everyone knows their sign." I wave her off.

"So you disagree that you're pessimistic, stubborn, observant, a little wild, and a dreamer, even if you don't want to admit it?"

I stare at her, spoon halfway to my mouth. She's not entirely wrong.

"You could name off any trait and say that it applies to a certain sign. A person who believes in it will accept that and feel found. It's all what you're willing to believe."

"And that's pessimistic."

I roll my eyes. Ever the eternal pessimist. On one hand, I admire Lottie's hope in every situation. On the other, she spouts off a lot of ridiculous things. But, hey, I could definitely have a worse roommate.

My bowl is empty and I glance around the dining hall. The wooden islands with marbled granite countertops are stacked with diminishing food items. Though there's not as many people here as usual with it not quite being the first day back, those that are here are still ravenous for breakfast. Leah, part of the Shirreff Hall cafeteria staff, hovers at the edge of the kitchen and dining hall, waiting to turn everything over for lunch. I wave. She smiles and gestures toward the remaining muffins. Lottie turns and catches the interaction.

"There's a double chocolate chip muffin calling your name," Lottie says.

"I'm sold," I say and stand.

Double chocolate chip muffins are my weakness. I grabbed one off the buffet table my first day at Shirreff Hall and fell in love.

"Hey, Leah," I say, once I'm close enough to the kitchen.

"Hey, Mare," Leah says.

Leah is the only person on earth who is allowed to call me Mare. During elementary school, immature boys started calling me *mére*, thinking it was so hilarious to call me mother. But Leah isn't from Québec and really only knows how to say hi in French, so this isn't a joke to her. I'd asked if she was calling me a horse, but she merely laughed and stated she was the furthest thing from a horse girl.

"You look like death today, girl," she says as she swipes my student card and charges me for the muffin.

Leah always looks fabulous. She went prematurely grey at twenty and has worn it with pride since then, as she's told me before. She's nearly fifty now, but apart from the hair, you could never tell. Besides, the long grey hair adds to her whole hippie vibe.

"Thank you, Leah." I laugh.

"Wild night?"

I shrug. "Something like that."

Leah tilts her head, a gesture I recognize all too well. It's her, I'm-going-to-read-you head tilt. The first time I met her she decided I was anxious and somehow guessed that I was worried about not making the swim team. And no, my hair wasn't wet, I didn't smell of chlorine, and I had no identifying swim gear with me. Lottie loves talking astrology with her while I nod along and pretend that two competent and generally cool individuals aren't acting like the stars have influence on their lives.

"I've never seen you question your sexual choices before," she says.

"That's because I don't."

"Then why are you? You're letting someone get to you, I think. Who's telling you what you're doing is wrong?"

I stay silent. The fact is no one except the girl on the fourth floor told me to stop. Lottie expressed her concern, but she never told me I was wrong or in danger.

"Am I that easy to see through?" I ask.

"Everyone's easy to see through if you know how to look at them."

I blink. "Okaayy."

She laughs. "I know that doesn't help you much. Just here to say, do what you want to do. Don't let people tell you what. You know, unless you're truly doing something stupid. Are you doing something stupid?"

"What if it's not that I'm planning on *doing* something, but that I already did it?"

"Then whoever said you were wrong is probably right."

I shake my head and take my student card. "Yeah, thanks, helpful."

"Was it Lottie?"

"No, someone else I know. Someone named Penny."

She pauses and frowns, so quickly I nearly miss it, then clears her throat. "New friend? Haven't heard you mention a Penny before."

"Yeah," I say. I almost don't want to continue, all instincts telling me that something weird happened. "Just met her. Are you okay? You look like you've seen a ghost."

She laughs, shrill and higher than I've heard from her before. "Unless you're the ghost, I have not seen one. But stumble around campus for long enough, you probably will."

"I wasn't being serious." I smirk and start to walk away.

"I know," she calls. "But I was."

I turn and begin to walk backwards, shooting Leah a raised eyebrows, half smile, yeah-right look. She waves me off and I face forward again. Lottie's staring at me, mouth open, amused. I crinkle my nose, break off a piece of the muffin, and throw it at her.

"What was that about?" she says, dusting chocolate crumbs from her blousy shirt.

"The muffin?"

"No. I'm used to that from you. I meant the conversation with Leah."

I pick a chocolate chip out of my muffin and plop it into my mouth. Lottie sits patiently, because, yes, I'm stalling. My Sunday has been nothing but weird conversations coming one after the other. This, no doubt, is going to be another one.

"You know how Leah is," I mutter around a mouthful of chocolate. "She talks to you about all your life's problems and then suddenly mentions the ghosts on campus."

Lottie smiles and leans in. "Okay, so what ghost stories have you heard?"

She shakes her head when I stare at her blankly. The answer is none. Her excitement triples with the added element of disbelief. I'm starting to believe in ghosts, because she's acting like she's possessed as she reaches into the tote bag she carries around everywhere and pulls out a somehow very pristine brochure.

"Are you recruiting me to the dark side?" I ask.

Lottie points a silver sparkly manicured finger at the brochure. "Look at it."

Ghosts of Halifax appears in bold letters at the top of the page. I unfold the brochure until I see an image of Dalhousie, then further down, Shirreff Hall.

"Where did you get this?"

"They gave it out on the frosh tour," she says and blushes when I raise my eyebrows. How she kept that paper so perfect for half a year, I'll never know. "We have a bunch of ghosts here. There's one in Shirreff."

"And yet, I've never seen it, have you?"

Lottie rolls her eyes. "That's not how it works, Maryl. You can't decide that because you've never seen it, it doesn't exist."

"That's exactly how it works."

"Have you ever seen oxygen before?"

"Lottie..."

"I get it, you're all *woman of science* and this isn't science, but, like, isn't it? Science is all about discovering things that don't exist. Do you think people believed that radium existed before Marie Curie found it?"

"That's such an oddly specific examp—"

"The point is," she interrupts, louder and with authority, "people don't believe things until they see them, but that doesn't mean they aren't real."

"You sound like a walking cliché."

"At least read the story."

When I hesitate, Lottie gives me the glare. I know better than to question it at this point. I bow my head to read.

Legend has it, a Dalhousie student had an affair with a professor almost twenty years ago. Their affair ended disastrously when the student found out she was pregnant and the professor denied her any support. So despondent, the student killed herself. In Shirreff Hall. She came back to the residence and hanged herself in Old Eddy.

"You finished?" Lottie asks.

"This isn't real, is it?"

"Of course it is," she says. "This is why I never want to go up there with you. It's so eerie. I have friends on that floor who've heard rustling in the middle of the night. One time, they heard someone crying and when they went to check, no one was there."

I chew on my lip, attempting to come up with some excuse for rustling and crying in the middle of the night. I try to ignore what all signs point toward. Because it's completely illogical and makes no sense and I don't believe in any of this and yet... And yet, I can't reconcile the coincidence of a ghost being named Penelope and a girl I just met in that exact spot telling me her name was the same.

Penelope, the brochure said. The girl in blue.

"What?" Lottie asks. Her brows furrow. I usually have a good poker face, but apparently not today. "What's wrong?"

"Nothing," I say. She waits, all wide eyes and high expectations. "It's just this girl. When I was up there earlier, she got really intense with me. She said I was talking to myself, then explained she'd had an affair and nothing good comes of it. I—it was weird and I've been thinking about it."

"You think you saw the ghost?!"

"Or someone pretending to be a ghost. It wouldn't be hard to pretend and freak someone out if you know the story and say your name is Penny."

There. That's the explanation. Silence falls between us. Lottie's face is so blank that I can't read her.

"Maryl, you don't talk to yourself. I've never seen that happen and, well, I didn't see anyone up there with you."

"Don't joke, please."

"I'm not joking," she says and sticks out a pinkie. "I swear. You saw the ghost."

"I did not see the ghost."

"What did she look like?"

"The *girl* I saw had blonde hair and super green eyes. She also had on this really thin sundress that was way too cold for winter."

The intensity comes back into Lottie's eyes. "That's her. Everyone says she's wearing a blue dress. Was she wearing a scarf? People say she's wearing a scarf."

I pause and sigh. "Yes," I admit. "A really flimsy orange one, but why would a ghost dress that way?"

"She died in, like, 2000, do you want her to wear a pioneer dress?"

"Well, no, but I've never seen a ghost dressed so modern."

"Implying you've seen a ghost before."

I roll my eyes.

"This is so exciting! We have to go back up there and investigate."

"No, I'm not ghost hunting. Someone's playing some stupid joke and probably pretends to be this ghost girl for everyone. Didn't they do that during frosh week on the tour? Someone dressed up as a ghost over by Howe Hall and jumped out at all of us."

"Yes," Lottie says. "Because they're playing off all the legends. OH! Oh my God, Maryl!!"

"What?"

"My horoscope said this!" She pulls out her phone and scrolls to her horoscope app, courtesy of *Cosmopolitan*. "See! Look!"

Legends prove to be true, reads the first line.

I shrug and stand. I grab my coat off the back of the chair and slip into it. Lottie pouts.

"Congratulations on taking your horoscope very literally today."

"As always," she says and puts her phone away. "See you for dinner!"

I nod and walk away. True to myself, I need some time to process things. Contemplating the fact that you might have seen a ghost is a big moment for a skeptic. Of course, there's nothing that really proves I saw a ghost apart from a girl with no fashion sense and a coincidental name. I should probably be focusing on the more pressing issue of how to convince my TA I didn't sleep with him for blackmail purposes.

My phone buzzes and I jump. I stop just outside the Shirreff Hall doors. I reach into my pocket, realize I'm still holding a muffin wrapper, and throw it into the food waste bin. Garbage free, I pull my phone out.

Stephen

Happy first Sunday back!

Maryl

what's so happy about it?

Stephen

Uh oh! What's wrong with you?

Maryl

I see dead people

Stephen

Lol I know.

I laugh and return my phone to my pocket.

Chapter Four

LOTTIE AND I WALK into the lecture hall for the first Introduction to Creative Writing class the next morning. Our professor, Denver Keyes, has taught here for twenty-five years. I've never taken a creative writing class in my life. I don't think I've ever really written much outside of an English class. During first semester, Lottie convinced me to take this with her. I switched around another elective that would have filled the same requirement and added this one instead. It's one of the most popular first year courses and I was waitlisted until the day before New Year's Eve. Which is probably why I had no idea who the TA was. But that's another story.

"Do you see him?" Lottie whispers.

"Shut up," I hiss back. "No one needs to know. I'm not even going to look."

We find a spot near the middle of the lecture hall. I shrug out of my coat and hang it over the back of the wheeled desk chair. Winter lectures with bulky coats are always so awkward. There's even less room to squeeze by. I pull my laptop and Dalhousie Tigers water bottle out of my whale-printed backpack and place them on the white table, then stash my bag under the desk. A generic white dude with dark brown curls watches as I settle down in the chair and adjust its height. Lottie sits to my right and makes eye contact with him. I keep my gaze level with the front of the classroom, making it seem as though I'm not watching, and notice the boy do everything in his power to pretend he wasn't staring. I hold back a laugh and turn to Lottie.

"Remind me how you got me here again," I say.

"Because you love me and I'm the best roommate ever," she replies. "But you also didn't seem to need much convincing."

"I really didn't want to take Intro to Philosophy, so never mind, thanks for this."

Lottie laughs. Honestly, I'm kind of thankful for Lottie and her band of pre-journalism girls. My friend, Sadie, decided to stay with Philosophy, and let's just say it didn't end well...

"Do you know why this class is in the Life Sciences building?" I ask.

Lottie shrugs. "They all are."

"Did I hear you say you're in LifeSci?" Mystery Boy speaks.

I swivel in my chair and actually look at him for the first time. He's definitely trying to be like one of those cool action movie guys. Not only does his wavy dark hair brush his ears, but he has stubbly cheeks and an even stubblier moustache. He brushes a hand through his hair and smiles, one that I note, doesn't quite reach his hooded, dark eyes.

"No," I say. "I'm a biology major, focusing on marine animals."

"Of course."

His eyes stray to the whales on my backpack. He's about to speak again when several screeching girls interrupt. I jump as Lottie's friends appear in front of our table.

"Lottie!" one, who I think is named Hannah or Jessica or Nicole, says. "Come sit with us! You can't sit alone! Denver Keyes is supposed to be THE BEST professor and he's hot too. Come. Come sit! We're right up front!"

Lottie looks at me hesitantly. I try to hold back the bewilderment on my face. Her friends had a good idea making me switch classes, but they're also a little... much.

"Oh!" Hanessicole says. "Your friend can come as well."

I shake my head. "That's alright," I say. There's no way I'm sitting at the front. "You go ahead, Lottie."

Lottie gathers her things slowly, eyes clouded with worry that she's somehow offended me. I pull her bag from beneath the table and hold it out to her, smiling. Hanessicole and company have returned to the front of the lecture hall and hesitation creeps through Lottie with turtle speed.

"Seriously," I say to her. "I won't be caught dead in the front row. Go sit with your friends. I'm here for a credit, not a hot guy."

Lottie's head jerks up at that, a smirk playing on her lips. She scans the front of the lecture hall and lingers on a man in a tweed jacket. Well, fuck, she found him. Her eyes meet mine, wide and inquisitive. I raise my eyebrows and shake my head, then nod to tell her to go. She puts a finger to her lips.

I snicker.

"See you later," she says.

She walks down the steps to the front of the lecture hall and sits almost at the end of the aisle, next to her friends. Lewis Pickering walks from the table at the front of the classroom to the seat beside Lottie. He pulls papers out of his briefcase on the chair next to her, then hangs his jacket over the back. Lottie turns in her seat and finds me. Her eyes shift between me and Lewis. I wave her away.

"I'm Hale, by the way," Mystery Boy says.

"What?" I say and snap my gaze away from Lottie's shenanigans. "Sorry, you said your name..."

"Hale," he says. "Hale Butler."

"That's an interesting name."

"It's a family name," he tells me. "My grandpa didn't want to let it go."

"Your grandpa named you?"

"Kind of." He shrugs. "It was before he died. My parents kind of liked it."

"Well, Hale, whose parents kind of like his name, I'm Maryl."

"Your parents must have liked the actress."

"Or French."

I provide the usual Meryl Streep story and inform him that it's spelt completely different, while fidgeting with the top of my water bottle. Conversation stilts after my anecdote. I glance down at my phone. Two minutes until class starts.

"So why are you taking this class if you're in LifeSci?" I ask, if only to kill the awkward silence.

"My mom encouraged me to try a number of different courses. That whole broaden horizons thing. My mom and dad met here so they both know what Dal is like."

"Or they did like, twenty years ago, right?"

"Oh, yeah. I'm sure a bunch has changed since then, but it's good advice. You're taking this to fill a credit, I gather?"

"I am. I've got my life here all mapped out."

"Already? You're only a semester in. What do you want to do?"

"I'm going to be a marine biologist, so naturally, I'll take all the biology courses until I can switch into the Marine Biology stream. That's not till third year, though. I'm going to minor in French so I won't even have to think about it. And then I'll keep swimming."

"Okay... So you're from Québec, then? I thought I heard a little accent. And on the swim team?"

"Everyone has an accent here, but mine's not east coast so it sticks out a little. But I am from Québec. Montréal, specifically. My parents wanted me to stay in the province, but I had to come here for the program. Plus, I've always wanted to live by an ocean. Which has to do with the swimming thing. I wanted to grow up and be a mermaid. My grandma always said I was one in a past life."

"That's sweet. She sounds like a lovely person."

I smile, about to nod and pretend like talking about her doesn't stab at my heart, but the lecture hall hushes as a man in jeans and a blazer stands at the podium. I've never seen a room quiet so fast. Denver Keyes commands the space. He stands perfectly straight and looks over the crowd of first year students. He exudes a quiet dignity as he strokes his full salt and pepper beard, a contrast to his deep umber skin. The black rimmed glasses pull his scholarly look together, with knowledgeable eyes maximized behind the lenses.

"Good afternoon." His voice booms, projecting without a microphone. "Welcome to Introduction to Creative Writing. This is one of the most popular courses here at Dalhousie and it is, as always, an honour for me to be here and teach you all. There is a long waitlist for this course, so I'm going to get into this right away. There are people who want and need to be here, if you do not fall into this category and are not going to take this class seriously, I ask that you please leave now."

No one gets up.

"I don't expect anyone to leave immediately. Only once has a student left after that part of my speech. But tonight, when you go home, please consider why you are here and if you're taking a spot away from someone else. There are still twenty people on the waitlist right now. A few people typically drop after this lecture, and a few more after first assignments are marked. I'm very upfront so you can make informed decisions. The syllabus is already up, but I'm going to go over it now so there is no confusion."

Lewis grabs the pile of papers he took out of his briefcase and hands a stack to each row of the lecture hall. I keep my head down in case he looks my way. This course is intense. We have to submit seven short stories over twelve weeks, the first of which is due next week. This is in addition to any exercises we do in class or have to take home. I mentally calculate the pages of extra work I'm going to have to do for this course. I roll my shoulders and resolve that I won't quit at least until after the first assignment.

"Any questions?" Denver asks after finishing his explanation of the syllabus.

Hanessicole raises her hand and Denver nods. "Yes," she says. "So these stories that we submit throughout term, what are they supposed to be about?"

"Anything."

"Anything?! There's no guideline?"

Denver chuckles. "This is the beauty of creative writing. It can be about anything. There are no guidelines because guidelines hinder creativity. Just write. Take inspiration from around you. What inspires you? What scares you? What interests you? Ask yourself questions and write the story you need to write. There are endless possibilities. Open your eyes and you will find them. This seems like a good time to take our ten-minute break. We'll do a writing exercise once we get back."

Professor Keyes walks away from the podium and stations himself at the front of the classroom. A few students hurry to his desk and chat with him.

Hale whistles. I snap my head in his direction and raise my eyebrows.

"He's intense," Hale says. "Makes me unsure about staying in this course. My roommate told me it was a bird course."

"Where did your roommate get that information?" I ask, scanning the classroom.

"His brother," he pauses. "Which, I guess, would explain it. Probably messing with him."

"Is he taking this course too?"

"Who? Blake?" Hale asks. I shrug, annoyed by his presumption that I'm supposed to know his roommate's name. "Yeah, but he got plastered last night and was sleeping when I left."

"It's 3 p.m."

"He didn't get back till 8 a.m."

"Oh God," I say. "Lottie would hate him so much more than me."

Hale drops his pen. It rolls off the edge of the desk, onto the floor, and continues down the incline of the hall. We both stare at it until it stops beneath someone's foot. He clears his throat.

"Lottie is your roommate?" I nod and he continues. "She hates you?"

"No, not at all. We get along really well. I just know it's annoying when I get back late."

"No offence," he says, and I brace myself to probably be a little offended. "But I feel like she can't be annoyed at little things like that when she ditches you for other people."

I laugh. "Oh. It's cool. She can have friends outside of me. I really don't want to hang out with the pre-journalist crew anyway. They're always on their phones and buzzing about things online. It's tedious to be with them all the time."

"What res are you in?"

"Shirreff Hall."

"Oh, no way!" he says, mouth lifting into a half smile. "Me too."

"We're in Newcombe and I'm assuming you're not."

Hale laughs and looks down. "Definitely not." He glances at the front of the classroom where the line of students at Denver's desk is dwindling. "So have you met the resident ghost?"

I exhale a little more forcefully than intended. "Why is everyone talking about that?"

"Why wouldn't people talk about it? Ghost stories are the coolest part of living somewhere old."

"Ghost stories are overrated."

"You don't believe in them?"

I pause, thinking of my odd encounter with Penny, then shrug. "I have a healthy amount of skepticism."

"So you've never seen Penelope, then?"

"Have you?"

"No," he says and I have to hold back a laugh. "But Blake swears he did. He wants to do an investigation of the place. Grab a Ouija board and those weird cameras people use on ghost shows."

"Wouldn't that debunk the Ouija board?"

Hale shakes his head. "Oh, ye of little faith. Come on! How cool would it be to find a ghost? Especially this one. You know Penelope hooked up with a prof, right? I keep looking at all my professors, wondering if it was them."

"And your opinion of Denver?"

Hale looks up again. The remaining fan club of students have gone back to their seats, leaving Denver alone. He takes a sip of water, then walks back to the podium, standing at attention, his authority radiating silence across the lecture hall.

"Now he's a possibility."

Class ends a little after the allotted time. I stand and shuffle into my coat, ready to make the icy trip back to Shirreff Hall. I exchange numbers with Hale and say goodbye as Lottie waves me down to the front. I hesitate. Lewis has vacated his seat, but he's still here. I wave at Lottie to come up to me. She draws her eyebrows together as if she can't possibly understand why I would want to be anywhere else but next to the jacket I peeled off Lewis's shoulders a few nights ago.

But, of course, our interaction and the fact that people are exiting left and right, leaving me as one of the only students at the back of the hall, draws more attention. And suddenly, I'm making eye contact with Lewis Pickering.

I put on my poker face and hope I am devoid of emotion by the time I get to the front of the lecture hall. I sidle up next to Lottie, pretending like I never even saw him.

"Sorry," Lottie hisses.

I glare at her while her friends chat, oblivious to the situation.

"Excuse me," Lewis says.

I don't turn around because I know he's not speaking to me, but I also know he's leaving his conversation to come over. I close my eyes as a figure brushes past me. It's Lewis. When I open my eyes again, he's not even looking at me. But he's so obviously not looking at me that I know exactly why he's come back to rustle through his briefcase.

"You ready to go?" Lottie asks. I nod and turn to leave with her friends.

"Hey," Lewis says. The girls stop. He's looking at me. He's seen me naked. Fuck. "Did I have a class with you last semester?"

Lottie's friends walk away, uninterested. She goes with them, but motions she'll wait outside. I can tell from his eyes that that's not really the question he's asking me.

"I think we did," I say, playing with a short lock of my dark hair because my hands are fidgety and I need to do something to keep myself from running out of here.

"Maryl, right?"

"That's right," I say. "Lewis."

He nods and smiles. His smile was one of the reasons why I trusted him, why I left with him. He seemed so approachable.

"Well, I look forward to seeing more of you this semester, Maryl."

Something in me relaxes. He doesn't think it's a big deal, and maybe it wouldn't be so bad to entertain the idea of him.

Chapter Five

SNOW HAS HIT HALIFAX almost every day since I've been back, blanketing the pathways and grey bricks in crystals of ice. Montréal gets more snow and below freezing temperatures than the Maritimes every year, but a Halifax winter is punctuated by dampness and fog, which somehow makes it worse. The cold seeps in through the back of my shirt at my spot on the fourth floor, permeating through drywall and insulation. It's either freezing rain or snowing again, but I refuse to look.

My first Cell Biology lab got cancelled. There was no reason for a lab after an introductory lecture. Cell Bio is stupid early. My only 8 a.m. class, luckily on the only day I can have an 8 a.m. class. I would probably die trying to get changed and run across campus after swim practice otherwise. Especially now with the ice.

I debated going back to the dorm and sleeping, but I figure I'd better get some work done. So here I am, doing what Denver Keyes told us to do, trying to find inspiration to write that first assignment. But as I stare down at my very very empty page, I realize, more truthfully, I feel as though something pulled me here. It's not like I'm expecting my new friend Penny to show up... but...

Students in sweatpants and university sweaters roam the halls. The lucky students who didn't have to wake up for the dreaded early class, and question how the hell we woke up this early in high school, head downstairs for breakfast. My stomach grumbles, despite having eaten only two hours ago. No one takes note of me. No one ever does when I'm here. This isn't the busiest part of the residence, but there are still dorms on either side. My only theory for invisibility is that no one likes being around here for long enough to notice. Everyone except me finds this little alcove creepy.

I click the top of my pen absently, the noise filling the now empty hallway. I tried to write on my laptop, but nothing. I'm not a writer and I have no idea why I took this class. I probably should have thought it through before jumping ship. Lottie suggested I write on paper. It helps, she claims. I don't know what's more intimidating; a blank Word doc or a literal blank page. Well, not entirely blank. I have managed to draw some very pretty flowers, zig zags, and stars.

"I used to do that too," a voice beside my left ear says.

I turn and, of course, see nothing.

"This is getting old," I say.

I face forward. Penny gives me a little wave as she takes a step toward me. A smirk plays on her lips. The baby hairs on the back of my neck rise. She sits down in front of me and points a finger at the flowers on my page.

"Classic procrastination," she whispers.

I stare at her, uncertain now. She's either totally real and thinks I'm weird, or I'm hallucinating and I *am* weird. She slips her hand away and stands. An insurmountable, crushing feeling of sadness settles over me. I try to shake it off, but it all melts away when I realize she's gone. Again.

"Wait!' I say. "I'm confused." Nothing. "I don't know who you are or what you want, but I know you have something to do with this place. Or maybe I'm crazy. There's a high possibility of that too."

Nothing.

I sigh and turn my attention back to my doodled page. I trace over one of the blue lines across the page, then another, then draw triangles between the two. The line fills up. My pen is going to die long before I even start on the assignment, long before I get any answers from whoever the hell Penny is. Sadness weighs on my shoulders once more. The unsettling sense of eyes on me comes with the sadness. I look up.

Penny.

She leans against the wall across from me, crossing her legs at the ankles. "Tell me about yourself."

"I—wait, what?" I stumble.

Penny shrugs. Something about her isn't right. Maybe I wasn't looking before, but I can see it now; an almost imperceptible flicker of her whole body when she moves. I rub beneath my eyes and recall the moment I put my contacts in this morning. The hologram-like effect to her has nothing to do with the blur of my vision and everything to do with... her.

"Tell me about yourself," she repeats. "I know you slept with your TA, but there has to be more to your story than that. There was more to mine."

I stare at her again. Words work their way through my brain but don't come out. I don't know what to say to her. I don't know if she's even real.

"Past tense?"

She startles. "Yes. I'm glad you caught that."

"What does that mean?"

"It means that my story, as it was, as people want to believe it, is over. It's static. There's nothing I can do about that."

I place my notebook on the floor and lean forward, resting my elbows on my knees and propping my head in my hands. "Why can't you do anything about that?"

"Do I seem like I'd be capable of that?"

"Anyone's capable of changing their story."

She laughs, unbothered. "Until you're dead."

She stalks toward me, one eyebrow raised. I'm torn between fear and curiosity. Something tells me she won't hurt me, she won't do anything bad. But... she's dead.

I shake my head. "That's impossible."

Another laugh. There's an edge to her laugh. Harsher than when I met her on Sunday. Angrier, sadder, so much more bitter. Infused with more malice than it was just moments before. I open my mouth to explain myself, but she beats me to it.

"You know what," Penny says. "I'd think that too if I were you but since we're here, you have no choice but to just go with it." She sits next to me again. "Besides, I have this suspicion that you're not here by accident."

"I live here."

"Here," she says and widens her eyes, gestures to the space around us. "Where I died."

I grab my notebook and slam it shut, then get up on my knees. When I whip around to tell her off, she's merely sitting there, arms crossed, that smile on her lips again. My stomach twists and I can't quite pinpoint why, but it sets me off further. She simply watches as I push myself off the ground and back away from her slowly.

"This has gone a bit far, don't you think?" I ask her, a mix of disbelief and indignance creeps into my voice, masking the fear that I really feel.

"Look, you came back to talk to me. You've been up here since you arrived in September, even though your room isn't on this floor. I know you weren't coming to see me then, but something made you come up here. Maybe you haven't realized it before. Maybe you've been too afraid or too logical, but I swear to God, you were drawn here. I know that some people can sense things and I think you might be able to sense, well, me. Maryl, you can see ghosts."

I grip the strap of my backpack, slung loosely over my shoulder. I've never known what it feels like to be in a horror movie, but as far as moments go, this is one. My body reacts by backing up until my shoulder bounces against the opposite wall. The breath is stolen from my lungs. Penny stares.

"I have to go," I say.

Her face falls, as if she expected different, but to her credit, she doesn't say anything more. I walk away from her without looking back.

I'm not a pacer. Lottie is. She paces to solve problems and I've never understood it until now. Because now, I'm pacing. There is no possible way I was talking to a dead girl, and yet... And yet, what's the other explanation?

I fidget with my phone. I want to call Stephen so badly and get his opinion, but his last text about this was him saying *he knows* I see dead people. And now that I've had this weird experience with Penny, I'm starting to doubt that was a joke. I've always teased him about ghosts and monsters, but he's never cared. He's always told me that once I see something, I'll believe it, as if there's something to see.

"Stephen," I say after he picks up the phone.

"Hello to you too," he grumbles. "Can this wait? I'm with a client."

Stephen is a physiotherapist. He found his calling after tearing his rotator cuff during a swimming competition in high school and needing extensive physio. I know I'm supposed to give my brother shit, but I can honestly say that the world of sports injuries is better with him in this role.

"Yeah, it can wait," I say, but the jumpy agitation in my voice betrays me.

He sighs and mutters something to his client. "What's happening, kid?"

I bristle at the nickname. He's only six years older than me and he insists on calling me kid. Always has.

"I wanted to know what made you believe in ghosts."

"What?" He laughs. "This is why you're interrupting my workday?"

For lack of anything better to say, "Yes."

I can almost picture him laughing at me. His face breaking out into a grin, and eyes crinkling as he draws his shoulders back for a hearty laugh. I'm giving him fodder to make fun of me for years to come.

"Okay. Well, since I'm already on the phone with you... It was with Mamie. We were cleaning out her house before she went to the old folk's home and Papi's things kept flying off shelves. Specifically, his things. Nothing else."

"But you've never seen anything?"

"I guess not," he says, pensive. "I'm not like you."

"What the hell does that mean?"

"Mamie always told me you saw dead people. You literally just told me you did two days ago, kid."

"That was a joke. What does Mamie know?"

"She told me that you saw things. She said our family has always seen things."

"That's not real."

"Then why are you calling me?" I don't have an answer. "Oookay... I have to get back to work. Call me later."

I stand in the dorm with the phone still to my ear, listening to the dial tone. *Our family has always seen things.*

My phone remains at my ear until Lottie walks in. I immediately put my arm down, as if she could somehow read my mind. And, nonetheless, she still raises her eyebrows.

"See some ghosts again?" she asks.

"No," I say too quickly.

Lottie laughs as she places her keys in the key bowl—her idea—and strips out of her coat. I ease myself down onto my bed and fold my legs underneath me. She turns to face me, hands on hips, hair back in ponytail.

"So, yes?" she says. "Someone's playing a trick on you."

"What?" I almost scoff.

I stare at her. She breaks eye contact and crouches to her bag. I watch as she rifles through, silently searching for God knows what. Eventually, she pulls out a small journal.

"Lottie, you're the one who told me about the ghost."

She shrugs and opens the little journal. I squint and recognize it as her agenda. Her second one. She has a big one that she writes down her timetable, assignments, and extracurriculars, and this small one for anything social. Lottie doesn't do much social outside of the newspaper, photography club, and historical society, except the occasional date with her boyfriend Gray when he's in town. Her journalism friends are in the same clubs as her, so she doesn't need to schedule much friend time outside of me and her boyfriend.

"I was wrong," she says, simply.

"So you're going to sit here and tell me that there's no such thing as ghosts, but the fucking stars are guiding your life?"

"Well, that makes more sense than a spirit floating around. At least the stars actually tell me things."

"And a ghost can't?"

"You're talking like you believe in them now."

A beat passes between us. "Maybe I do."

"Nicole says that ghosts aren't possible. If they were, they'd probably be great sources and solve murders."

I nearly scream. "Stop listening to the journalism twits. They all parrot the same thing."

"You told me it wasn't possible two days ago. Pick a side, Maryl."

Okay, I'll pick a side.

The rational part of me knows I'm being stupid coming back here. I'm trying to convince my kooky roommate of something I don't even believe. And why?

Because something tells me it does exist.

"Are you convincing yourself of that or do you actually think so?"

Penny, blue dress flowing around her, hair in perfect ringlets, scarf wrapped loosely around her neck, the same as I've always seen her, appears.

"That depends," I whisper. "Are you messing with me or will you actually talk?"

"A question for a question," she says. She walks toward me and I notice for the first time that her black heels don't make any noise. "Alright. Let's talk."

I stare at her, waiting. But of course I get to talk with a reluctant ghost. Penny scoffs.

"Can you read minds?" I ask.

She shrugs. "I don't think you realize you're doing it. You *are* talking to me. Just not out loud. You're projecting it."

I nod and she sits beside me. What's the limit on batshit things you can hear in one day? I've barely learned anything but I think I'm reaching that limit. Her movement brings a sudden rush of cold air, raising goosebumps on my arm through my sweater.

"No one ever talks back, though," she mumbles.

"You're joking," I say.

A girl that lives in the dorm a few down just next to where I'm stationed exits and raises her brows at me. I grab my phone off the floor and put it to my ear.

"Sorry," I say, intentionally much louder. "You surprised me and I dropped the phone!"

Penny laughs again. "Ridiculous."

"You don't have to worry about what anyone thinks of you," I hiss, phone still at my ear.

"Okay," she says. "Stay like that then."

She watches me and I do the same with her. I keep the phone at my ear, then slowly lower it. She smiles, showing me her perfect teeth. My mind tries to form something to ask her, but I really don't know. I've never sat in front of a ghost before and tried to get information.

"Well," Penny says. "That's only half true. You've been near ghosts before."

I purse my lips. "And how do you know that?"

She tilts her head as if it's obvious. "You must subconsciously know."

"But why you? If I've supposedly been around a bunch of ghosts, why are you the first one to talk to me?"

"Maybe others have and you didn't realize. Or maybe this time is important."

I glance at her from the corner of my eye. She fiddles with the tassels on her scarf, then runs her hands up and down the length of it. A thin line of worry forms between her eyes.

"What?" I ask. "Do you need me to help you cross over or something? Go into the light? Be like *Ghost Whisperer*? Does that even work with suicide?"

Penny whips her head toward me, worry line fading into anger. She snickers. "So you've heard my story, then? Think you know everything?"

A challenge, but still, I continue. "You killed yourself. You had an affair with one of the professors here and he got you pregnant. He didn't want anything to do with you, so you hung yourself in the rafters."

I point above us, though there's nothing but flat, speckled roof. Her gaze follows my finger, then she shakes her head.

"No." A short and simple answer, leaving me to debate whether I should apologize or ask more. "But points to you for listening, I guess."

I bite my lip. The edge in her voice makes it very clear that listening was not a good thing.

"It's a rumour, you know," she says. "Jilted lover committing suicide apparently sounds a lot sexier than the truth."

I remain silent for a moment, processing.

"Okay," I say. "So what's the truth?"

"I was murdered."

"With your baby?!" My voice screeches. I notice after the fact and glance around to make sure no one heard.

Penny shakes her head. "No. I had my affair and child years before. I never told him. I left and didn't come back until a few years later. Look what coming back got me..."

I try to make eye contact with her, but she won't look at me. She's achingly quiet. So quiet that if I look away, I believe she won't be here when I look back. I only hear myself breathing. Goosebumps cover my flesh as I realize what her words mean.

"I think it is very possible that the man I had a child with killed me."

Chapter Six

I SLICE THROUGH THE water in powerful strokes. My arms and legs propel me further and further away from the starting line to the other end of the Olympic-sized pool. My body glides beneath the surface and cuts through the top, desperately clawing to the finish, intent on beating my teammates in the opposite lanes. I push every derelict thought from my mind, my only focus on the blue tile sneaking up on me, preparing for the turn. I dive under and flip, forcing my feet against the wall just strong enough to take the lead.

And that's where it all falls apart.

Suddenly, I lose focus. My thoughts hover over the words I haven't let myself process since Lottie flip-flopped on me for believing in legends two days ago.

It's possible the man I had a child with killed me.

My limbs freeze under the water and for a moment I sink, sputter. Then, I regain my senses and propel myself forward. It's no use. I've lost the race. I can't make up for the momentum I lost. But in an effort to not lose my spot on the team, I try to regain my speed and finish strong.

I finish fourth. Out of five swimmers.

"Laine!" Coach Jaffee yells as I surface and rip off my goggles. I stare at him, waiting for him to continue, not fully trusting myself to speak. "What happened out there?! You froze!"

"I didn't realize," I mutter and climb out of the pool.

"You didn't realize?!" he screeches. I'm used to the screeches. For all the love our team has for this man, we also know he's prone to turning red when things don't quite go his way. "If you can't get that under control, I might not play you at the next race."

"Oh, come on!" I groan, shaking out my swim cap, busying my hands so I don't busy them on his face. "It was one time! And I recovered!"

"Prove that to me next time."

I stalk over to the bench and plunk down beside Sadie, a fellow rookie. She throws a towel over my shoulders.

"I thought you did very well," she lilts in her almost English accent. I thought it was an east coast accent at first, but Sadie was actually born and lived in England for ten years.

"I froze."

"Yes," she chirps, "but you recovered."

"You should be the coach, then," I say.

I sit silently, arms crossed, full pout, next to Sadie for the rest of practice. Coach doesn't call on me again. He calls around me. Anytime I catch his eyes, I glare. He smirks. He's dealt with my bullshit before.

"Stop," Sadie hisses. "You want to get kicked off the team for good?"

"He hasn't done it yet."

"One of these days he's going to get tired of your sulkfests and then I'm going to be stuck on the team all by myself."

I laugh. "You have, like, thirty other people to be friends with."

"But I don't like anyone else from our year."

"There's always Riley," I say.

"Riley's graduating."

I shrug and go back to playing my staring game. I track the swimmers in the pool. Coach loves playing games at the end of practice. I've never lost colours, the game currently being played. And yet, we're debating my merit and speed while some other rookie gets caught not even halfway to the other end of the pool.

"So what's really bugging you?" Sadie asks as she gathers her long red hair into a ponytail.

I always wanted red hair instead of the indistinct brown I actually have. Her hair is the mermaid dream I wanted as a kid, even if it's because she dyed it bright red from black. Sadie is basically the Little Mermaid, just a British-Indian combo instead of German.

I shift and groan. How much do I say? How many people need to know I've lost my mind? I settle on a lie.

"Nothing," I say. "The semester just began and it's what, the tenth? I'm already overwhelmed. This stupid creative writing course is more work than my labs. We have to submit a story almost every Friday and the professor is this ridiculously fast grader who turns them around by Monday, so he clearly also has no life. The first one is due next Friday and I have no idea what I'm doing."

"Well, hey, it's Keyes, right? I've heard he's a cutie."

"He and the TA have this whole scholarly vibe on lock," I say and smirk. "There were girls lined up at their desks every break."

"That is my kind of vibe. You know my Psych 101 prof? Super fit, too."

I sigh. "Doesn't help the situation, much, though."

"Okay," she says and watches another swimmer fall victim to the game. "What are you going to write about? They say write what you know, so you could always write about your angsty behaviour at the pool."

I shove her arm and she dramatically falls off the edge of the bench. Coach looks over at the commotion and we both smile innocently. I wave for good measure. Sadie plops back down and grins.

"What's your idea, then?" she asks.

"You ever heard about the Shirreff Hall ghost?"

"Ooh, exciting," she says and rubs her hands together. "My best friend purposely looked up all the ghosts here. So yes, I do know about her. She's the one who killed herself twenty years ago, right?"

I nod. Penny's words play in my head once more. "Yeah, something like that."

"That's such a fun story! Or well... Not fun for her, but you know what I mean. Fascinating? She was on the swim team, you know."

"What?" I shriek.

Sadie laughs and places a hand on my shoulder. "Calm down, girl. I can show you if you want."

I stare blankly at her. She smiles, showing me all her teeth, the perfect top row and slightly crooked bottom. She tilts her head to the side and pushes up off the bench.

"Where are you going, Westmount?" Coach calls.

Sadie turns back and raises her eyebrows. "I'm not in the pool and it's 8 a.m. Practice is over."

Bold. He waves her off and the few stragglers on the bench follow her lead. I stand, gather my goggles, cap, and towel, then join her. Sadie waits at the edge of the pool, just in front of the change rooms. She yanks on my arm, bypasses the change rooms, and rushes along the edge of the pool.

"Laine! Westmount! Slow the blazes down!" Coach yells.

Sadie slows, but barely. She makes a beeline for the exit and I hesitate, not entirely keen on being outside the pool in a swimsuit while everyone else is in winter coats. But another yank on my arm keeps me going. I see where she's guiding me. A wall filled with awards and headshots of each swim year appears in front of us. Our faces will be added to this wall by the end of the season, hopefully with a trophy in the case, as well. Sadie points to the gold framed 1993–94 swim season. I step closer.

"Okay so that's Coach Gleeson, she was here before Jaffee. That's Holly Tamiko, she was captain of the team, and Elora Hale, she was the rookie of the year... Oh! This is Kathleen Reign, she's the one—"

"That broke the record for fastest 500 metre."

"Exactly!" she says. "Okay... And... Her! Right there is Penelope Walsh. She's your dead girl."

I swallow. *Penelope Walsh.*

Long blonde hair falls in waves that frame her face. Her smile looks easy, practised, but genuine. And then there are those piercing seafoam eyes. She's the spitting image of the girl I keep seeing. The only difference is that instead of her blue dress and scarf combo, she's wearing a Dalhousie Tigers jacket.

"Gorgeous, right?" Sadie says. "For reference. So you can write about her."

I nod. "Thanks," I say, half-heartedly.

Because now I can't deny it. She's real.

Chapter Seven

THE DAY PASSES IN a blur.

I picked up my phone multiple times, intending on calling Stephen, and interrogating him on whether there's a history of mental illness in our family, or the less likely scenario that he actually had talked to Mamie about ghosts and my supposed gift. But each time I picked up my phone, I put it right back down. Neither option is all that appealing to me. I'm either Haley Joel Osment or Haley Joel Osment from a different movie, probably. And if I accept the whole dead people thing, I'm accepting a fact that science cannot prove.

I shrug into my red puffer, yank my black pompom toque onto my mess of a lob, and brace for that blast of cold air after my useless French lecture. I stuff my hands deep into my pockets and prepare to make the trek from the Marion McCain Arts and Social Sciences Building across campus, past the grey bricks and pointed arches of the Henry Hicks building, around the back of Wickwire Field, before finally arriving on South Street, which leads directly to Shirreff Hall.

I trudge through the generically modern halls of the McCain building, ignoring the flurry of students around me. I have to call Stephen. That's the only way to stop my thought spiral. But stuck between a throng of bodies and the knowledge of Lottie sitting in our dorm, I don't know where I can make the call. It's moments like these where I wish I brought my car here instead of leaving it back home. But in my defence, I didn't realize I'd be having an identity crisis.

"Maryl!" a voice calls from somewhere on University Avenue. Several heads turn toward the source of the voice. I squint through white blankness, regretting the moment I left my glasses on the bedside table this morning, and notice a man with shaggy dark hair making his way toward me. "You okay?"

He steps closer. "Hale," I breathe out. "Hey, yeah, I'm fine."

"You sure?" he asks. "You look kind of sick."

"Wow, thanks."

"Oh, no, no!" he backtracks as I continue walking. "I meant you don't look on your game."

I blink, struggling to figure out how that's any better. "You've seen me once in your life, how, exactly, do you know what my game face is?"

"I can't say I know, entirely. But I do know you wouldn't be defensive if I hadn't struck a nerve."

"What a fucking ballsy statement." I roll my eyes.

He makes a high pitched noise that I've heard boys make when they realize they've dug themselves a hole. I smirk. Eventually, he shrugs.

"Alright, start over?" he says. "What's up?"

I bite my lip, eyeing the trees at the edges of Wickwire Field. How much of a hypocrite do I want to turn into? I hate liars and I'm here debating another lie. But Hale is new. He knows next to nothing about me outside of a creative writing classroom. If he thinks I'm immature or out of my mind, it doesn't matter if he leaves. I care about both Lottie and Sadie. Hale... Well, maybe he can take it.

"You know the ghost?"

"Oh my God!" A voice booms behind me. I jump. "Which one?"

I turn to find another man following us, his blond hair messy and flaked with snow.

"This is Blake," Hale says, taking in my shock. "He's my roommate."

I stand there for a moment, steadying my heartbeat. Right. Blake, the drama major. I turn and start back to Shirreff. Both boys continue to follow me.

"The one at Shirreff," I say.

"Oh, yeah! I know all about her!" Blake says. "I stole a Ouija board from the prop closet to contact her."

I laugh. "You what?"

"I never used it. But I had this awesome idea to contact her last semester and then I never did. I can't remember why, though."

Hale brings two fingers to his mouth and pulls them away, breathing and causing steam to come out, just like smoke. I giggle again.

"We should do it," Hale says.

"Excuse me?"

"The Ouija board. We should contact the ghost."

"Dude, that's the best idea you've had since I moved in!" Blake shouts.

An hour later, now with glasses and my hair pulled up into a small, tufty ponytail, I sit on the floor of Hale and Blake's dorm room. It smells strongly of fried food and Axe deodorant, one wall covered in movie posters, the other completely bare, save for a few photos of what I assume is Hale's family. Hale sits on his bed as Blake meticulously reads the instructions for the board. I draw my legs to my chest and question every decision that led me to this point.

"Okay," Blake says, finally putting the booklet down. "I think we're good to go."

"So tell me, Blake," I say. "Why does the drama department have a Ouija board?"

Blake says nothing and takes the board and planchette out of its box. I've seen several horror movies make use of the board, but I've never seen one in person until this moment. My mind tells me that I should be afraid. That I should feel some sort of intuitive spookiness by looking at it, but I don't. All I feel is a deep seated question about what the fuck I'm doing and why I chose to go to the room of two boys I barely know.

"Do you guys know how to play?" Blake asks.

I shrug. "I guess. I've seen enough movies."

Blake narrows his eyes, then stands. "Well, forget those. We're not summoning demons or some shit like that."

He walks to his dresser and opens a drawer. Hale raises his eyebrows as Blake digs through what I can only assume is a bunch of junk from the clamouring noises. Finally, he turns triumphantly, candles in hand.

"Where did you get candles from?" Hale asks.

"You didn't bring candles with you?" Blake asks, shocked. "What are you going to do if the power goes out?"

Hale laughs. "Use yours."

Blake scoffs, then walks to the window. He pulls on the shade, our only dwindling source of light at 4 p.m., then hesitates. He grins mischievously. "It's not too late to back out."

Neither Hale nor I speak. Blake pulls the shade down and plunges the room into darkness. A tiny bit of light seeps in under the door.

I hear Blake stumbling back to his spot as my eyes adjust to darkness. He produces a lighter from somewhere on his body and lights one of the five tea lights, then another until they're all lit. He places them along the top of the board, illuminating the letters. The sun and moon etchings on the top corners take on an otherworldly glow in the flickering light.

"So, two of us are going to use the board and one of us is going to write down what it says. Hale, you should be our recorder." Blake hands Hale a piece of paper and a pen. "It works better if a dude and chick touch the planchette."

I reach forward to touch the pointed piece of wood and Blake stops me.

"Not yet," he says. "Just want to make sure you're both cool with this." We nod. Blake grins. "Okay, Maryl, you can put your hands on the planchette. Two fingers from each hand." I do and he does the same. "Now, we move it around in a circle twice." I press my fingers against the wood and follow his lead. "Great. I'll ask the questions tonight."

"Blake, don't do anything stu—" Hale starts.

Blake snaps to attention. "I'm not doing anything. I know more than both of you about this. Let me do the work."

Hale nods. I breathe out. Goosebumps form on my arms and I want to rub them away, but I realize with a disappointed jerk that I'm too afraid to remove my hands from the planchette. Blake returns to the board.

"We ask for the spirit of Penelope of Shirreff Hall to come and join us tonight."

What the hell am I doing here? With a prop from a play. With full knowledge that it probably won't work. Blake sighs, then closes his eyes. I don't know what he's doing. He looks almost peaceful, meditative.

"Penelope," Blake says. "I apologize for calling on you so abruptly, but we really would love to talk to you. Please, show us a sign."

I jump as the wooden block moves underneath my fingers. I go to lift them, but Blake shoots me a sharp glare. The planchette moves to *Hello.* The rational part of my brain knows that Blake moved it. There's no real other option. But the rational part of my brain has also, kind of, accepted that ghosts exist.

Blake grins. "Hello, Penelope."

"How do you know it's Penelope?" Hale asks.

Blake gasps. If his hands weren't on the planchette, I could see him dramatically clutching his chest. I know the question I want to ask would be more insulting.

How do you know this is even real?

"Stop your doubting!" he says.

"Then carry on," I say.

Blake clears his throat and flips a blond curl out of his eyes, "Penelope, is it true you died in Shirreff Hall?"

A cold hand touches my neck and a chill shoots through my body. But I don't jump, I don't make a sound, because no one is behind me and I'm not admitting that I've been swept up in this. I'm not admitting it, even as the planchette edges its way away from *Hello* and over to *Yes*.

Blake clears his throat. "Thank you, Penelope."

For a split second, I can picture her sitting right next to me. Her hands reach toward the board, a bemused smile playing on her face. For the first time, I notice a red, angry bruise around her wrist, hiding beneath a scrunchie. But as fast as I see her, she's gone.

"Penelope," Blake says, and this time I startle. Hale's eyes narrow. "Is it true that you killed yourself?"

"Blake!" Hale hisses.

"We need to know." Blake inhales deeply, then exhales dramatically. "Did you commit suicide in Shirreff Hall?"

My hands grow cold as the planchette moves. I close my eyes momentarily, but still somehow know where it landed.

"No?" Blake questions. "Was it somewhere else on campus?"

I open my eyes. The planchette circles *No* once more. Blake makes a puzzled noise, then clicks his tongue.

"Were you murdered?"

The planchette moves along the board, stopping at certain letters, moving too quick for my buzzing mind to figure out.

"Maybe," Hale whispers, after it returns to *Hello*.

"You don't know if you were murdered?" Blake asks.

The planchette doesn't move, but confusion envelopes me at the same moment as invisible hands encircle me. I gasp as a hanging body fills my field of vision, accompanied by the sound of running footfalls reverberating through an empty hall.

"Maryl?" Hale asks.

I snap my eyes open. "Yeah?"

"Are you okay? You seem kind of spaced."

"I'm fine."

Blake smirks, but doesn't comment. Instead, he asks, "Do you haunt Shirreff Hall?"

The planchette zips across the board to *Yes*, then returns to *Hello*. I no longer want to do this, but I don't know how to get out of it. Something feels wrong.

"Do you have a message for us?"

Once more, cold shoots through my body, from my head to toes. A sharper, starker cold than I've ever felt during a harsh winter. My soul feels chilled. And I can't say I've ever thought too long and hard about my soul or whether that concept actually exists. But today, in Blake and

Hale's dorm room in Old Eddy of Shirreff Hall, I feel cold right down to my soul. I don't even realize the planchette moves. Or that it stops. The only knowledge I have of that is the frantic scratching of Hale's pen and the full sense of tugging on my arms. Other than that, all my senses are encompassed by cold. Frozen solid, dead, immovable, hearing those echoes of someone running away and a ringing cry of a young child.

"Whoa," Blake says.

I take a breath as though I'm resurfacing from water and glance down at the board. The planchette now rests on *Goodbye*.

"Fuck," Hale says. His eyes are wide. He rushes to the window and opens the dorm provided curtains, then flips on his bedside lamp. "That was..."

"What'd it say?" Blake asks. "I caught some of it, but I wasn't sure..." His eyes slide over to me.

"I think I got everything," Hale says. "Jade. Blessing. Moth. Eyes. Old. Name. Picture. Get out, Maryl. Get out. Mistake. Stop now. Get out. Maryl."

I back away from the two boys in the room. Nausea settles deep in my stomach. Hale thrusts the note paper over to me. I reluctantly take it, then slowly stand. They both look at me with wide, unfiltered gazes. Eyes tinged with confusion and rimmed with fear. Their stunned looks convince me that this wasn't a joke. Blake may be an actor, but you can't fake the white hot swallow of fear.

I grab my backpack and slam their door shut behind me.

Chapter Eight

The paper Hale gave me falls to the floor beside my bed the second I climb into it. The words are nonsense, mostly, but also a warning. I don't know if the boys are playing a trick on me. I'd like to believe it is all fake, but they both seemed too bewildered to have done it.

I run my hands over my face and sit up. Darkness has clawed its way into the room. I grab my glasses off the bedside table and glare at Lottie's alarm clock. 8:26 p.m. *Where is she?* I debate calling her, but the door opens before I make the decision. Lottie steps through, hip nudging the door, sun-kissed hand reaching out to the light switch. I flinch as the lights turn on. She jumps at the sight of me.

"Jesus, Maryl!" she says. "What are you doing in the dark?"

I stare at her. I don't have a good answer to that.

"Are you okay? Are you sick?" She unwinds her fluffy white scarf, plucks off her red knitted Canada hat, shrugs out of her beige Sherpa coat, and drops her messenger bag to the floor. Concern creates lines on her forehead. "What's up?"

"You're going to think I'm insane."

She laughs. "I already think you're insane. What else is new?"

"The fact that I very well may be," I answer honestly.

I sit up and dangle my legs over the side of the bed. Lottie plops down next to me.

"What'd you do?" she asks. "Is this about Lewis? I told you to stop texting him."

I flush. He'd slipped me his number as I left class on Monday. I'd taken the bait and texted. What's a little harmless flirting?

"It's not about him. And I am still texting him. I'm not going hook up with him again or anything, but he's cute and he seems to like me, so even if he's a pretentious little shit, I'm okay with texting..." I explain. Lottie raises her eyebrows, a hint of judgement lining her lips. "But that's beside the point."

"Okay, it's not about him. What is it then?"

"The ghost."

"The ghost?" she holds back a laugh.

I groan and flop back on the mattress. "You cannot laugh at ghosts and religiously believe in horoscopes!"

"I'm sorry! I've never seen one!" I stare straight ahead. She sighs. "Okay. I'm sorry. What about her?"

"I'm sorry too." She waits for me to continue. Finally, I sigh. "Remember Hale?"

"I can honestly say I have no idea who that is."

"That guy who sat next to me in Creative Writing." I wait for her to nod. "We were talking about the ghost and he seemed really interested, so me, him, and his roommate used a Ouija board to contact her."

"That's like the start of a horror movie," she says. I bite my lip. I almost feel like it is. "It's not like a horror movie, is it?"

I shrug. "That's what it said."

I gesture at the piece of paper on the floor and she picks it up. Lottie's face drains of colour. I wouldn't have believed such a drastic change if I hadn't seen it myself. I push myself up and stare at her.

"You don't... Do you believe it?" I ask.

"Oh my God," she says.

Her hands find the oval gemstone necklace hanging loosely against her sternum. Her eyes meet mine for the briefest of seconds, then close.

"What?" I whisper. "What is it? What does it mean?"

Lottie reaches up and undoes the clasp on her necklace. She pools it in her hand, then sighs, running her thumb along something on the back. I crane my neck to see it, but she closes her fingers over it.

"When I was adopted, my parents were given one thing that belonged to my mother. When I turned ten and became interested in where I came from, they gave it to me." She opens her hand. "And I've worn it every day since because at least it's something, you know?"

I nod. She extends her hand and allows me to look at the necklace. I take it from her and stare at the pastel green teardrop stone. I've seen it on her neck every day since moving in, but never up close. On the back, set in gold, is an inscription that reads *Blessing* and below that, an engraved moth.

"Is this jade?" I ask. Lottie nods. "What does this mean?"

"I don't know. I've never seen those words strung together so... so... intentionally. Jade, blessing, moth. You can say one or two, and maybe I wouldn't make the connection, but all three?"

"The moth really sells it," I say, running my finger over the engraving.

"I don't... What *does* this mean? What do I have to do with this?"

I shake my head. "You've never met the guys before, right? It can't be some stupid prank?"

"No, and I never take this necklace off anyway. Only when I sleep. I don't think Gray even knows there's something on the back."

Lottie picks at her nail polish. Part of me wishes I'd never shown her the piece of paper. Part of me wishes I'd never run into Hale today. But then there's the part of me becoming more and more invested in this mystery. She stares at the necklace in my hands and I pass it back to her. We briefly lock eyes and I connect another part of the message. Eyes. I'd never seen anything like them before Lottie was my roommate, and then I met Penny. Seafoam green irises, with deep, dark blue ringing the outer edges—like the ocean before a storm.

"Your eyes," I say, weakly. "The girl I've seen... I can show you her picture. It's outside the pool. Your eyes are exactly the same."

"You're joking, right?"

"I wish. I don't get it. Your eyes are so unique. They're the first thing I noticed about you and the first I noticed about her." I bite my lip and hesitate. She looks freaked out enough, but also curious. A classic Lottie the Journalist look. "What do you know about your family?"

Lottie sighs, dramatically, but not intentionally dramatic. "I know some things. It's incredibly challenging. My adoption was closed, so all of my records are sealed. I can't ask for them, even though I'm of age and want them. They're private. I struggled with that for a while. I thought that meant my parents wouldn't want to know me even if I wanted to know them."

"Lottie."

She holds up a hand. "I know. I've done a lot of growing since I was fifteen. I had to realize it wasn't about me. There's a story somewhere about why they gave me up, I just don't have it yet. I've dug through archives. I've talked with genealogists. I've done Ancestry DNA in case someone related to me did theirs too, but I only have dead ends. Every time I think I have something, it goes dry. If anyone's prepared to be a journalist, it's me. I'm not giving up on this."

"What do you know?"

"For certain? What my parents have told me. I was born in December 2000 and given up for adoption in May 2001 when I was five months old. There was a period of time when I lived with my birth family. I had a brother. I don't know what happened with him. I don't know if he was also adopted five months later."

"But this. The ghost?"

"I haven't considered the fact that my birth mother might be dead."

"I'm sorry."

"Don't be," Lottie says and pins me down with those eyes. "It's a new lane to explore. And maybe... Maybe it does have something to do with here. With her." I nod. "Show me the swimming photo."

Chapter Nine

I SLIDE DOWN THE chilly wall and pull my legs to my chest, my normal study pose. In the three days I've religiously returned to Penny's domain, I've seen no ghost. I still haven't started my story for class and I'm running out of time. Every other assignment I have? Yeah, they're all done. I'm the best student in every class that doesn't have a pressing deadline. But how do you even write a story? I feel like SpongeBob meticulously doodling out the word *The* for over an hour, looking busy, but making absolutely no progress.

I need guidance, but Denver Keyes refuses to give any. All of his guidance comes from in class exercises meant to teach us the basics and get us inspired. Lewis offered to help me, but a) I feel like that's cheating and b) I feel like his offer was a thinly veiled booty call. Even so, I've been texting him, asking for tips.

I glance down at my phone and find his name on the screen.

Lewis

You just have to let it all flow out of you!

Helpful. I exhale and stare at the white beam above me. A shiver violently shoots through me.

"I thought I told you to stop talking to him," Penny says.

I startle and rub at the goosebumps on my arms. Penny seats herself next to me, grinning in satisfaction.

"Where have you been the past few days?" I hiss.

"Listen," she says. "You'll know nothing of this until you kick the bucket, but it takes a ton of energy to do the whole board thing and come out with a coherent message."

"Coherent?"

"Okay, I tried."

I look her over, noticing how similar she and Lottie are and wonder how I never saw that before. Their hair is almost the same shade and falls in the same waves. They're both petite. They both have the same straight, bright white teeth and the same sun-kissed tan. And then, those eyes. They even have the same mannerisms.

"Where'd you get that?" I ask Penny, gesturing to her right arm. Red welts line the skin of her wrist. I'd seen it during the session. I can't believe it took this long to notice.

"Where I got everything else," she says and shrugs. "It's from the night I died."

I drop her gaze as I ask the next question, "Will you tell me about it?"

Penny laughs lightly. "I guess I don't have much of a choice at this point, right?"

"You always have a choice."

"That's a nice thing to say, but sometimes you don't." She smiles sadly. "It's okay, though. I'm not blaming you. I've just never told anyone before. How can I?"

I sit on this. How can she? How can she even be telling me now?

"Stop fretting about it. If you want to know how I died, I have to start years earlier. I can't say for certain, but I think it's linked." I nod. She continues. "When I was nineteen, I started dating one of my professors. You already know this part. He was twenty-eight and new here. Just finished his PhD, totally fresh and doe-eyed, but so handsome and so intelligent. The university tried so hard to snag him. He was this young guy who already had his life together. Already had several publications under his belt, already won a few writing awards... He was a catch in more ways than one."

I flip a page of my notebook and scowl. Uh oh.

"We met before classes started. A bar off campus. It was the start of my second year. I was there with some friends and called him over because he looked cute and lonely. And it went from there. It didn't matter that a few days later I found out he was my professor. We discussed it and I decided to drop the course since it wasn't my major. No conflict that way.

"We stayed together for almost a year and then I got pregnant. It was at the end of that school year. I was twenty and terrified. My best friend, Elle, convinced me that I shouldn't tell him. No one but her and another friend knew I was dating him. In hindsight, it was stupid. I should have said something, both to him and to others about the relationship. But

I went back home, told my parents I was pregnant, and I had the baby. I never finished my degree. I figured it was better to provide for my son than to go back and face what I'd done." She draws her features up into a cringe. "Stupid, I know."

I shrug.

Penny takes a deep breath, then continues. "I came back a few years later. Well, five years later. It was after I had my second child, a girl this time. I brought my son with me so he could meet his dad. It was an extremely bold move. I mean, to spring a child on someone? I don't know what I was thinking."

"What happened?" I ask when she goes quiet.

"I died instead," she whispers. "I told him about Sam. He was shocked, but seemed almost happy, you know? That's what I thought. We hadn't seen each other since I left. So it was a shock to see me and then a shock to meet this kid. But I also told him I was moving. I guess that sort of soured things. I can see that now. Like, here's your kid! But I'm moving away! What was I thinking?"

"Whatever you were thinking and whatever you did wasn't a reason to kill you."

"I know. I thought I left on good terms. I said I'd keep in touch, then I left. I came up here because I used to live here. I wanted to say goodbye one last time. The next thing I knew, someone wrenched my wrist behind my back, grabbed my scarf, and pulled. Then I was here, forever."

I exhale. "You have no idea who did it."

Penny shakes her head and wipes a tear from her eye. "I don't have any proof because I didn't see it, no. Sometimes I wonder... It's horrible, but sometimes I wonder if my son remembers. He had just turned five. He could have seen something or someone. I don't know if they did something to him too."

"I'm sure they didn't," I say, then pause. "Who do you think they are?"

"There's only one person who knew I was here."

"The professor."

"Not to sound like a game of Clue, but yes, the professor."

"But he loved you, didn't he?"

Her breath comes out in a shudder. Or is it really breathing when you're dead?

"I thought so. I loved him, too. I had a funny way of showing it, but I did. I did a really stupid thing. People kill for less than that."

"Why would he kill you after you came back?"

"I don't know how the mind of a murderer works, Maryl."

Silence fills the hallway as I digest everything she's told me. The affair. The pregnancy. The babies. The professor. The death.

"Who was he?"

She looks at me like I must already know, then sighs.

"Denver Keyes."

Chapter Ten

Denver Keyes stands at the podium in front of the lecture hall. He's finished his lecture and today's assigned exercise—an overheard story. My Word doc has a total of one hundred words, much less than other students who spoke up and volunteered to read their story. I'm a slow writer and I damn well know it.

"Thank you all for being vulnerable and reading your stories! That was a wonderful and productive class today," Denver grins and I can see how easy it would be to fall in love with him. He enchants the room with that smile. "Now, we've come to the end of class and I have a treat for all of you! Your first stories are graded. Lewis and I worked hard on them over the weekend. There are some very, very talented authors in this room."

Lewis wanders away from his seat and writes groups of letters on the chalkboard, then places assignments under each one. A-C, D-F, G-I...

"Lewis is setting the stories in alphabetical groups. Find the group with the first letter of your last name. Your assignment will be somewhere in that stack. Have a good day, everyone, and as always, my office door is open if you need to talk about anything or have questions about the assignment."

Everyone around me gets up, but I stay in my seat. I'm in no rush to leave, nor do I have anywhere to go.

"You coming?" Hale asks.

He sat beside me today even though I moved to a different spot, so I guess he's my buddy now, especially considering Blake dropped the class.

I crinkle my nose. "To go where? I'd rather wait for the crowd to pass than be jostled through it."

Hale hikes his orthotic backpack up on his shoulder, but hesitates. He scans the approximately three hundred people huddling around the front of the class and crowding the aisles. He sits down again.

"Yeah, okay," he says. He drums his fingers on the table, then meets my eyes. I can hardly tell the difference between his pupils and irises. "Hey, I wanted to apologize."

"For what?"

"For Blake," he explains. "He's forceful and thinks he knows everything. And I know we did the Ouija board thing almost two weeks ago now, but I still wanted to say I'm sorry for it. I kept thinking about it last class. Don't know why I didn't say anything, but, yeah, I'm sorry."

"You have nothing to be sorry for," I say, shaking my head back and forth, feeling my tiny ponytail against my neck. "It was just a game."

"Yeah, but I think we freaked you out and that was mean."

"What? You made it say that?"

He pauses. "Well, no... But... No."

I laugh. "Okay, thanks."

"I wanted to make sure that we're good," he says and before I can answer, "Hey, isn't that your friend?"

Lottie grabs her assignment from the first group of papers. I read it and thought it was such a beautiful love story. So much better than what I wrote which came in about five hundred words under the limit because I am extremely well-written.

"Yeah, that's her. Why?"

"Weird she doesn't sit with you," he says.

"I don't sit with her." I snicker, then stand. The crowd thins around us. "I don't like her friends."

Hale stands and files in after me. "So long as she's not being mean to you."

"I can handle myself," I say.

I glance behind me and see him smirking, so I raise an eyebrow. He grins. Not many people remain at the front of the classroom. A few grab their stories and go, a few more hang around to talk to Denver or Lewis, and a few loiter in the room, talking to friends. Hale heads to the left of the classroom where the *A–C* section lies and I hold true to the middle for *J–L*. Three assignments are left in the stack and mine lies on top with a big, fat, red D.

"What?" I whisper.

I look over my shoulder and see only one student talking to Denver. Okay, maybe I was being a little bit bold writing about a professor falling in love with and killing his student, but isn't that the whole point of a story? Isn't there a disclaimer at the front of books that says no one is actually real here? How is it my fault if he saw himself in some creep?

Hale comes up beside me and I smile, but hold up a finger.

"You want me to wait for you?" he asks. The room grows emptier, leaving me there with two men I don't entirely trust, plus Hale.

"That'd be great," I say.

My heeled riding boots make uncertain clicks as I walk toward Professor Keyes. It reminds me of those footsteps I swore I heard while using the Ouija board. He shoots me that enchanting smile once I stand in front of him.

"Um, I had a question about my assignment," I say.

He holds out his hand and takes my assignment. His eyes skim over my name, the red marks, then land on my face.

"Ah," he says. "Miss Laine."

"Professor Keyes."

"Denver," he says with an unmistakable edge. He runs his fingers along his greying beard. "What's the question?"

"Why?" I say, before realizing that's not at all specific. Creases form at the edges of his eyes. "I mean, why is this so low? I didn't think it was that bad."

Denver leans against the blackboard. "Well, to be frank, I thought it was unrealistic and more work could have been put into the writing."

"You thought it was unrealistic? *You* did?"

His brows draw together and arms cross. "Yes, *I* did. I can't say that I know any professors who, as you say," he says, pointing at a specific spot on my paper, "are out to ruin their students."

I mimic his pose, arms crossing over my chest. "You said we could write about anything. I never said it was real, I just wrote."

"So you did." He hands the assignment back to me and begins tiding up. "It didn't work. If you'd like to visit me during office hours, I can explain what needs work and how we can fix those issues."

"I'd really rather not be alone with you," I say, then freeze.

I spoke before my brain thought it through. His hands pause on the groups of papers he's reaching for. He stares at me. All his enchantment has disappeared and I can see fire in him.

"What was that, Miss Laine?"

"I'm not sure I want to be alone with someone who doesn't have the best track record around female students."

"What did you say?" his voice is barely above a whisper, his body rigid.

I stand there and debate how far I want to dig this hole, but since I'm already in it...

"I know what happened the last time and how her life ended. Walls talk, you know."

His face falls. "I'd advise you not to believe every rumour you hear, Miss Laine." His voice comes out clipped and strained. A muscle ticks in his neck. "Those are some dangerous accusations you're making and I would hope you have something other than walls talking to back yourself up. I would also advise you drop this class if you intend to pass your first year. Now, get out of my classroom."

I stumble backward, knowing I've pushed too far in my own haze of stupidity and hurt feelings over a grade on a story that clearly touched a nerve, when I was intending to do exactly that. So basically, I brought this on myself. I watch Denver gather the rest of the papers, shove them into his briefcase, and stalk out of the lecture hall. I breathe.

"Hey!" a man's voice says. I jump. "What the hell was that about?"

I pivot slowly on my heel and find Lewis leaning against a table in the front row, brows drawn together in confusion. I take a breath and then another, as if I can't get enough oxygen into my lungs. Because I can't. The edges of panic settle over me, a feeling I'm not accustomed to, but I know how badly I've fucked up.

"Nothing," I say. "Just a bad grade."

He nods. "You know, I can try and get your assignments from now on if you'd like. It's unfair of him to say he's going to fail you."

"I'm good, thanks," I say and shake my head.

I realize how bad I've miscalculated my decisions in this moment. I've accused Denver of being in a relationship with a student (and also maybe killing her), while standing in front of a man who is definitely involved with a student (me).

"You sure? I'd never give you a D." A smirk. "Well, not in grade form, anyway."

I cringe. "I'm fine getting marks on my own, thanks."

I watch as Lewis reacts to my rejection. His head slips slowly back, straightens from his casual lean, and his mouth drops open. He closes his eyes and shakes his head, then turns back to his own things.

"I was just being nice," he says. "No need to be a bitch about it."

I don't give him the vindication of a response. I walk out, letting him hear my shoes click bitchily in my wake. Hale waits in the hallway. He opens his mouth to say something. I keep walking, my head held high. Eventually, Hale falls into step with me and I realize that's a good thing because the next stage in my dramatic exit is yelling and screaming. And yes, once I get somewhere I can do it, it's going to be at Hale.

Chapter Eleven

As it turns out, screaming is not the choice I make.

I stalk through the thinning halls of the Life Sciences building, wracking my brain for somewhere close and private I could go and yell about the dumbass mess I've gotten myself into. I step out onto the slushy walkways of campus. The cold air hits my face and even though I'm prepared for it, I'm still shocked at how frigid the wind can be. I zip up my coat and run my hands along the puffy red material until I find the pockets, then shove them in deep.

The Wallace McCain Learning Commons sticks out like a sore thumb smashed in between all the old, stone buildings. I could complain to my heart's content in a study room, but I run the risk of being overheard by everyone and I'm not quite ready for that yet. I change course and decide Shirreff is probably the best option.

Hale trails behind me as I stomp my way across campus. He jogs to keep up, eventually grasping my shoulder and whirling me to face him.

"What was that?" Hale asks. "What's going on? Are you okay?"

There's part of me that wants to tear his hand away and take my self-inflicted anger out on him, but that part melts away when I meet his eyes and see genuine concern in them. I swallow what's left of the anger and close my eyes. Wind whips at my cheeks and I wince.

"Sorry about that," I open my eyes and finally say to Hale.

He takes a moment to respond and I realize that I didn't actually answer his question. "Don't worry about it. We've both apologized, so now we're even."

"So it seems."

"What was that, though?" He runs a hand through his hair, further messing up his unruly curls.

I shrug and continue walking. "I got a bad mark."

Hale laughs. "You must be a real perfectionist, then. But that really seemed like more than bad mark talk."

"Yeah," I say and pull on the door to Shirreff. "You're right, it was."

We track snow in through the entryway, then trudge up the stairs. He doesn't say anything, just follows. I glance at him and see he's biting his lip, almost as if he's hesitating on his next words. I don't prompt. I pause outside my dorm room. Lottie affixed a white board to the door and wrote our names in loopy script. Other girls in our wing have done the same. Sometimes I erase our real names and replace them with obviously fake ones. Today, I erase them with the sleeve of my sweater and pluck a dry erase marker from the side pocket of my bag. I replace our names with *Ghost Hunter* and *Astrologer*. I draw a little ghost beside the first and stars beside the second.

Hale raises his eyebrows as I open the door and invite him in.

"What was it then?" he asks.

Lottie looks up from her cross-legged position on her bed. I can't tell what she's reading, but I know it's a book for one of her many English classes. Her eyes sweep across me, to Hale. We have a rule that no sex happens in our dorm. I know she's gauging whether or not to subtly remind me of this.

"Hey, Lottie," I say. Hale startles and looks to me for guidance. I notice her assignment resting on the end of her bed. "How'd you do on the assignment?"

She smiles politely. Lottie is all kindness and rainbows for new people. "I did well," she says, which means she did more than well and probably got a fabulous mark. "How about you?"

I wave Hale further into the room and he closes the door behind me. Might as well kill two birds with one stone and update both of them. I hang my coat up in our tiny, overflowing closet and kick off my boots. Hale hesitates once more.

"You can come in," I say. I gesture to my uncomfortable, school-provided desk chair. "Sit, stay a while."

Hale obeys, shrugging out of his coat and sitting down. I plop down on my bed and fold my legs underneath myself.

"I did something stupid," I say. "Want to hear about it?"

Lottie closes her book. Ironically, *Lolita*. "Always!"

"So, I basically accused our professor of murdering Penny."

Lottie gasps. "You're joking!"

"I am very stupidly telling the truth. You read my story. You knew I was poking the bear. He failed me and I had the audacity to ask why even though I knew why. He told me the story was unrealistic."

"Wait," Lottie says. "How do you know she had an affair with him?"

"The ghost? It's Keyes that she was fucking?" Hale asks.

I close my eyes and take a breath. "She told me."

Lottie had come around a tiny bit more on the idea of ghosts after seeing the picture of Penny. It bothered her so much that she hadn't looked Penny up further. I thought research would be a good idea, especially if Lottie was related to her, but I respected her wishes.

"When did she tell you?" Lottie asks at the same time as Hale chimes in.

"You're talking to ghosts?"

I hold up a hand. "Last week. It was the last time I was up there. She told me and it freaked me out enough that I had to sit back and digest for a bit. Then I wrote that stupid story... And, yes. Just her, but... Yeah... Ghosts."

"Cool," Hale says. "Can you introduce me?" He smirks, but part of me knows he genuinely thinks it's cool.

"Okay, so she said he was the one she had a relationship with... Is he the one who killed her? Did she say that?" Lottie asks.

"She thinks he may have because he's the only one who knew she was here, but she was attacked from behind so she really has no idea."

We all stay silent for a moment. My face grows hot. They may or may not think I'm full of crap. I have nothing to verify this, no evidence of what I've seen and heard. It kills the scientist in me to say these things without any proof. But apparently the scientist in me went on vacation the second I decided to write a story based on the word of someone no one else can see.

"Have you looked into this?" Hale asks. "I mean, I have no idea how you would, but I'm sure there's a record of her death or her life or something."

My eyes slide over to Lottie. I understand her hesitation in moving forward. It's such a huge part of her life to end this way. Lottie meets my eyes for a moment, before staring down at her constellation comforter.

"Uh," I say. "Yeah, we haven't gotten to that step yet."

"Why not? Let's do it! Let's figure this out!"

Lottie touches the jade stone around her neck. I swallow and smile at Hale. "I'm sure we will eventually." I pointedly look at the clock. "I have a biology test tomorrow. I should probably start studying. Thanks for the help today."

I stand as Hale does. He bundles his coat and backpack into his hands and walks toward the exit. I open the door for him and step into the hallway.

"Seriously, thanks for being there."

He waves me off. "Is your roommate okay? Does she not believe you or something? She got pretty uncomfortable and, I don't know, kind of shady."

"No, she's fine," I say, clipped. "I'll let you know what we find."

Hale nods, then walks away. I wait until he turns into the stairwell to close the door.

"You okay?" I ask Lottie.

Her eyes are closed now, hands still clutching the necklace. She shakes her head. "I could say yes, but that would be a lie. I didn't expect to feel this way about what you've been seeing. I'm kind of ashamed because I promised myself years ago that I would be okay with whatever I found. And now I'm not."

I stride across the room and sit on the end of her bed. I reach out and grip her knee. She glances up at me, green eyes shining with tears.

"You don't have to be okay with this. We don't even know if this *is* actually happening."

"She looks like me, Maryl," she says. "I've never seen anyone that looks so much like me. You know I'm always on the lookout and this is the first person I've found that could actually be a genuine link and they're not even living."

"It's okay," I say. "But you can't dwell on it without even knowing if it's true."

"How would I find out?" she asks. Then she laughs, embarrassed. "What if I don't even want to find out?"

"You don't?"

Lottie shrugs. "If she's dead and she was my mother, then that's it. I have nowhere to go from there. My parents were told that they had no paternal info. They don't know who my father is. All these years I've been looking for a woman and if that woman's dead, then that's it. I have no way of knowing anything else."

"There must be some way," I whisper.

"I don't know. I might feel able to look into it someday, but it's not today."

Chapter Twelve

AGAINST MY BETTER JUDGEMENT, I go to see Penelope the next day. I'd avoided her for Lottie's sake, and also because the thing about Denver really freaked me out. Not enough to stay quiet about it, but still.

I don't pretend to study this time. I couldn't sleep, so I dragged myself here at 3:14 a.m., the witching hour. Campus is silent, dim, and not at all as vibrant as usual. Wisps of snow blow in the yellow streetlight of the courtyard outside Shirreff Hall. This is supposed to be the last storm for the next few weeks. It'll be gross, greyish slush by morning, but I get to catch the brief moment of peace and purity as the flurries fall. I stop my pacing and stare out the window.

It takes a minute for me to realize that I'm not alone. I see a flash of blue in my peripheral vision. Penny stands beside me, also watching the snow. She drifts closer to the window, nose almost touching the glass.

"I can't fall through, if that's what you're wondering." She smiles. "Ghostly misconception."

"You can't travel through walls?" I ask.

"I have a hard time travelling anywhere," she replies. "This is basically my home."

"Really?" I ask. "So you're stuck here?"

She shrugs. "Not stuck, no," she says and finally turns to face me. Her brows are drawn together and she hesitates, as if not sure how to explain ghost physics to me. "Just mostly stuck. I can go other places, but it takes a lot of energy. This is basically my home, but Shirreff is pretty easy to travel around. If I want to go any further than that, though... Now, that's a problem."

"So you could come to my dorm to chat if you wanted."

"If I wanted to, sure. It's easiest for me to be me here. If I go elsewhere I'm just a voice or touch."

I nod, though I'm not sure I understand why or what rules stop her from doing these things. I slide down the wall once more and sit on the cold floor. I should start bringing a chair with me.

"So it's late, Maryl," she says and slides like I did. "What are you doing here?"

"I had no plan to come up here," I start.

"Clearly," she snorts. "You've been avoiding me."

"I've been uncomfortable, I guess. So yes, I have been, but it's not because of you."

Her eyes narrow and she studies me. I try to imagine what I might look like to her. My hair stands up on end, doing its little flippy thing when it's that awkward length between fresh cut and three months of grow out. My eyes are smudged with makeup I hadn't bothered to take off because I hadn't bothered to change out of the leggings and T-shirt I'd been wearing all day.

"You gonna expand on that?"

"You said you had two kids?" I ask, unwilling to come out with all my theories, knowing they're pretty jumbled.

"Yes, why?"

I hesitate. I have to know, but at the same time I'm pretty sure I'm breaking Lottie's trust, somehow, by even asking. If she doesn't want to know, then why should I dig? But I know there's more than Lottie's involvement in this that's bugging me. It's my own.

"You said you had a girl?"

"My oldest is a boy and youngest is a girl."

"How old would they be now?"

She clucks her tongue. "It's 2019, right?" I nod. "Then he would be almost twenty-three and she would be eighteen. He's my Valentine boy and she's my Christmas girl."

"She was born on Christmas?"

"Just before." Lottie's birthday is December 20th. "But why do you want to know about my children?"

I take an unintentionally shuddery breath. "I think I know one of them. And if I do know one of them, then I have some questions."

She smiles and closes her eyes. Waves of joy radiate off of her, then suddenly dissipate into a deep sort of sadness. Her shoulders shake in a silent sob.

"It's torture to be here and not know," her voice is barely above a whisper. "I've thought about them for years."

"What's your daughter's name?" I ask.

"Charlotte. After my great grandma. We used her old nickname too." Another wistful smile. "Lottie."

I don't gasp. I don't make a sound or turn my hand. I don't want to draw conclusions or make my conclusion *the* conclusion, but I know that this being a coincidence is a slim margin.

"My roommate's name is Lottie," I say. "She was adopted when she was five months old. She doesn't know her birth parents and they have no information on her father. I'm not one to jump to things, but..."

"But that would be quite a huge coincidence. I've seen her, I think," Penny says, those eyes wide and bright. "She's met you here a few times. Blonde hair, kind of artsy?"

"That's her."

I grab my phone and navigate over to the photos app. I swipe through until I find the last picture I took with Lottie, after my win at the University of New Brunswick swim meet this past weekend. I'm slimy and flushed from the pool and Lottie is radiant; waves of hair fluffed around her face, cat eye applied perfectly, emerald green sweater complementing her ocean eyes. I turn the phone for Penny.

"Oh."

She reaches toward my phone screen, longing to touch Lottie's perfect face, but she pauses before her fingers make contact. Her face floods with unabashed emotion. Tears fill her eyes and tiny cries escape her lips.

"That's her," she whispers. "That has to be her. She looks a lot like my mom."

I stay silent for a moment, getting my thoughts together and trying to respect Penny's emotional state. Ever since the whole Lottie connection began, I've had questions. I still don't get why I'm the go between when Lottie is right here.

"Penny," I say. "I'm sorry. I don't really know what to say, I'm caught in the middle here. I don't understand why this is happening."

"Why what's happening?" she asks, suddenly sharp.

"Why are you coming to me?"

Penny raises her eyebrows and giggles, almost shocked. "Look, I can't say I know how all this works because I'm not in charge of the spirit world. I can't say that a ghost has ever had to do this but, Maryl, I'm coming to you because I *can* come to you."

"What do you mean?"

"Not everyone sees me. The people with dorms just over there, they don't see or hear me when I'm around. Some people hear me walking or crying, but I'm disembodied noises sparked by rumours for them. I'm not a full-bodied apparition that people talk to. I've been here almost twenty years, and in those years, only three people have talked to me. The first two thought I was alive and we had a casual conversation. You're the only one who's seen me multiple times and kept talking."

"That doesn't make any sense."

"I thought you were like the other two when I first met you. I don't know if you remember, but you were here studying one day last semester and you noticed me because I was watching you. I said hi and you did too, then I left. I didn't talk to you again until a few weeks ago and that's when I realized what you can do."

I blink at her, unsure if what she's saying doesn't make any sense or if it's way too early and I'm way too sleepless for my brain to comprehend this. Penny stares at me earnestly. Her hands cover her mouth and her eyes grow wide.

"You truly didn't know," she whispers. "I'm sorry. I feel like that's not something you just tell people."

"What do you mean? What can I do? What are you telling me?"

She laughs again. "You tell me. You're talking to a ghost. What can you do?"

I open my mouth and nothing comes out. *I'm talking to a ghost.* I've struggled with that from the second I realized what she was. Because it doesn't make any sense and it doesn't have any basis in reality and now she's telling me that this is something I *do*? Like this is a power that I have? I run my hands over my face and settle my head in them. My breathing comes out fast and hard.

"Have you never noticed this before?" she asks. "I mean, have you never talked to anyone else before? Like, maybe you were in a graveyard and saw someone who no one else could?"

I shake my head wildly. This has never happened before. This isn't happening. This doesn't make any goddamned sense.

And then, Stephen's words come back to me. *Mamie always told me you could see dead people.* Did Mamie ever tell me? Mamie always drew me pictures. She created a mermaid illustration I want as a tattoo. She painted a portrait of me every year of my life until she died last spring, each a different colour depending on how she saw that year. The last portrait she painted was for my birthday last year. It was all in shades of green and violet. She told me violet holds spiritual power and green is all about healing and helping others. The odd thing is that her portrait predictions were always true. My years, whether influenced by this idea in my mind or otherwise affected, always followed what she set out in her colours. And now, here with Penny, violet and green doesn't seem wrong at all.

So what was Mamie really seeing? Stephen said he'd seen and felt things while around her, and I'm starting to believe he isn't crazy for thinking that.

"Something's happened before, hasn't it?" Penny asks, interrupting my wayward thoughts.

"I don't know," I admit. Because I truly don't anymore and the more I look back at my life, the more I think I may have brushed a lot off.

I remember having an imaginary friend when I was younger, but he only appeared at my grandparent's house. Mamie always asked if I was playing with Matthew. I don't remember ever telling her that that was his name. I remember going to my neighbour's funeral when I was twelve years old and seeing someone wearing a bright red dress at the memorial service. She looked so out of place that I told Stephen about it. He had no idea who I was talking about. I remember leaving my prom in tears because my high school boyfriend thought that the last dance was an appropriate time to break up with me. I thought he was the one following me when I heard footsteps after I left the banquet hall, but it was a lovely old woman making sure I was all right. She left almost too quickly when my best friend found me a moment later.

Light filters into the corridor as the sun begins to rise. I startle and notice Penny still sitting next to me. Her eyes are closed now and her breathing is relaxed, but she's still here. Rainbow prisms of light flicker on her cheek. She turns her face and gazes at me.

"Are you okay?" she asks.

"I don't know," I answer. I glance down at my phone. 7:12 a.m. "I think so. I should go, though. I didn't mean to be here all night."

"Hey," she says. "At least you've figured some things out."

I nod and head out, a little too shaken for a proper goodbye. I pause in the stairwell and pull out my phone. It's an hour earlier in Montréal, but I know Stephen will be up. This is when he exercises before work. I dial his number without another thought. He answers.

"So, you say we see dead people?" I ask.

"I didn't say *we* did. Mamie said you did. I've only ever felt things," Stephen tells me.

"How did Mamie know this about me?"

"I don't know. You'll have to ask her."

"How the hell would I do that?"

I can hear the smile in his voice as he talks. "It's a joke, kid, chill. I think she saw the same things as you do, even if you didn't realize it. It's a shame you didn't get to ask her this stuff."

I wish I did. She'd know more than Stephen does. Maybe she'd be able to calm my frazzled nerves. I'd give anything for one of her hugs right now.

"Why are you asking? What's going on?"

I start the long and winding story that led me to this moment. I tell him everything that's happened this semester, and then the fuzzy, vaguely ghostly details of the past eighteen and three quarter years of my life.

"I think you have to figure out who killed this Penny girl. If you can help her, then why not? There has to be some reason you stumbled upon her."

I know he's right. But the thought of pursuing this thing further scares the shit out of me.

Chapter Thirteen

"You did it again, didn't you?" Hale asks.

"Did what?"

He shakes his head. "Don't play me, Maryl, you know what I'm asking."

I stare straight ahead at Lewis writing those same alphabet groups on the board. Yes, I'd poked the beast again. I'm not creative minded enough to come up with a different narrative. My only other idea was psychic Maryl's horrible ghostly life discovery. And I didn't exactly want to put that on paper when I could barely even admit it to myself.

"I wrote another story. Doesn't mean I did anything," I say, not making eye contact.

Hale watches me. No, he probably didn't deserve my crabbiness, but to be fair he was the one who started it. He *did* just make an assumption instead of asking me what I wrote about. I can feel his eyes boring into the side of my face and I ignore him. Instead, I gather all of my papers and supplies and shove them into the deep pocket of my backpack. I trace the pattern on one of the humpback whales beside the zipper.

"What did you write about?" I finally turn to him.

His eyebrows raise, but he answers. “I wrote about a conversation I overheard in the washroom.”

“Oh, yeah? Juicy one?”

“I guess someone on my floor cheated on their girlfriend. She doesn’t go here but the girl he’s sleeping with does so it’s this whole thing because his girlfriend is visiting this week.”

"Yikes.” I cringe. “But update me if you find out more.”

He nods. “What’d you write about?”

“Murder.”

“So you did it again, then?”

I don’t answer him directly. The crowd of students collecting their assignments thins to an acceptable point. Hale rises with me and mutters a good luck. I bite my lip to hold back the nervous laugh that threatens to escape. The fact that I’ve done this a second time fills me with so much dread that I question why I even did it in the first place. I know what mark I’m going to get. I know I’m going to fail the class, lower my GPA, and lose part of my scholarship. Professor Keyes said so. And yet, I made the choice because Stephen is right and I have to help Penny.

I grab my paper, ready to confront Denver Keyes, ready to fight for something better. A giant red F is scrawled at the top of my paper. I turn on my heel and he’s already behind me. To anyone else, it wouldn’t look weird or draw attention, but he knows what he’s doing. His eyebrows are drawn together behind the rim of his glasses. His eyes are dark and angry. It’s a glare that sets my teeth on edge. It dares me to come and talk to him, say something about this ongoing narrative I've created. It stops all of my thoughts immediately and I walk away from him instead.

I don't have a lead. I don't have a confession. I don't have anything but the word of someone who is dead and didn't even see their killer.

I walk into Lewis.

"Whoa there, honey," he says.

And I finally laugh. Nervous energy giving way to anger. He shakes his head as if he can't understand my reaction, and quite frankly, I can't either. I'm confused and tired and know I'm in the wrong, but I want to keep fighting for the truth.

"Are you okay?" Lewis asks. He jerks his head toward Denver. "I've seen his marks for you in the system. I don't think they're fair."

"Oh, they're probably extremely fair."

He cocks his head and touches my elbow. I glance down at his hand, then around the classroom. No one's looking at us, but that could change quickly and I've realized over the last few days how much I don't want to go down this road. I may have liked his attention and flirty texts, but I can't do this. I slip out of his grasp.

"Listen," he says, lowering his voice and drawing his head close to mine, "I bet I can convince him to give you a better mark. I offered the last time and you refused. I respect that, but think about it. You don't want to fail a class in your first year. If you wanted a better mark, I could arrange that."

My eyes narrow. "Arrange what?"

"You could come to my apartment again," he says. "We could have a drink, have a little fun, talk about writing. Would you like that?"

I take a step away from him. "Excuse me?"

"You didn't seem to mind a few weeks ago." A smile. He bridges the gap. "It would be the best thing for you."

I stay frozen to my spot. I've played a dangerous game and I can see it all burning down now. I close my eyes, take a breath, then turn on him.

"Delete my number and never talk to me again if you want to keep your job," I say and run out of the lecture hall.

I don't stop running until I reach Shirreff Hall. I don't know when Hale left, but he was gone by the time I stepped foot outside the classroom. He's not here either. Barely anyone is, and I'm glad because I'm pretty sure I'm going to start crying at any moment.

"Hey!" Leah calls. "You okay?"

It takes me a moment to focus, realize where I am, who's talking to me and why. Leah stands in front of me, out of her uniform, smiling in a motherly way. She reaches a hand out to me and I don't know what to do with it at first. When she touches my elbow as Lewis did, I flinch.

"Whoa." She takes her hand away immediately. "What's going on? Walk with me?"

I nod and she guides me back through the doors. We walk around campus in silence for a few minutes. I take in the slushy banks along the sides of the walkways and kick at stray ice chunks. Patches of green grass and salty stones peek through the melting snow.

"I'm in a weird situation," I finally say.

"You know," Leah says. "I had a friend in a bit of a weird situation back when I was your age. You kind of remind me of her."

"What's she like?"

"She was feisty and confident. Really knew what she wanted most of the time and would go for it. Didn't care what other people thought. I admired those qualities in her."

"I don't know if it's good or bad that you're comparing me to her. Are you still friends?"

Leah pauses. "I think we still would be if she were alive."

"Oh," I say. "I'm sorry."

Her eyes slide over me, as if judging my reaction for her next response. She stops walking. I get a few steps ahead before noticing. I stop, turn, and meet her eyes.

"I do think you know her, though," she says.

"Penny." The name is on my lips before my brain has a chance to filter it. Leah nods. I almost laugh again, but stop myself. Leah is too serious for my hysterics. "You don't see her?"

She shrugs. "I hear her, sometimes. I hear a lot of things. But that's about where my gift ends."

"So you...?"

"I have a form of mediumship. I've always been able to hear spirits talking to me, though I can't fully manifest them. I don't tell people very often, but considering what you've been doing, I figured I should talk to you."

"Did Penny tell you?"

"She may have whispered something," Leah says with a wink. "Look, Mare, I can't tell you if you have a strong gift or if Penny appears to you so definitively because you're like minded, but I can tell you do have a gift."

"Some gift," I scoff.

"Yeah," Leah says. I can tell from the shake of her head that she's been here. "It really feels that way when you first find out. But trust me, it's not a bad thing. I've brought a lot of people peace with what I do."

"And what do you do?"

"Well, I work here. You know that part," she says. "I've also done private readings for at least fifteen years. Penny encouraged me to do it before she died. I didn't get around to it until a few years after."

"Do you and Penny still talk?"

"Sometimes."

"Then why haven't you helped her?"

"She's never asked." Leah shrugs. "I think she was waiting for someone like you to come along. I'm not inquisitive or focused enough to solve a murder. I think she trusts you."

"That's a lot of pressure to put on someone."

"It is, but I think you're up to the challenge. Aren't you?" I don't know what to say so I stay silent. "Just be careful, okay? Don't put your trust in people that aren't worthy of it."

"How do I know who is and isn't worthy?"

Leah smiles and taps her temple. "You'll figure it out soon enough. That TA of yours? Not him."

Chapter Fourteen

I TAKE STEPHEN'S ADVICE and start looking up the literature around Penny's death. My first search is simple: her name. Unfortunately, Penelope Walsh is a bit too common. I get several hundred results for Penelope or Penny Walsh social media profiles, none of which can be her unless she's running a page from beyond the grave.

In the hours between Lottie being in class and coming back to our dorm, I search. I haven't asked her if she wants me to. I haven't asked if she wants to help me either. My journalistic skills are definitely lacking in comparison to hers, but I make do.

I balance my laptop on my bent knees. I've stared at it for hours without a breakthrough. Just an old obituary. There are probably thousands of leads I can take from her obit, but I stall, overcome with such a strange sadness for someone I didn't get to know in life but I've come to know in death. I never would have met her if she'd stayed alive. My life would be virtually unchanged and the same as it had been in January. Maybe Lottie wouldn't even be my roommate if Penny had lived.

I rub at my eyes behind my glasses, then reach up to redo my bun. Penelope's obituary is still on my screen. I sigh and read it for a third time.

Penelope Charlotte Walsh

Penelope Charlotte Walsh, 26, died on Monday, April 9, 2001. A devastating loss for the family, just seven months after her mother, Christine Walsh's death. Penny was a vibrant young woman. Her resiliency and strength throughout the years were admirable. After attending school at Dalhousie University, Penny focused her energy on raising her son, Samuel, to the best of her ability. There was not one day without laughter from her son. She raised him through pure joy and art. Penny was a talented painter and teacher. Her landscapes have been featured in two gallery shows and she was the founder of a club for young artists within the Halifax community. She is survived by her father, Elliot, and two children, Samuel and Charlotte. Her spirit will live on in her paintings and philanthropy. A memorial service will be held at St. Paul's Anglican Church on Sunday, April 15, 2001, from 3–5 p.m. All are welcome to come share memories and celebrate the life of Penelope Walsh. Memorial donations may be made to CMHA Halifax.

A picture is attached at the top of the obituary. Penelope stands next to a gorgeous landscape painting of a hiking trail outside of Halifax. Her hair is long, golden, and blowing in a light wind. She grins from ear to ear, the spark in her smile reaches her eyes and literally shines. I can see why they chose this photo for her obituary—it's perfect.

On a whim, I search *"Penelope Walsh art."* One of her paintings is in the collection at a local art gallery. I have half the mind to go and check it out, but I don't know what, if anything, that'll give me. I study her paintings. Most are of landscapes, a few are more abstract. I'm no art critic, but even I can recognize the pure vibrancy and talent in her work. They're all so natural, so clean, so incredibly moving. It takes ten minutes of me switching from painting to painting, studying their lines and colour, for me to realize that they're attached to articles also related to her death.

I click on the first. It's dated April 10, 2001, the day after she died.

Tragic Death at Dalhousie University

Monday evening, a student at Dalhousie University was shocked to discover the body of Penelope Walsh, 26. Police have stated that foul play is not suspected, but a further autopsy will provide more details. Shirreff Hall, the residence where Walsh was found, has been blockaded on the fourth floor. Students are asked not to cross police tape at this time unless otherwise directed.

Penelope Walsh was a former student at Dalhousie University. It is currently unclear why Walsh was on campus. She was a talented painter and will be remembered as such. The Art Gallery of Nova Scotia recently acquired one of her pieces (pictured below). Hers is a great loss to the Halifax art community.

It's short and sweet, without detail. I click on the photo of the painting. Another landscape, this one focuses on the anchor of the Bonaventure, monumented at Point Pleasant Park. The water crashes against the rocky shore in powerful waves; the sky dark in the distance, a storm threatening to come out of the painting.

I scroll down and find another article related to this one. It was published the week after her obituary.

Postpartum Depression Cited as Cause of Death at Dalhousie University

Police have confirmed that there was no foul play involved in the death of Penelope Walsh. Walsh's body was found in Shirreff Hall at Dalhousie University. After an investigation and autopsy, her death has been ruled a suicide. Walsh was a mother of two and gave birth to her daughter five months ago. She suffered from postpartum depression after the birth of her first child and it is believed she was suffering until her death, as well. According to Statistics Canada, postpartum depression affects around 23% of Canadian mothers each year. In Nova Scotia, this number is closer to 31%. It is suggested that young mothers are more likely to feel and report poor mental health during this time period. Postpartum depression can appear within days or weeks of birth and last for months or years. Suicide is the second leading cause of death in postpartum women and is most common between nine and twelve months after birth. If you or a loved one is experiencing signs of postpartum depression, reach out to your doctor or the organizations listed below.

A chill runs through me. I scroll down further, hoping for more articles about Penny and her death, but I stop in the comments. One strikes me as odd and aggressive: *This is irresponsible journalism!! She was NOT suffering from postpartum depression. This is a bogus claim, conveniently made because she gave birth, but it is entirely unfounded. Her life could have been saved if she wasn't KILLED.* I shudder. It's anonymous. Anyone could have written it.

My phone buzzes and I jump.

Hale

BioChem test tomorrow. I have a study room. Want to study with me?

I suck in a breath. Shit. I forgot about that. I close my laptop, article on Penelope still open, and stuff it into my backpack. Lottie walks in as I'm packing up.

"Where are you going?" she asks. Her face is flushed from the cold, but another emotion obscures her features.

"I have a test tomorrow so I'm going to go study with Hale," I explain. She purses her lips. "You okay?"

She nods. "Gray's coming over."

"Oh, okay," I say and smile. "I'll leave you guys to it then. Is he staying the weekend?" Another nod. "You good?"

"Ghosts on my mind." She laughs, but half-heartedly. "I wanted to talk to him in person about my mommy issues. You're amazing, but he knows all of me so..."

"Yeah, I get it," I say. "I hope you don't mind that I've been doing some digging. I haven't found much because I don't have your skills, I just needed to know."

Her face remains impassive, but her eyes shift slightly. I can see something in them. Not quite hurt or anger. She swallows and nods, then lets me know it's all good. I pull out my phone and text Hale about meeting up.

Maryl

Text me the room and I'll be there.

He does. I grab my coat and head off to the Killam Memorial Library. It's quite possibly the ugliest building on campus with its concrete slab exterior, but the atrium at the centre of the building is gorgeous. Windows into the library surround the atrium on all four floors, complete with a skylight shining natural light throughout the open space.

I trudge up to the second floor of the library and smirk as I pass the illustrated whiteboard sign about laptop theft. It's been five days since a laptop was last stolen here. Yikes. This place is like a tornado drawn to a trailer park with how many computers have been stolen.

It doesn't take long for me to find the study room. Hale sits at a round table meant to seat six, his papers for our BioChem class spread out over the surface. He looks a little frantic, a lot unprepared. And even as I take in his mood, I know I'm not coming in to study. Maybe that makes me a bad person, but maybe I'm not in charge of what he chooses to do next.

"Hey," I say and he says it back.

I take off my coat and hang it on the back of a chair, then plop my backpack onto another. He eyes me as I do all of this. I sit down and pull out my laptop, then smile.

We talk about Penelope for the next hour.

Chapter Fifteen

I EMERGE FROM THE pool, victorious. My teammates rush toward me as I beam. It's the beginning of February and the end of swim season: The Atlantic University Sports Swimming Championship. The end of my first year as a Dalhousie Tiger and I couldn't be more proud of myself. Coach Jaffee says if we do well here, we may be invited to a "for fun" competition in Toronto next month. I've just killed the Women's 100m Breaststroke Final.

"Maryl!!" Sadie yells above the cheers in the DalPlex Aquatic Centre. "That was amazing! I think you beat a record!"

My eyes grow wide and I whip my head toward the judges who have my time. The AUS record for 100m Breaststroke is 1:09.65 and hasn't been broken since 2013. And if I break it as a rookie?! *Holy shit.*

"You're joking!" I yell.

I rip off my swimming cap and shake out my hair. There are five events after mine, so I shuffle away and join the rest of the team on the bench. Riley throws a towel at me as he stands to get ready for his event, the Men's 100m Breaststroke.

"Nice one, Maryl," he says. "Shots on me tonight."

Sadie cheers as he walks away. I can't stop smiling. Adrenaline pumps through my veins like it always does after a race. This is the high I chase every year, every season, my whole life.

"Ladies and gentlemen," the announcer says, briefly quieting the excitement in the stands. "It is with great pleasure that I announce the Women's 100m Breaststroke record has been broken. Maryl Laine from Dalhousie University swam an impressive 1:08.97!"

Thunderous cheers erupt throughout the stadium once more. I cover my face in shock as I grin so hard my cheeks hurt. Sadie holds up my left arm in victory. My teammates nudge me, slap me on the back, and roar in celebration with everyone else. Riley's booming screams echo from across the pool. Coach pulls me to my feet and propels me slightly away from the mass of swimmers.

I stand amongst the cheers, trying not to cry out of pure joy, until the announcer moves onto the next race. Sadie pulls me back down next to her, but only for a moment before she tells me to go phone my parents. This was my last race of the day and I don't swim again until Sunday, so I'm technically free to go. I wait and cheer for my team instead.

Once the event ends, Lottie sprints down from the stands and hugs me. She's dressed for a party: blousy chiffon tank tucked into leather pants, and bombshell waves. She was overly confident I was going to crush it today.

"Oh my God, Maryl!" she cries. "That was incredible. You won that race by a mile!"

"Well, not a mile." I flush.

"It may as well have been," Sadie says, dripping dry from her final race of the night. "You were so far ahead of everyone else."

I shrug, but pride swells in my chest.

"Okay," Lottie says. "Go get changed and then we'll head to the pub. I'll meet you outside the change rooms."

"Riley's going to hook us up," Sadie whispers, conspiratorially, eyebrows waggling.

Riley works at the on campus pub, conveniently located within the Student Union Building. My birthday's in a month and I'll legally be able to drink then, but for now, he'll have to sneak us a little something. He's been doing it since I joined the swim team, probably was before I even got here. The first time he did it was when I confessed I thought he was hot. And then I kissed him. Because I make the worst decisions when I'm even mildly tipsy. Riley shrugged it off, didn't push any further while I was drunk, and asked me about it later when I was sober. Lottie thought I was stupid for my "no swim team" rule after hearing me moon over Riley. Maybe it is a dumb rule, but I'm still keeping to it.

Sadie and I change into our celebration outfits. Hers is a lace body suit, dark jeans, and seasonably inappropriate open toed heels. Mine is a skintight black turtleneck, snakeskin print mini skirt, and thigh high boots. Some of the other girls around us have the same idea. Our swim meets usually end in parties if we don't have unspeakably early races the next day.

Sadie holds up two lipsticks, one that matches the deep burgundy of her hair and her signature taupe that perfectly complements her amber skin. I point to the burgundy as I apply a bright red to my own lips. After she finishes, she turns and faces me, smirking, raring to go. She's let her hair air dry in beachy waves, while mine has been blown sleek and straight.

I quickly put on my coat, then gather my things and follow her out of the change room. Lottie leans against the wall opposite the exit. Her features are drawn up into an almost sneer and when she sees us, her eyes widen, then shift to the right. I follow them and see Hale, looking equally, if not more, annoyed.

"Hey," I say and smile, trying my very best to be disarming. "What's up?"

"The results for the BioChem test are up," he says as if this means something to me.

I shrug. "Oh yeah, I saw that earlier today."

His eyes travel the length of my body, then roll. I close my coat and cross my arms.

"I see you're taking that really seriously."

"Excuse me?"

"Well," he says, about to spew some wisdom I'm not seeing, "you're dressed like that." As if it's a bad thing. "You're clearly about to go out and have some fun. Damn anything else because parties and mystery hunting are all that matters."

I laugh. "It's Friday night. You can go do whatever else you think is important, but tonight I'm celebrating a win and there's a zero percent chance I'm letting you take that away from me."

"Oh, of course not. I wouldn't dare take your time away from you because it's so precious. It's not like my time matters."

"When exactly did I take your time away?"

"Last Thursday when we were supposed to be studying and all you could talk about was some dead girl."

I groan. Lottie smirks and Sadie picks at her nails, impatiently. "Okay. So next time I'm wasting your time, let me know in the moment and don't come at me later. Cause I really don't care for retroactive complaints."

"Are you serious?" Hale runs a hand through his hair, then shakes his head. "You're too involved with this stupid ghost shit and it's affecting your studies."

"It's affecting *my* studies? Please, this is all about you. You're mad at yourself and instead of looking at where *you* may have gone wrong, you're blaming me. But I'll have you know I got an 87 on that test, so this has nothing to do with how invested I am in stupid ghost shit."

He stares at me, ugly and open-mouthed. I stare back with my chin held high. There is no way I'm letting a man blame me for his mistakes. I wait for him to say something, but he doesn't. He storms away.

"Who the fuck is that?" Sadie asks.

I laugh. "Hale. He's in two of my classes and that is the first time he's ever done that."

"I bet it's not the last, though," she says.

I shrug and follow Lottie as she walks away. For the first time since I've been back on campus this year, there's no snow. The stone pathways have chalky remains of salt, but no ice and no slush. I know we're several weeks from spring, but I'm so excited for the change in seasons. Our heels clack against the stone. Sadie complains about the cool air on her toes. The wind hits my face and I smile. Not even Hale can ruin the high I'm on.

Record breaker.

The thrill of those words race through my veins.

Riley grabs our swim bags as we walk through the door of the pub, almost as if he's been waiting for us. Half the swim team is here, combined with swimmers from the other Atlantic Division teams. Seats along the well-stocked bar are all full. When Riley's working, that's usually the best place to sit. He'll do shots with us from behind the bar. I catch his eye as he walks toward the back to put our stuff away, and signal which table we'll be at. A few metres from the bar, we settle into the picnic style table branded with Alexander Keith's name. I scrape the bench along the floor, but barely hear it over the buzz of students talking all at once.

"What can I get you lovely ladies?" Riley asks, sliding three beers in front of us.

Sadie and I order our usual post-competition meal: nachos, onion rings, mozzarella sticks, chicken fingers, and poutine. Lottie adds to our greasy pub fare and orders French fries. After we demolish the food and the beer, the shots come out. Sadie always makes sure that we've eaten enough before drinking so that we never get to the point where we blackout. I can hold my liquor fairly well, but I have my moments.

Tonight is one of them...

Several shots later, my head is swimming. I don't know if it's the elation of breaking a record or the huge release of stress the pool always brings me or the slightest bit of anger at Hale, but my body feels wonky. I find myself seeing double and losing my balance. Everything Lottie does makes me giggle. She and Sadie dance wildly with Riley and several other swim boys while I sip on a beer at our table.

"Hey, stranger," a man says and sits down next to me.

At first I think it's Hale. I swear I saw him a moment ago. My involuntary reaction is bile rising up my throat and a moment later, I realize why. Lewis.

"What are you doing here?" I yell above the noise. My giddiness doesn't apply to him. "You were supposed to lose my number."

"I did," Lewis says, eyeing me and my drink a little too closely. His gaze trails down my body and lands on my thighs. "But you're here now. I'm not texting you. You looked a little lonely."

"I also said leave me alone." I take another sip of beer for something to do, so I don't have to look at him. His hand moves to my knee. I brush him off and consider spilling my drink on him but I resolve not to because I don't want to cause a scene.

"But you didn't mean that."

Fuck. I know enough to not like how close he is. I'm not drunk enough to miss the look in his eyes. I scan the crowd for Lottie or Sadie, but can't find them. How did they disappear in the two seconds it took for Lewis to sit down?

"Leave me alone," I mutter, the lack of confidence in my voice shocks me. "I meant it."

I push myself up from the table and stumble, sloshing beer over the side of my glass. I curse and close my eyes. A hand appears on my arm, steadying me. I know it's Lewis from the too tight grip and I yank my arm away. A bemused expression plays across his face.

"Are you going to say thank you?" he asks. I don't answer. Just blink. His eyebrows shoot up and he laughs. "I see we're being very ungrateful today. But you can change that tonight, babe."

My head spins and I try to catch someone's eye, but everyone seems to be looking away, almost intentionally. I don't understand why anyone would look away when something so clearly wrong is happening. My thoughts stray to Penny. Did she feel this fear when she was alive? Would my affair kill me too? I see an idea flickering behind his eyes. He wants me and I don't think I'm getting away unscathed.

So I run. I don't grab my bag or my coat. I take off up the stairs and out the red doors of the pub. I run up, instead of out, hoping to confuse Lewis Pickering, and feeling so incredibly vindicated when I do. He dashes out, into the main Student Union building, then through the glass front doors. I close my eyes and catch my breath against the upstairs railing, but only for a moment because he comes right back inside. I duck down, praying that the shadows hide me. He walks to the back of the building. I make my next plan and bolt.

I don't stop running until I reach Shirreff Hall. Inside the safety of the stairwell, I text Lottie.

Maryl

Had a sitsustaiion. Back at the dorm

I get no reply so I go to the only place that's been on my mind since Lewis sat next to me. I need to talk to Penny. The tears come as I climb, realizing what I narrowly escaped. I trip through the doors at the top of the stairs and make a clatter that echoes throughout the hallway. Penelope waits for me, but so does a full bodied, fully alive man. They both jump.

The man in the floor length black trench coat turns. There's something familiar about him. My brain cannot compute why he's so familiar. It's the height, the confident stature, the thick rimmed glasses, the beard... Oh shit.

Denver Keyes takes a few steps toward me, confusion marring his features. Confusion that quickly turns into poorly concealed rage. He wipes away what I think is a tear, but I can't be certain.

"What are you playing at here? Making accusations against me isn't enough? Now you're stalking me?"

Chapter Sixteen

I DON'T KNOW WHICH situation is worse. Being cornered in a bar by your one-night stand or being cornered on the top floor of your residence building by a professor you've been harassing since the second week of classes.

Penelope stares at me, wide-eyed. She face palms as I move toward Denver instead of away. Yeah, me too, Penny. I don't know what I'm doing either.

"I wasn't," I say, though it comes out slurred and uncertain. "I promise—I promise I wasn't doing that. I live here."

His eyebrows raise. "Here? One of these rooms, then?"

"I don't feel super comfy telling you that," I say. "Which is so *not* me saying you killed someone or anything, I just don't tell my uh—my professors where I live, you know? I'm sure you know. I'm sure you don't have all the girls telling you where they live. Or you know what, actually, they probably might. Maybe they tell you that, but I, like, don't."

I shake my head and blink about a million times after I finish. I barely know what I said. I had a point and then, nothing. That was way too much speech.

Denver stares at me. Penny appears next to him and scrutinizes me too.

"I can't believe I'm being slandered by some drunk teen," Denver eventually mutters.

I laugh. It's out before I can stop it. I cover my mouth, but it doesn't stop me. I keep laughing until my eyes water. Denver shakes his head and pulls out his cell phone.

"What are you doing?"

"Well, I'm going to take a guess that you're under the legal drinking age, Miss Laine. And even if you're not, you're publicly intoxicated. Which is illegal. So I'm calling security."

He dials a number and puts his phone against his ear.

"I'm not drunk."

He laughs. "Hi, yes, I'm in Shirreff Hall and I've found a drunk, underage student. I believe she'll be fined for public intoxication."

Oh shit. "You can't do this. I'm not drunk. If you do this, I'm going to get kicked off the team and they'll be so pissed because I'm really important to them and I think they'll take away my win today. You can't do this."

He holds a hand up to silence me and I start to cry. His face falters a bit at my tears, but he stays on the line.

"Yes, I'm certain. From her behaviour and how she smells like a liquor store."

"Well, I'm sorry that your pervy TA spilled beer on me. That's not my goddamn fault. Please, I'll stop."

His eyebrows raise, but he continues to talk on the phone. My body screams at me to run but he knows me. I can't go anywhere because they'll find me or he'll continue to give me shit marks with no remorse.

"How are you calling the cops on me when you're the one who killed someone?" Okay, that's slander. "Me being drunk is so low on the scale of terrible things that people in this room have done. But I'm not even drunk. You're making things up about me. You're doing the same thing you said I was doing to you."

"That is her in the background, yes," he says. "Would you like to speak to her or can you tell from her ravings that she is, in fact, intoxicated?"

I shut up. There's no way I'm talking to the university security team when they're going to be on his side even though his side is one hundred percent invested in revenge. I stand there with my arms crossed, glaring.

And then, a smash behind us. I look around him and he turns fully. There, silhouetted in the window is Penelope. The large vase that's held an artificial fern for as long as I've been here is shattered. Turquoise glass scatters across the white tile. Denver freezes. I can't see his eyes, but his head is turned to exactly where Penelope stands. He doesn't say a word. The phone clatters to the ground.

He can see her.

Penny smiles, sweet and innocent. She takes a silent step toward him. He reaches out a hand and she does the same.

"Penny," he breathes.

"Darling," she says. "Don't blame Maryl for the things she's done. I may have accidentally misled her." She shoots me an apologetic glance, then seems to flicker. She told me how much energy this takes. "I love you."

Then she's gone. He stares at the empty space. Slowly, he bends and picks up his phone. A voice yells from the other end.

Denver clears his throat. "So sorry," he says, though his voice comes out faint and whispery. "I don't know who it was and she ran away. I'm sorry to waste your time."

He ends the call and turns to me, a question on his lips.

"So that's Penny," I say because I can't think of anything else.

I've never seen such sadness in someone's eyes. He looks like the shell of the man who usually stands before the classroom. His shoulders slump and his breathing comes out staggered, almost pained. He looks as though he's aged in a matter of seconds. Unseen lines of his face come out in full force. Sadness hits him like a tsunami. He shakes his head.

"I'm sorry," he says, then brushes past me.

I wait for another ten minutes before I'm certain Penny isn't going to return. Then somehow, I'm back in my dorm, my mind so far away that I don't realize I've done this until I'm unlocking the door. Lottie sits on her bed.

"I was just about to call you," she says, sounding completely sober. "You said you came back so I thought you'd be here."

I nod. My swim bag and coat are on the floor by the foot of my bed. "Thank you."

She waits for me to start talking. I tell her about the last hour of my life and how I'm certain Denver Keyes is not a murderer. His sadness was too great to mean anything other than utter heartbreak at losing his lover.

I know what I have to do now. I sit down on my bed and pull out my laptop. I spend the next two hours rewriting my third story for Creative Writing. I know I'll get late marks and maybe he won't even accept the new submission. But he didn't kill Penelope and I have to try to undo every wrong thing I've ever said about him.

Chapter Seventeen

SUNDAY GOES MUCH THE same as Friday, except this time my race is the last of the day. It's the Women's 4x100m Medley Relay. A group of four swims 100m, each doing different swimming strokes. I'm at my best when I'm doing the breaststroke, so I'm second to jump in and make up ground for the team that way. Before that is the backstroke, after is the butterfly, then freestyle. Sadie is our freestyle swimmer because she's tall, muscular, and fast. She finishes strong. And that is exactly what we do.

Sadie's heading to the pub again. I consider going since it's the last official swim party of the year, but the whole thing with Lewis gives me pause. He'll more than likely be there because his creepy ass probably thinks I'll be there too. So I pretend I have schoolwork to do and leave the change room before the rest of the girls, wet hair, sweats and all. It's only fitting that like last time, leaning against a wall outside the pool is Hale. I square my shoulders and inwardly cringe, not ready for another fight.

"Hey," he says as I try and fail to walk past him. "Maryl, please stop."

I do. I turn to face him, then run my hands through my hair. "Okay. What's up?"

"I wanted to apologize. You were right. How I was feeling wasn't about you and I shouldn't have blamed you for the bad mark."

I nod and laugh slightly. "Seems like you apologize to me a lot."

"Now you have to do something stupid and say sorry so we're even." He shrugs.

I wrinkle my nose. Part of me doesn't want to forgive him. I kind of just want to move on and not have to deal with someone who needs to constantly apologize. But he's here and it's dark and I don't want to walk across campus alone, so I say I forgive him.

We're halfway to Shirreff when he speaks again. "Hey, you want to do something fun?"

"Like what?" I eye him.

"Something to take your mind off my stupidity and all the ghost drama."

"I happen to like ghost drama."

"You do?" I nod. His brows furrow. "Does that mean you have more ghost drama?"

"Well, I don't think Professor Keyes did it anymore. I ran into him on Friday and some... stuff happened. But it's clear he wouldn't have hurt her. I've seen people be devastated by death, and that's exactly what this was and more. He looked absolutely gutted, hollowed out by grief."

Hale stops walking. I pivot and face him, tilting my head to the side as he studies me. The lights from the main buildings on campus silhouette him perfectly, looking bulkier than normal because of his winter coat.

The breeze blows his dark curls and that would probably be attractive if he didn't look sickly pale in the lighting.

"What?" I ask.

"It's just," he pauses and makes a somewhat exasperated noise, "I don't see how him being sad makes him less of a suspect. That doesn't prove anything."

"But what proof do we have that it is him?"

"Who else could it have been?"

I scoff. "Lots of people. It could have been a family member, another professor, Keyes's girlfriend, any of her friends, another ex, anyone jealous of her, someone from the art world, her other child's father..."

He starts walking again before he responds. "You *are* taking this too seriously, though. I know I said sorry, but I don't take back the part about you being obsessed. It can't end well."

"How, exactly, do you think it's going to end badly?" I ask, frustration creeping into my voice despite my best efforts.

"I've seen obsession kill people," he says with a sigh. "My mom has lived her life convinced my dad is cheating on her. It really drags everyone down. I can't remember a time when she didn't have a snide comment or wasn't searching through his phone."

"Okay, well, I didn't cheat on anybody and there's probably a reason why she's so insecure about that."

"That might not be the best example." His cheeks flame, finally bringing colour to his deathly pale skin. "I found a letter that suggested my dad had a fling while my mom was pregnant with me." I snort. "But she's still obsessed."

"She's well within her rights to be after of that!"

Hale goes silent. We walk until we finally reach the front doors of Shirreff. He places a hand in front of me before I open the door.

"So do you want to do something fun?" he asks.

"That offer's still on the table?" I joke.

He seems taken aback for a moment, but recovers well. "Yeah, why not? Are you dressed warm enough for a harbour walk?"

I nod. We drive down to the harbour since it'll take a good half hour to walk there. Hale has his car with him because his family is actually from Halifax. I assume they have money if he chose to live on campus. I wouldn't have if I lived this close.

The harbourfront is one of my favourite places. During the summer and fall, I gladly make that half hour walk to be here. The colourful shops and restaurants that line the sides of the boardwalk remind me of a fair. Bright red, yellow, blue, and green cover the siding on the little houses. At night, there's cute lampposts—my favourites being the totally functional art installation of the Drunken Lampposts at the end of the boardwalk, as one "pees" into the ocean, one is lying on the floor, and the final watches its wayward friends—and caged fairy lights on boats, alongside blinking lights from the Dartmouth side of the harbour. Chatter and folksy music weave their way through the crowds.

We walk past the Tim Hortons and stop in front of Cows. A hefty statue of a cow greets us. I suddenly want nothing more than a good ice cream cone, but the waterfront shop closes in the winter, so we walk on.

"So tell me about your marine biologist stuff," Hale says.

"Umm," I say. "I never really made a conscious decision. At least, not that I remember. I've always been an advocate for animals and I've been swimming all my life. My grandma used to joke that I was a fish in a past life and when I was young, I took that as meaning I used to be a mermaid."

"Oh, so that's what your pillowcase is about."

I blush furiously, glad it's hidden by my already cold, reddened cheeks. "I forgot you saw that. Yeah, my brother got it for me as a joke. I usually turn it around when people come over. It's purple on the other side."

"The mermaid is very cute."

"I guess." I shrug and continue. "I chose to come here because Dalhousie is the best school in Canada for marine biology. Also, the Bedford Institute of Oceanography is right here and I would kill to work there one day."

"Oh, my aunt works there."

"Really?! That's so cool. They've done so much for oceanography. They studied the effects of radiation in sea life on the west coast after the Fukushima Nuclear meltdown in Japan. I followed their findings religiously for a while. There's so much we don't know about ocean life and there's so much changing for them through climate change and environmental disasters."

"You said you advocated for animals. Have you done any of that out here too?"

"I have," I say. "I was talking to one of the marine biology professors last semester about whales and she let me see some of her research about right whales. Their numbers are declining because of boats traveling too fast, fishing entanglements meant for other animals, garbage in the water—all needless things. She was trying to organize an event about it. That was before Christmas. Things have been a bit busy since then..."

"You should talk to her again. Enough of the ghost crap. You should do something for your future!"

I laugh. "My brother thinks doing something for my future includes getting a tattoo."

"Well, why not? That's not at all related to this, but it is something you can do in the future."

"It's kind of related." I pull my phone out and show him Mamie's drawing. It's minimalist line work. A half-finished outline of a mermaid—fully drawn tail, curving up on the left side into an arm, and her profile, with her hair swirling in lines around her. "My grandma drew this for me. I have the original sketch back at the dorm, but I like having it with me just in case."

"That's really beautiful," Hale says after studying the image in silence for almost a minute. "Your grandma is really talented."

"She was," I say and smile. I add in my head, *I don't know why she hasn't come to visit me.*

"Oh, I'm sorry."

I shake my head as if it's no big deal, but I'm tired and it's been a long weekend, so I almost let the tears slip. He places his hands on my upper arms and makes me look at him. I almost think he's going to kiss me but he doesn't. He smiles until I do.

"You should get it," he says. "Double meaning. It'll be in her honour and it'll make all your mermaid dreams come true."

"That's really sweet." I pause. "And it's the perfect time to do it since the season is over."

"Do it!!" he cheers me on, then drops his hands from my arms and grabs my hand. "Let's go get something to eat. Do you do fish?" I shake my head. "Okay, then let's not get fish. We could get BeaverTails?"

Chapter Eighteen

"Oh!" Lottie says and shifts about a thousand papers spread out over her bed as I open the door. "I thought you'd be out later with the last swimming party."

"Didn't want to go after Friday." I shrug. "Plus, I'm sure there'll be more. There's the Athletic Banquet next month."

She nods and returns to her papers. She looks like she hasn't moved since I left this morning. Still in her loungewear, eyes slightly red-rimmed. I put my bag down and drop my coat on top of it, then curl up in bed. My laptop lies on top of my comforter, right where I left it this morning. I consider asking Lottie if something's wrong. I'm almost certain something is, but I don't want to make her talk if she doesn't want to.

"Where'd you go?" she asks.

"I went out with Hale," I say and when her eyebrows shoot up, I laugh. "I know. I don't know. We went down to the harbour and talked and he apologized for being a dick on Friday."

"I don't like him. There's something about him that just..." She shakes her head. "He gives me the creeps."

"Everyone I associate with gives you the creeps."

"I'm usually right! Look at Lewis! Or that guy last semester who kept following you around."

"Okay, he wasn't someone I was ever considering. He was an actual creep from one of my classes."

"Still."

I shrug and open my laptop. Creep or not, Hale had a good idea. I've wanted Mamie's work inked on my skin since the day she drew it. But I was sixteen and my parents didn't want me getting a tattoo. When Mamie died last year, the pull to get it was even stronger. I had a plan to graduate, get out of Québec and out from under my parents' watch, and get the tattoo. Six months later, I still haven't done it.

"Hey, Lottie?" She looks up. "What was that tattoo place you went to again?"

"Inked in Sin. They're the highest rated in Halifax. Are you getting a tattoo?"

I peer over the top of my laptop. I have her full attention now. Lottie loves tattoos. She's gone on and on about how delicate this kind of artistry is, and has two of her own. The Sagittarius constellation sits behind her right ear. Anytime she pulls her hair back into a ponytail, you get a little glimpse of the stars. A curve of vibrant wildflowers lies along the side of her left breast. This was actually the first of her tattoos I saw during Frosh week when she donned a bikini top for one of the events. Both have such beautiful line work that there's no question my tattoo would be done well.

I stretch across my bed, reach down into the drawer of my bedside table, and pull out a black leather-bound sketchbook. All of Mamie's drawings are in here, including the mermaid. I flip pages until I find it, then turn it toward Lottie.

"My grandma made this for me. I've always thought I'd get it along the inside of my arm."

"That's gorgeous," Lottie says. She gets off her bed and reaches out for the sketchbook. Reluctantly, I give it to her. She flips through the pages, her smile growing. "Your grandma was really talented."

"She was a woman of many talents, that's for sure."

Lottie returns to her bed and begins fidgeting with her camera, probably something for the school paper. I watch her from the corner of my eye, still sensing something off, but most of my attention stays on drafting an email to the tattoo parlour. There was a simple form on their website that I could have filled out, but they ask for emails if you have a picture for reference or additional info. I have both. After a few minutes of tweaking what I want and when, I finish the email off by asking if there's any availability on Friday, the day before I head back to Montréal for reading week. Then I send it. I close my laptop and stare at Lottie who is still aimlessly pressing buttons on her camera.

"Okay," I say and break the silence. "I've ignored it long enough. What's up?"

Lottie runs a hand over her face and clears her throat. She opens her mouth but nothing comes out, so she opens her laptop and turns it toward me instead. I move to the edge of my bed and squint at the screen.

"Ancestry?" I ask. "Haven't you been on there forever?"

She nods. "Yeah, but I can't exactly find much not knowing my birth family or a last name. I've done my adoptive parents' tree and I'm on that, but, like, a different sort of line, you know? Like these people are my relatives." Air quotes. "But they have no DNA link to me. So it's my tree, but it's not."

"What's new, then?"

"I did the Ancestry DNA test. It was one of my Christmas presents because my family knows how much I want to know where I came from and they thought this might help me find a link. I got an email that the results came in today and I haven't been able to open it."

"Lottie! This might be your answer. You might be able to find so much through this! You have to open it."

"I know." She swallows and stares at the wall. A moment later, she furiously wipes at her eyes. "I just can't."

Silence falls between us. I meet her eyes, anxiety and a sheen of tears rounding them, making them shine like the ocean at sunrise. I push myself off my bed and onto the floor. Sitting in front of her bed, I take the laptop. She doesn't fight me.

"Do you want me to look at it?"

"Would you?" she whispers. "You don't have to. I won't ask you to do it, but if you wanted to... If you think that's a good idea. If you—"

"Lottie, stop. It's nothing. I can do this for you."

She's already signed into the website, so I navigate over to her notifications, assuming that's where the answers will be. The notification takes me to the Ancestry DNA page. It shows me a breakdown of where she comes from and how much of her DNA belongs to what place. My stomach sinks as I realize that's it. There are no further links from her effort. No other leaves have come up. Nothing she can use to give herself closure. I try to keep my disappointment from her, but from her sigh, I know my poker face was unconvincing.

"You're 79% British," I say, trying to break the tension.

"Great," she says and takes her laptop back.

"Maybe your family hasn't done this. You're the first person I know who has."

"Maybe," she whispers and blinks away tears. "You know, I don't know what's worse. Finding something or finding nothing. I was so convinced I'd get a leaf from this. And now I don't know where to go from here."

I stare at her crestfallen face and try to think of some way to make her feel better. I pull my phone out of the pocket of my sweater and start to look up something, or rather someone, but pause.

"Can you search people on there?" I ask. "I've never done this so I have no idea, but that's how you add people, right? You search their names and add their leaves, right?"

"You can search people, yeah. That's how I've found some unrelated things. Why?"

"Search Denver Keyes. Maybe he has a tree. He seems like the type to—"

"I have."

That stops me. "What?"

Her lips quirk in a sad smile and she shakes her head. "You've been doing your ghost research and I've done some of my own, too. I looked him up on here last week. He does have a tree, but I guess I have no link to it."

"Has he done the DNA thing?"

Lottie shrugs. I type *Denver Keyes Ancestry DNA* into the search engine and miraculously, an article from the *Dalhousie Gazette* comes up. It's a year old, but it's exactly what I'm looking for, and more. I skim it, then pass my phone to Lottie.

Denver on DNA

It is with great pleasure that I take this opportunity as a guest writer for the Dalhousie Gazette. It excites me to be asked to talk about my thoughts and experience.

Ancestry DNA has gained popularity in mainstream media. Everyone seems to want to know where they came from. I'm uncertain what this means for many people, but I do see the merits, personally. I don't know where I came from. I do, in a purely biological way, but outside of that, in a purely semantic way, I do not. One of the foundational moments of my life was the one that set me on the path of becoming an author, a scholar, a researcher, and a professor.

This moment happened when I was sixteen years old and received news that I was adopted. You may be wondering how this set me on the writing path, but to me, it's quite obvious. I did what many people in crisis do: I wrote about it. I put all my emotions and more on paper to try and understand this loss of identity I was feeling. It helped, but I still cannot say that I have ever fully processed this revelation. Nonetheless, I am grateful for it because of who I am today.

Today, I am a man who is still trying to make sense of his life. With Ancestry DNA, I believed I could make further sense of my desire to know where I came from. Would it link me to people I had been missing in my life... my past relatives, my future relatives? Would it reveal people I didn't know about? Would it reveal people I did know about? Questions upon questions ran through my mind and I could not shake the feeling of hope. I'm certain it's a feeling many adoptees work through.

When my results came back, I was pleased to discover a biological brother. This was not something I expected. It may not look well on me, but what I expected to find was a child. Much like everyone else in life, I am not perfect. When I was young, I fathered a child, but I did not learn about this until much later in my life. Every revelation of mine has come years after it should have. To this day, I still do not know where my child is, but I have never given up that hope of finding him.

Someday, much like I found my brother, much like I found my familial link all spelled out in a nice little tree, I will find my son.

Lottie drops my phone onto the bed after she finishes. She closes her eyes and sighs. I don't know what to say and she clearly doesn't either. Minutes pass before we make another sound. I count the flowers on the garland around the mirror.

"He's like me," Lottie whispers. "He's like me and he's looking for the same person I am. Why can't we find him? What if he doesn't exist anymore?"

"Penny seems to think her son is still alive. She feels like she'd know if he were dead. That makes sense, right? Like, a mother would know."

"How do I find out if Penny's my mom? How do I find out if these are the same people? If Denver is my brother's father... Who is my father... Where do I begin?"

"Have you searched for Penny on there? Penelope Walsh?"

"She's nowhere on here. At least, not that I can find. Someone hasn't input her records."

Lottie pulls her hair up into a bun and the stars come out. I study the lines of her constellation before meeting her eyes. She stares, unfocused. Her fingers run over the jade stone around her neck. I want to reach out and steady her, but I know there's nothing I can do for her immense disappointment and it's all my fault.

Chapter Nineteen

NERVES ATTACK ME ALL throughout Creative Writing. The anxiety is tenfold. There's the most recent story I submitted that may or may not confuse Denver Keyes even more considering it was a love story, the fuckwad that is Lewis Pickering, and Hale who decided it was cool to ask me on a Valentine's Day date when I walked into class this afternoon.

"I'll let you know about Valentine's Day soon," I say to Hale as we make our way down to the groups of papers at the front of the lecture hall. "Definitely before Thursday."

Hale grimaces, but quickly rearranges his face. We split. My submission is sitting on top of the pile with a bright, red B+. I stare at it in disbelief. Beside the red mark is a comment in red marker. *Very moving. Marks off for being late.*

The knot in my stomach slips away along with the chatter that once filled the room. One student is talking with Lewis, another with Denver, and three wait by the door. As my eyes travel around the room, they meet the now kindly eyes behind Denver's glasses. He nods toward me. I wait for him to finish with his student. Not even a minute later, Denver is in front of me, his movements slow and measured, hesitant.

"Miss Laine, if you're comfortable, I'd like to talk to you about your assignments in my office," Denver says. I absently wonder what this interaction looks like to anyone still watching, but I agree and follow.

His office is the standard of every other professor's office I've been in at Dal. Stark white walls, cherry wood desk, large Mac monitor, degrees hanging proudly on the wall, bookshelves lining the free space. Denver's bookshelves are a little different. Instead of science textbooks and research dossiers that I'm used to in the science offices, his shelves are lined with creative writing texts, classic English literature, modern fiction, the school journal which he helps produce, and a few of his own books. Hanging up above his desk is not a whiteboard or bulletin board like so many other professors have, but a painting. A lighthouse at the edge of the world and waves crashing against the rugged dark rocks on a sunny day. A young woman in a blue dress stands in the wind next to the lighthouse, dress and hair wild. An unsettling feeling falls over me. It's Penny.

Denver closes the door and notices me staring. "After Penny died, they held a fundraiser for her children. Part of it involved her paintings being sold. I bought one to show my support and have a piece of her with me."

"It's gorgeous. All of her paintings are," I mumble, entranced for a moment. "Why did you just buy a painting?"

"Instead of getting involved in my son's life?" he asks and sinks into his desk chair. "That's a good question. I have half answers. None of them are the best. All of them have my regrets."

I pull the chair by the window closer to him and sit down. I wait for him to say more. He removes his glasses, revealing the lines and hollows around his eyes.

"I never thought I had much of a choice. Penny never told me about her pregnancy. You were right in what you wrote. One day, she left and I had no idea where she went. This was the 90s. I couldn't just look her up like you guys do now. I was lost and didn't understand why she did it, still don't. Then, as suddenly as she disappeared, she returned. It was a quick little meeting. She sat down, introduced our son, then asked me for money because she was leaving."

I gasp. She hadn't told me that. My eyes find their way to the girl in the painting again.

"It was the best and worst day of my life. She came back to me and I had a son. It was everything I wanted when we were together. I tried to convince her to stay. I tried to make her feel that everything was going to be all right and I wanted to be in their lives, but she was terrified. She was so scared and so sad and I was stupid and in love. I did not understand why she was doing this. I was blinded by myself and couldn't see she was in danger until it was too late."

"What do you mean?" I whisper.

"I've never thought she killed herself."

He lets that sit for a moment. He may have thought that but he never did anything. Why would he let her murder go?

"I didn't want to become a suspect," he says, answering the question that sits between us. "Which I know was incredibly selfish. I sacrificed a life of knowing my child because I didn't want to admit that I loved Penelope. But I knew I'd be risking my job, and my future if I said anything. The optics… well, I'm sure you can imagine. I figured I'd leave it up to him. If he ever found me or, if by some chance, we both happened on each other it would be okay… But I knew she was afraid that day and I thought she was afraid to tell me about him, but I realized how wrong I was when she died. I couldn't come out and say that I was the last person who saw her alive. Which, again, I have regretted every day of my life since I made that choice, but I thought that was the only thing I could do in the moment. The version of the truth where she killed herself was harder for me to live with in innumerable ways, the rumours surrounding that version of events… But I knew the truth that she was murdered would be even worse. I had to take a year's sabbatical after her death. I couldn't function knowing she was gone and maybe I could have stopped that."

"I'm sorry," I say, because I am. "I don't know what to say to that. I mean, I believe you. I saw you on Friday and I don't think you could fake that emotion when you saw Penny."

"What was that?" he asks. He leans closer to me, his hands coming up below his chin. "That was really Penny? I've never seen anything like that."

"I know. I don't know if you'll believe me but—"

"I'll believe anything at this point."

"I've been seeing her this whole semester. I didn't believe it at first, but she's told me a lot that no one else would know and Leah told me that I probably have—"

"Leah Easton?" I nod in response to his question before he continues, "Leah was one of Penny's best friends."

"Leah works at Shirreff Hall now," I say and Denver makes a noise of acknowledgement. "She told me I have a gift, if that makes sense. I don't know. I'm figuring it out as I go right now too, but I want to help her. Penny. I want to help Penny."

Denver shakes his head, but smiles. "I will do whatever I can to help you. I don't fully understand what's going on either, but I think I owe her this. If you'll let me, I'll help."

"Penny!" I yell when I get to the fourth floor, no longer worried or ashamed that people might hear me. "Penny, where are you?"

Penny taps my shoulder and cold spreads through the right side of my body. I turn and she stands there, hands worrying the edges of her frayed scarf, studying me.

"You have to tell me more," I demand. "I know basically nothing about you and I can't assume Denver was the one who fucked you over, so give me something to go on. Give me other people. Give me a reason why someone might kill you."

"Okay," she says and sits down with her back against the windows like usual. She waves me over and I sit with her.

I stare at the wall and passing students as she tells me about petty things she did while she was alive, things I fear have no influence on this case.

Like being pregnant for a second time while her best friend and former roommate, Elle was pregnant with her first child. Joint baby showers and birthdays just days apart for their kids. An upstaging, I guess, one Penny claims might be bitter enough to kill over. Or how Leah likely resents her for sticking around Shirreff, forcing her to stay, as well, as some form of loyalty to her dead friend. Which, sure, maybe. But you can't kill someone *again*.

She tells me about catty swim team girls, of which, I am familiar. But killing someone because they were better than you or flirtier with the boys or left the team is so far-fetched. Maybe I'm naive but I can't imagine someone wanting me dead because I broke a record.

Jason is the only name I take note of. Penny's ex-boyfriend from her first year of university hated her after their nasty, messy breakup, despite it being his fault. She claims he was too possessive and prohibitive, not something you want during your first taste of freedom. Or ever. Jason accused her of moving on too quickly when she got with Denver a month later. Then, when he found out who she was dating, he threatened to tell the school. Penny had to blackmail him, threatening expulsion, so he'd stay silent.

And then, she tells me about her father, Elliot.

"My mom died a few months before Lottie was born. She drowned on my dad's boat. It was horrific. None of us saw it coming. We were all devastated, especially my dad. I've never met two people more in love than they were, so her death broke him. He was never the same after. He started... slipping. I don't know what was happening. I was pregnant and grieving and still trying to be a mom for my son, so my dad was on the backburner. I didn't realize how bad it got until April 8th."

"You died the next day," I mumble.

"I know." She gazes far off into the distance. "He told me that someone wanted to kill me. He was convinced. He had all this evidence and I was exhausted, and quite frankly, I was depressed. I wanted an out, so I believed him. I went to Denver and told him I wanted child support money. But I could see he didn't believe me. He could see how afraid and worn out I was. He tried to convince me to stay and let him help, but I left." She laughs. "I left without any money because I couldn't do it and I came here to cry."

"Shit," I say. Penny repeats the sentiment.

Someone lured her here. They made it look like suicide and used Denver as a scapegoat just in case.

Shit.

Chapter Twenty

EVERYTHING BECOMES A DEAD end. Lottie and I spent the week researching, finding limited results. Elliot Walsh is a retired fisherman, still in the house where he lived with his late wife, his daughter, and his grandchildren. Old university friends have moved on or moved away. People have successful lives and no second thought of the girl who died nearly twenty years ago.

The only morsel of dirt we find is Jason. Jason Ives is exactly who I expect him to be. He looks like an overgrown frat boy, and seeing as he's a lawyer, he probably is. Artificially tanned skin, slicked back hair, and a grin just as slimy. He still lives in Halifax, so he's my only potential link at this point. Him, and his coworker Elle. It's shocking. I didn't expect to find Penny's best friend working with her ex, but I intuitively know the second I see her scowling face listed on the law firm's employee page. Penny confirms when I show her the site.

A theory takes root that, maybe, they worked together to kill Penny. I have no proof. I have nothing, but I intend to find out.

Just...next week once I'm back in Halifax.

I meet up with Lottie after my BioChem class. Hale avoided me today because I blew him off last night. My research with Lottie was more important.

"Hey!" Lottie calls when she sees me enter the pub. A giant, decadent salad sits in front of her. "You eating first or do you have to go?"

"I have to head out soon, but I'll sit with you a sec," I say. "Did you find anything?"

She shakes her head. "Not yet. Penny *would* give us the hardest people in the world to find. I think our best bet is to talk to Jason and Elliot since we know more about them. Maybe her friend as well. We can ask Leah."

"You think that's smart?"

She shrugs. "Dunno. But we have all reading week to decide whether or not it's a good idea."

I agree with her, then check the time. My tattoo appointment is in a half hour. It's time for me to head out and get inked. My anxious energy eats at me, but I'm more excited to have a piece of Mamie on me forever than worried about any potential pain.

"I'm sure I'll be back before you leave," I say.

"Of course you will be," Lottie replies. "I'm not going home until you show me the tattoo!"

I take a taxi to Inked in Sin. The tattoo shop is a few blocks from the Halifax waterfront, situated right in the downtown core, and sandwiched between Argyle and Barrington Street, near all the bars and restaurants. Inked in Sin sits in a corner building, next to a burger joint. It's a blink and you'll miss it sort of façade. A sign on the door with the business name, phone number, and a neon *Open*. I understand why when I walk inside: there's several businesses within the building, divided into three separate hardwood floored hallways with Inked in Sin being straight ahead.

Light blue walls greet me when I walk in. The walls are adorned with framed intricate tattoo designs and business awards. I turn and face the long reception desk, if you can call a glass desk filled with piercing jewelry a reception desk. A pale woman with blonde and pink hair, nose, lip, and eyebrow piercings, and tattoos down both arms looks up as I approach.

"Hi, love," she says. "How can I help you?"

I open my mouth to say I'm here for my appointment when the door swings open and a tall Black man with the nicest looking curls I've ever seen in my life barges in and booms, "Sorry, I'm late and I know we hate that, but I'm here now!"

"Shut up, Sam," the girl at the front says with a laugh. "McKenna is ready for you. She's excusing your lateness because it was your birthday."

"How nice of McKenna," Sam says and rolls his eyes. "I'm sure she said that not at all begrudgingly."

"You know Ken hates everyone's birthday, not just yours." Then, as if on cue, they both notice me. "Sorry, love, it's the Sam show here even on his day off."

"You know you like the Sam show," he says and throws his coat on a coat rack, revealing a forearm arm with a prominent compass tattoo and the other with a line of what I can only assume are dates. He's the least tattooed person to work at a tattoo shop.

I draw my attention away from Sam and back to the front desk again, then smile. "Yeah, I'm here for my appointment."

"Okay, let me guess," she says. She clicks something with the mouse and looks me over. "You are Maryl Laine."

Once more, I'm about to respond when Sam speaks, "Marill is a Pokémon."

"What?" I say and almost manage to stifle the laugh.

He pauses, literally just freezes all body movement. "Pokémon. You know?"

I flush. "I never played. I mean, I downloaded Pokémon Go when that was a big thing, but I never watched the show."

"You're joking!" he groans. "How do you have the name of a Pokémon but you don't like it? You can't tell me I'm the first person to say that."

"You are, actually. People usually ask if I'm named after Meryl Streep."

"Are you?"

"No."

"Then you're a Pokémon." He grins and it disarms my entire being. His teeth are entirely too straight and the gap between his front teeth is just imperfect enough that it makes his smile somehow perfect. He lingers, a beat too long before walking away.

It takes a second for me to tune back into normal conversation. The receptionist shakes her head at me knowingly, then tells me to wait for my tattoo artist to come out. My mind whirrs through bits and pieces of information I've learned this week, but keeps coming back to this guy I just met. Something about him feels so familiar and my brain can't quite reach it. As I'm pondering this, a large middle-aged man with a full scraggly beard and tattoos covering every inch of his skin apart from his pink-tinged face approaches me.

"Hi there, Maryl," he says and shoots out his hand for me to shake. "I'm Paul. We've been speaking over email."

"Hi Paul," I say with a smile and shake his hand.

"Come on, come back." He turns and expects me to follow, so I do. "We'll talk placement and size."

He walks me to the back of the shop where little booths separate the tattoo stations. His is at the very end on the right. He tells me to take off my coat and get comfy while he gets ready. I decided on a T-shirt for this occasion and my skin erupts in goosebumps when I shed the coat. I rub them away and look around at the inks on the shelves and the tattoo gun Paul prepares. The process is fascinating and a lot more detailed than I would have expected. My eyes roam around the back of the shop and I notice Sam in the booth next to mine. He's alone and in shorts now, revealing yet another tattoo on his right leg, something I can't quite make out obscured behind the tattoo chair.

"We meet again, Pokémon," Sam says and I jump.

"Samuel," Paul says, a joking lilt to his frustration. "No harassing customers on your day off."

"Oh, but I can harass them when I'm working?" He flips himself onto the chair and stretches out his legs. I squint and attract his attention again. He twists and shows me the tentacles stretching down his leg. "It's a kraken. My first tattoo and honestly, probably why I started working here."

I study the blues, greens and purples of the kraken and finally place this man. I've seen him on campus. He was the guy I saw crying during my first few weeks at Dal.

"Did you go to Dalhousie?"

He flinches. Or it may have been my imagination, but he moves quickly and his face closes up for a moment before the good-natured smile returns. "No, I never did."

"Sorry. You look like someone I know."

"Someone looks like Sammy?" a curvy white woman with short blue hair, holding bottles of ink and a drawing of what may be a butterfly asks. "Impossible. No one looks like our Sam."

"I'm one of a kind." Sam winks and gives me that grin again.

I look away and turn to Paul. His eyebrows raise as he studies the interaction. I blush and train my eyes elsewhere. My mix of emotions, nerves, and hazy brain take away my usual snippy ability. So I swallow all thoughts other than the fact that I am doing this for Mamie.

"You good, Maryl?" Paul asks. "First tattoo, right?"

"Ooh we got a virgin!" the blue haired girl, who I can only assume is McKenna says.

Paul eyes the two of them, like a silent code to shut up.

I laugh. "No, I'm fine. You don't have to get mad at them. They're kind of taking the edge off."

Paul shrugs and lets them off the hook. He flips my arm over and asks how I want the tattoo. He pulls out a few sheets of paper that somehow transfer onto my arm. One is tiny, maybe about two inches and would only cover one side of my wrist. The second is midsized, one he says that we could centre on my arm. The final is the one that draws me. My original idea. It's the full-size version of Mamie's drawing and fits along the length of my inner forearm. I choose that one and he tells me to sit back and relax while he prepares my arm.

"Paul, you gonna tell her about how much that hurts for a virgin?" McKenna asks.

I open my eyes and look over at the other booth. Sam nudges McKenna with his foot and shakes his head. She flips him off.

"Doesn't everything hurt for a virgin?" I ask. It's only half a joke.

"Inner arm hurts." She shrugs.

Sam holds up his left arm, the one with the series of dates scrawled down it. "I lived. My second tattoo. She's right, the skin is thinner there so it's a place that does sometimes hurt more for people, but it all depends on the person and their pain tolerance. Some would say I bit off more than I could chew getting a huge, fully shaded and coloured kraken for my first, but that doesn't matter. The only thing that matters is what you want."

"That felt like an after school special," I say and smirk.

"What kind of after school specials were you watching that advocated for getting tattoos?"

I laugh again and he joins in, easy, booming, but not overbearing, just like his voice. McKenna sits down in front of his left leg and begins to work. From his wince, I can tell she's started.

"That did not hurt," he says in reassurance. "McKenna didn't tell me she was starting."

She snorts and gets back to work. Paul runs his hand along the special transfer paper he placed on my arm. It pulls off to reveal a blue copy of my grandma's drawing. He tells me to stand and look in the mirror to see if it's the right placement. The mermaid's hair snakes down my wrist, the tail ends just before the crook of my elbow. It's perfect. I pivot and face Paul again, a watery smile on my face, and find Sam's eyes on me again.

"Can I see that when it's done?" Sam asks.

And because the cliché seems like the only correct response here, I say, "I'll show you mine if you show me yours."

He smirks. I keep my eyes on Sam as the first pinprick of pain touches my skin. It hurts, but I've felt worse. It's a sting, more tender near my wrist than my elbow. I exhale and watch McKenna work instead of Paul.

"Is that a butterfly?" I ask.

"It's a moth," he says. "My mom drew it. She had the same tattoo. I had this weird memory of it for years and I wanted it. It actually should have been my first, but I couldn't get it right from drawing it and I couldn't find any photos of it until about a month ago."

"Why didn't you ask her about it?"

He hesitates and smiles, but this time with tight lips. "My, uh, my mom's dead."

"Oh my god, I'm so sorry," I say. "I should have realized. You said 'had.' I'm sorry."

He gives a thin lipped smile again and runs a hand through his tight curls. "No worries. I've had a lifetime of those reactions. Doesn't really faze me anymore."

I want to believe him, but I think a lifetime of that would be worse than anything. That's not a death you come back from unscathed.

"Moths are cool, though," he says, moving on. "They represent vulnerability, attraction, intuition, afterlife, transformation... I think that's why my mom got it."

"You sound like my roommate."

"Your roommate's a loon too?" McKenna asks.

"Fuck off," Sam chuckles. "I get deep and you insult me."

"You're just trying to impress a girl, Sammy boy."

Heat creeps up my chest and I avert my eyes. I study the ink on his skin and think about the stories they tell. "What about the others?"

"Well, the kraken is because I've always loved the myth. They've always been one of my favourite animals and I think they're pretty cool. I went to the Maritime Museum one day and saw their giant kraken and kind of made the decision then and there." He holds up his right arm and shows me the compass on the outside of his forearm, with the North and South points stretching from the base of his pinky to his elbow. "My grandpa's a fisherman, or he was until he retired, so this is for him. He basically raised me and I wanted a tribute to him somehow. He cried when I showed him because I based the illustration on a compass he once owned." Then he holds up his left arm again. The three lines run along his inner wrist. He points, line by line. "This one is my grandpa's birthday, then my mom's, then my sister's."

"You gonna tell her the part about how you barely know your sister or is that a story only I get?" McKenna asks.

"McKenna Louise Douglas!" Paul admonishes. "That's enough."

McKenna snorts. "Pulling the dad card on me. Great. I thought we wanted to get the full Samuel Walsh story."

Paul sighs and I freeze. "I'm sorry for my daughter. Can't fire family."

I assure him it's totally fine, but my body's gone cold. Okay, it's a common enough last name. I mean, there's probably hundreds of people with that last name in the province. But I stop and study Sam. Really study. Like stare an uncomfortably long amount of time. He'd notice if he wasn't still telling me about how his grandpa couldn't take care of two kids after his mom died, so his sister was put up for adoption. He was only five. She was a baby.

I start at his feet and trail up his body. He's probably over six feet, confident and he knows it. His posture is statuesque and open, reminiscent of another man I've come to know recently who can also command a room. He's muscular and looks like he'd be good at sports. I wonder if he was ever a swimmer like another woman I know. His skin tone is a mix of these two people—Denver's dark umber with Penelope's sun-kissed, freckled skin—to create a golden brown with a smattering of freckles over the bridge of his nose. A nose that I've seen on a man who broke down crying earlier this week. Eyes that I've looked at every day since fall semester began.

Oh fuck.

The eyes. The seafoam green with the dark blue around the edges.

How did I not clock that earlier?

"So, yeah, I don't know her, but she's important to me," Sam finishes.

McKenna stares at me, her eyebrows drawn together. "Sammy, look, you've weirded out the poor girl."

"I—no, no you didn't." I scramble for ways to grasp this link. "Sorry, just your eyes."

"The eyes!" McKenna shrieks and rolls her own.

Sam laughs, but I note a hint of confusion in it. "Yeah, I get that a lot too."

I smile and my eyes go back to his date tattoo. I squint, but too obviously. He holds his arm up again. His eyes question me and I question myself.

"When was your sister born?" I ask.

"December 20th, 2000."

I wrinkle my nose and turn away. Oh shit.

Chapter Twenty-One

I WALK BACK TO Dalhousie, hoping the cool air will soothe my thoughts. Sam and I exchanged numbers after I stopped acting weird. My brain screamed at me to tell him about Lottie, but that seemed so forward and normally I have no problems with that. But this is in a whole other realm that I've never dealt with before so I can't blurt everything I think I know.

But categorically, it's all too much to not fit together.

Samuel Walsh lives in Halifax with his grandpa who raised him after his mother died. Samuel Walsh's sister was born December 20th, 2000, which is also the exact date that my roommate was born. Both Lottie and his sister were put up for adoption. Samuel Walsh has striking eyes that I've only ever seen on two people before and those two people happen to be related. And, of course, his last name is Walsh.

There's no way he's not connected to all of this.

I'm still thinking about it by the time I get back to Shirreff Hall. I consider going straight up to Penny, but I figure I owe Lottie the courtesy of my discovery.

I stand in front of our door, staring. *Can* I tell her? Her loopy handwriting on our door's whiteboard makes me question myself. She probably needs a break from this semester and that's on me. I'm the one who started this and made her consider her mom might be dead, does she really need a brother on top of it? Or at least, does she need one right now? I'll tell her later, not the second before she goes back home for a week.

As I turn the key and open the door, I know I'm not going home for reading week. I'll call and tell my parents something came up. It's not entirely untrue. Something did come up, it just happens to be a person named Sam.

Lottie flutters around the room as I enter. A small bag filled to the brim sits on her bed. Grayson is coming to take her back home to Lunenburg. They're going to have dinner by the waterfront before making the winding journey down the coast. She packed earlier this week, but I gather those things weren't enough as she searches through her drawers when I walk in.

"What are you doing?" I ask.

Lottie jumps, too in her own world to notice I unlocked, opened, and closed our door. "You're back!" She smiles at me and I can see the genuine excitement pulsing off of her. "I'm looking for a specific dress but it doesn't matter. Show me the tattoo!!"

I plop my backpack on the floor and gingerly shrug out of my coat. The cold and whirring thoughts appear to have numbed my arm, but I can feel it now. It's not a terrible pain, much like the tattooing itself, just a sting. Though it's a sting the length of my forearm that twinges in pain depending on how I turn. I hold my arm out to her and show her the tattoo below the clear Saniderm bandage, the line work thin and delicate, exactly how I pictured it.

"Oh, wow!" she says. "It's actually better than I thought it would be. It suits you so perfectly!"

"It does, doesn't it?" I say, marvelling in its beauty for a moment. "He did a really good job."

"Who did it?" she asks.

"Paul. I think he owns the place."

"Oh, yeah, he does. I've had his daughter for both of mine."

"She seems like a real treat," I say and fall back onto my bed.

Lottie laughs. "Yeah, she's a bit mean? Kept calling me a tattoo virgin and implying I couldn't take the pain. But she does good work so I don't mind the attitude."

"She was doing a moth tattoo for someone while I was there. It was really well done, I'll give her that."

Lottie's hand subconsciously goes to her neck as she searches for her dress again. I ask if she left it at home but she's certain it's here, so I go back to staring at the ceiling. Part of me wants to look into Sam, to be sure that he's related to Elliot and everyone else, but I don't want to do it in front of her. I realize I'm fidgeting, knocking my feet together, when Lottie comes and sits beside me.

"What's wrong?" she asks. "Do you not like the tattoo?"

My gaze slides over to hers. The jolt I get when I see her eyes makes me uncomfortable. There are too many puzzle pieces.

"No, I love it," I say.

"Then what?"

I pause, Samuel Walsh's name on my tongue. Instead, I say, "Nothing."

But seeing as we've lived together for about six months, she knows when I'm being not entirely truthful. She continues to search for the dress, eyeing me as she moves around messes she's made. When she finally finds it and stuffs it into her bag, she turns to me.

"This is about Hale, isn't it?" she states.

"What? This is not about Hale," I say, somehow insulted. My words come quick and harsh, making it seem like a lie.

"What did he do that's making you all weird?"

"Nothing."

She rolls her eyes and zips up her bag in a harsh swish that lets me know she's annoyed with me and whatever I'm not saying.

"Then what are you hiding?" she asks and stares me down. We're minutes away from her starting to pace. "If not Hale, then what?"

I bite my lip and don't speak because I don't have a good enough lie. I know if I start to say something I'll spill all the details. I'll ruin her date with Gray. I'll ruin her week.

"Nothing," I say again. Irritation, more at myself than her, creeps into my voice.

Lottie huffs and pulls on her coat, then hoists her bag onto her shoulder. "Well, when you want to tell me the truth, let me know. Have a good reading week, I guess."

"You too," I say, my voice coming out small from my curled up position on my bed.

Lottie opens the door and breathes out a laugh. On the other side is Hale, his hand poised to knock. Lottie doesn't even stop, doesn't even say hi, she just turns to me and stares as if this proves her point. I immediately sit up. I look back at her and raise an eyebrow. I refuse to be the one to break eye contact. I win when she walks away.

Hale enters the room hesitantly and closes the door, even though I didn't invite him. I can tell from his face that he can feel the tension between me and Lottie. Just like the last time he was in my room, he sits at my desk chair. I do nothing more than watch him.

"What was that about?" Hale finally asks.

I shrug. "Roommate things."

He wrinkles his nose. "Really? That felt like more than roommate things."

"Yeah, well," I say. I look down at my hands and see the edge of the bandage on my right wrist. A slight stab of pain slips back to me.

"Seriously. Sounded like she was mad at you for no reason."

I exhale. "Can we not trash my roommate, please?"

"I'm not trashing her, just saying that she sounded pretty intense and I don't like that."

"Says the boy who yelled at me for a bad mark."

He grimaces. "I'm sorry about that. You know how school can be sometimes."

"Yeah."

I don't say anything more. I stare at Hale's fidgeting hands until he decides to break the awkward silence. "You don't seem like the usual Maryl."

"Marill is a Pokémon, did you know?" I ask.

"Yeah, it's a water/fairy type." Hale says this like it's obvious and I let that odd detail sink in. "Why does that matter now?"

"It doesn't."

"Your roommate sucks."

"Lottie doesn't suck."

"She made you feel like this. She sucks. Good people don't tear you down and apologize after the fact."

I swallow and eye him below my lashes. He seems proud of himself, but I don't know why. Every time I've ever talked about Lottie he's mentioned something he doesn't like about her. She seems wary of him as well. I wonder if they have a secret history. I run a hand over my face and nod.

"Yeah, she sucks," I say just to shut him up. Just to see his reaction.

A smirk appears on his lips. I don't like that.

"What're you doing for reading week?" Hale asks.

"I'm going to Montréal," I lie.

He frowns like some asshole asking *where's my hug*. "Too bad. We could have finally gone on that date."

“Yeah, that’s too bad,” I say. “We could do dinner now, I guess.”

Not because I want to, but because I want to do anything but stay in this room and think about the Walshes.

Chapter Twenty-Two

SINCE MY MOM HAS always been in love with swimming and pushed me and Stephen into her favourite sport, I figured a swimming lie would be the best lie. I told her we were practising over reading week and I totally forgot until now. Somehow, she bought it.

I've never been a good liar. Lottie saw right through me yesterday. My brother can spot my lies two provinces away. But my mom accepts them. I'm never certain if she knows and allows it or she really is that clueless. Either way, my lie got me what I wanted. I arranged a time to meet up with Sam and make his brain explode with everything I have to say. Which is why his text doesn't surprise me on Monday morning.

Sam

Hey I gotta cancel tonight

And just like that, I want to throw my phone against a wall the second I wake up. After spending all weekend thinking about how I wanted to introduce him to the concept that his sister is my roommate and his dead mother is my friend, he cancels. I know I have no one to blame but myself.

I consider going to talk to Penny about her son, but I don't want to bring him up until I'm certain, even though I'm at a strong 95% right now. I also don't think she'd have any insight apart from showing me a moth tattoo that I've somehow never seen on her before.

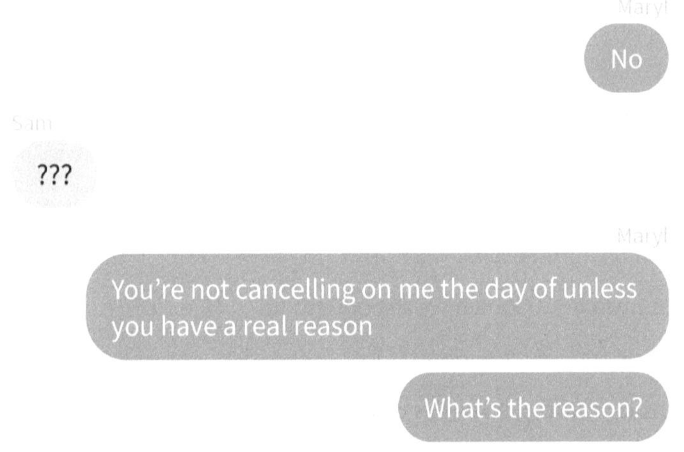

I watch the dots appear and disappear at the bottom of my screen. When they disappear for good, I roll my eyes, finally sit up in bed, and call him.

"Look, I'm not a stalker or anything. I just have info you might want to know," I say the second he picks up.

"Damn, Pokémon, you sound like a spy," Sam replies, his voice scratchy and slow.

I pull my phone away from my ear and check the time. 9:03 a.m. He probably woke up and sent the text.

"I'm not," I say. "At least not the professional kind."

He exhales. "What's the info?"

"Come to coffee with me."

"Really? I get nothing?"

"No. I'm keeping you hanging in the hopes it'll bring you there."

He laughs. "I have time before work now. You free?"

"Oh, so you're anxious for information, eh?" I joke, then stop myself from getting too cocky. "Yes, I'm free."

Half an hour later, I reach Uncommon Grounds. I chose this specific coffee shop because it's halfway between Dalhousie and Inked in Sin. I walk down the steps and into the building built into a hill, like so many businesses in Halifax. The inside is roomy and homey. It feels like stepping into Central Perk. Slate tables with white chairs line most of the windows and the left side of the shop. On the right is a section with plush armchairs and a long olive-green couch. An online review called it "basement chic," which I thought was hilarious, but is actually a pretty appropriate way of describing the vibe.

I join the line at the display counter. Their menu hangs above all the goodies that make my mouth water. Shining pretzels with crusted salt sprinkled on top, golden cinnamon rolls with icing dripping down the sides, brownies with all kinds of decadent toppings from caramel to maple to chocolate covered cherries, flaky, buttery scones that come with housemade cream.

Once I get to the front, I order a Nanaimo bar and blueberry muffin with dark hot chocolate. My new life goal is to try everything here. I grab my to-go box and cup and look around the coffee shop for the best spot.

"Hey, Pikachu!"

In spite of myself, I turn. There's no good reason why I should respond to or even think that I'm being called when someone yells out Pikachu, but I still look. Sam sits in one of the comfy armchairs, his back to me, but his head turned. I shake my head and watch him smile.

"That's not the kind of Pokémon I am," I say.

I settle down in an armchair across from him. I slide my phone into my Betsey Johnson mermaid satchel, a purse with a super subtle lilac, aqua, and white scale pattern. Sam appraises it and smirks.

"I know," he says with a chuckle. "Just wanted to see which ones you knew." I roll my eyes. "What's in the box?"

I open it and show him my treats. He gestures to the half demolished cinnamon roll lying on a white napkin in front of him.

"Solid choice," he says.

There's a nervous energy about him, and I get it. After he said Lottie's birthday at the tattoo shop on Friday, I basically stopped talking. Or, well, I stopped talking and pretended I was invested in watching my tattoo being done, but I just felt sick with information overload and watching needles being driven into my skin made it worse. Near the end of my session, I asked how he was doing with the tattoo and we lapsed back into easy conversation until I left. Obviously I didn't weird him out too much if he gave me his number. I know I'm not helping myself by telling him I have information but not saying who or what it's about.

"I like your glasses," he says after I've eaten half the muffin. "They're different than what people usually wear. I like the clear frames."

"Thank you," I say, my hand in front of my mouth so I don't spray crumbs all over him. "They're new. Got them when I went home for Christmas."

"Good choice." He smiles again, but it doesn't quite reach his eyes.

I take a deep breath. If I'm uncomfortable, then he's double that amount. I take a sip of hot chocolate like it's a shot.

"I'm so sorry for bringing you here and being a total idiot and making you uncomfortable, but—"

"No, stop," he says and puts his hand on top of mine, forcing me to look up at him instead of the table. "I may not know why you're here or what you're doing, and yeah, I did think it was really odd and that's why I cancelled, but I admire persistence and know that important things sometimes take a lot of courage. I think this might be important, otherwise you wouldn't keep hounding me."

"Well, I'm sorry for hounding you," I say it totally genuine, but can see the joking glint in his gorgeous eyes. "And I'm sorry everything I'm about to say is not going to make any sense."

"Lay it on me, Charmander."

I laugh. "You're going to have to stick to one Pokémon."

"Marill."

"Do you believe in ghosts?"

He pauses, a thoughtful look coming over his features. It's more thought than I would have put into the question. Two months ago I would have automatically answered no, but it's different now and it clearly means something to him. Eventually, he shrugs, feigning nonchalance, but I can see hesitation in how he fidgets with his coffee cup. He's seen something.

"I think it's possible."

"What would you do if I said I've been talking to your mother? Penelope Walsh."

He sucks in a breath through his teeth, opens his mouth to speak, but says nothing.

"Do you know anything about your father?"

He shakes his head. "My grandpa never told me anything. I overheard him talking about an affair once and I think it was in relation to me."

"What's your sister's name?"

"Charlotte. Lottie. Closed adoption, I've never been able to find anything about her."

"What if I told you I knew both of them?"

"I'd think you were joking."

"My roommate's name is Lottie Arthur. She was born on December 20th and she's eighteen. She's been searching for her birth family her entire life, but can't find anything because, as you say, her adoption was closed. And she has your eyes." Sam makes no move. His eyes shut and his hands go to the side of his head. I push on. "I also think I know your father. There's a professor at Dalhousie who's admitted he was involved with Penelope. The professor told me that he met you the day your mom died. You were five years old. I don't know if you'd remember that at all, but if you do—"

Sam moves quickly. He grabs his coat and gathers his belongings. He's up before I can say anything more. "I have to go," he says, his voice gruff and shaking. He doesn't look at me.

I watch him climb the stairs and leave the coffee shop. I've blown it.

Chapter Twenty-Three

Sam won't return my texts or calls and I don't blame him, but I'm still so ridiculously frustrated that my one lead won't help. So I decide to pursue a different lead. I sit at the Starbucks in front of Jason Ives's law firm instead. I sip on some intricately named coffee drink that I copied from the woman in line before me. Admittedly, it tastes good. I drum my fingers below my misspelt name.

I looked up Jason's socials and committed his face to memory. I'm working under the assumption that Jason might get his lunch here. So far, he hasn't. I peer overtop of my laptop anytime someone enters the coffee shop. Several businesspeople have come in, grabbed a drink and some food, then left. No Jason. I wonder if I'm wrong, if I should go, when the door jingles.

A man who looks strikingly similar to the photos I've studied walks in. Beside him, a woman with long, flowing curls points aggressively at a stack of papers. I don't get a solid look at her before she turns and saunters up to the counter, but I do get chills from her very distinct sneer. Could this be Elle? Two birds, one stone?

I close my laptop and catch Jason's eye. He glances at me briefly, then holds my stare. Jason is the complete opposite of Denver. While Denver commands a room easily, looks well read and neatly groomed, and reels you in with his charm, Jason exudes smarminess with his slicked back blond hair, too thin face, and guarded body language. I break eye contact and look down at my phone. Still nothing from Sam. I shove my laptop back into its case, then into my bag. I shuffle through the pockets of my coat for something to do.

Jason orders while his female companion waits at the back of the store. When he heads back to join her, I stand.

"Excuse me, are you Jason Ives?" I ask. I pull something out of my pocket in my haste and plunk it down on the table without looking.

Jason raises an eyebrow, scowl lessening just slightly. "I am. Why?"

"No reason, specifically," I say and bat my lashes. "A friend of mine showed me a photo of you a few days ago and I thought it was funny that you'd randomly appear."

"Why was a friend of yours showing you a photo of me?" he asks, the raised eyebrow morphing into a furrow of confusion.

I shrug. "You were in the background and I asked."

"Who's your friend?"

"Her name's Leah."

"Leah?" He smirks. "I'm not sure I know a Leah, sorry." He tries to push past me.

"She's older than me," I explain quickly. "We work together. I assumed you guys dated when she showed me the photo, but she said you were her friend's boyfriend."

"When was this?"

"Oh, over twenty years ago," I say easily. He smiles at his friend behind me. I glance over my shoulder and see the woman grabbing her drink. "I think her name was Penny?"

Jason sucks in a sharp breath. "Oh."

I try to read his expression, but it's guarded. The shock is evident along with something almost like grief, almost like Denver's reaction to seeing Penny.

"I'm sorry," I say.

"Don't worry about it," he says, though he says it with a distinct edge of pain. "She was the one that got away, you know?" He looks me over and takes in how young I am. "Or maybe you don't know. She died while I was away at law school. I got home that summer and found out. We hadn't dated in years, didn't end on the best of terms, but still a gut punch." He pauses. "I don't know why I'm telling you this."

"Sorry," I say again.

His friend appears next to me, and though her face seems tighter and more pinched than any of the photographs I've seen of her, it's unmistakably Elle. She narrows her eyes, then turns her glare on Jason. It only lasts for a moment once she takes in how distraught he is.

"What's going on?" Elle asks, voice shrill. She leans against the table, angling herself between me and him with her arm. "Is this *girl* bothering you?"

Jason shakes his head and touches his friend's upper arm. He guides her away with a shy smile my way. "It's nothing, Elle, just talking about an old friend."

They head back to retrieve his order and I have no choice but to walk away. I shrug into my coat and hang my bag over my shoulder. I glance at the back of the shop. Jason seems to be convincing Elle of something. She shakes her head and shoves her coffee free hand deep into the pocket of her leather jacket. Jason speaks to her and whatever it is catches her off guard. She meets my eyes for a brief moment, then they flicker away.

I store the interaction in the back of my mind. It's another thing I'll have to tell Lottie when she returns, even though this might not go anywhere.

Chapter Twenty-Four

I HEAD UP TO Old Eddy when I get back to campus. Somewhere between Starbucks and Dalhousie, I lost my keys. Security told me they'd have a new key in an hour if I had twenty-five dollars. Penny sits on the floor, arms folded and eyes narrowed.

"When were you going to tell me you stayed on campus?" Penny asks.

"Why? Did you miss me?"

"I don't miss people who avoid me."

I get it. I've been so preoccupied in drama about her that I forgot to actually include her.

"I got a tattoo," I say.

She takes my arm and studies the healing mermaid. It's an odd sensation as she runs her fingers along the delicate line work. I can only feel the touch once she moves her fingers away, like a sharp, cold aftershock. By the time she's done, my arm is covered in goosebumps.

"You're the reason he came to visit me then," Penny whispers.

"What?" I ask. "Who?"

"Sam."

We both stay silent. The news sinks over me. My words made him come here. He's come here before. I saw him at the beginning of last year in this exact spot and didn't think anything of it, but it clearly means as much, if not more, to him as it does to me. Which means he probably remembers something about the day his mom died and this is where he feels connected to her.

"He can't see me," Penny says. "He comes here every few months. It's his last connection to me."

"You told me you weren't sure if he was even alive."

"Well, I lied. I wasn't sure about Lottie, but I knew with him. He's always been my little secret and I guess I've taken that with me. I didn't want him involved, okay? I never wanted him involved in this."

I nod. Bingo. I fucked up all three of these relationships in under a week. Where's my award now? I close my eyes and lean my head back against the wall. I don't know where to go from here and there's no one I can bounce ideas off of. It's just me, alone with a ghost and an empty university. I should have gone home. I shouldn't have cared about the damn moth tattoo or the dates. I should have left it alone.

I'm about to leave when Penny speaks. The tone in her voice makes me stop and look. "I appreciate you," she says. "I don't want you thinking I don't. What you're doing is wonderful and I don't want you to stop, okay?"

She waits for me to acknowledge what she said, but I don't know how. I'm so tired. Pursuing dead leads for almost two months really takes it out of you.

"What if I want to stop?" I ask.

"Do you really, or are you just discouraged?" She studies me. The prickly feeling in my nose tells me that I'm close to crying and I don't know why. "Do you want to see my tattoo?"

I stare at her, wondering if that's even possible. If she's damned to wear this outfit for eternity, how can she show me something I can't already see? She turns her back to me and piles her hair to one side. Peeking out between her shoulder blades is the same moth that Sam described as a foggy dream. The moth is in shades of black and grey, with its wings spread, each tip touching an edge of her shoulder blade, but as I look closer, it seems like an omen of death. In the centre of the moth's body is a subtle skull.

After a suitable amount of time, Penny drops her hair and turns back to me. She notices the colour drained from my face. Pieces keep fitting together and I don't like them.

"I know it's an odd choice. I drew it and the moth totem has always meant a lot to me, so I got it after Sam was born as a kind of rebirth for myself."

"Sam just got that exact tattoo."

"He did?"

I nod and as if summoned by the moth, footsteps sound throughout the hallway. Penny looks up at the exact moment I do. Sam stops when he sees me on the floor. He hesitates, then confidently saunters up to me and sits down. Penny sighs. She stands and runs her hand along her son's cheek. He lifts his own hand to where hers was moments before. Then, resigning herself to the fact that I've gotten her son involved in the search for her murderer, Penny leaves.

"Your mom was just here," I whisper.

"I know," Sam says. His eyes focus on a space down the hall, as if he doesn't want to look at me. Or maybe he's waiting for Penny to return. "Sometimes I come here when I want to feel close to her. I can't quite explain what this place makes me feel. I've always been told that she died here... Well, not specifically here, but this is where I'm drawn to so I guess I assumed. You said I was here the day she died and it's like I remember, but I don't. It feels like a fever dream I've probably buried."

Sam's face is drawn tight. I hate myself for making him feel this way. I barely even know him, but there's something so genuinely sweet about Sam that I feel like I've crushed him. He looks down, sniffs, and runs a hand over his nose. I don't say anything.

"I can picture her hanging and I don't know if it's something I saw or something I've made up based on what people tell me. I remember her shoes, they were these black heels with open toes. Maybe that's all I could see? I also remember hiding. There's a little alcove over there—" He gestures further down the hallway. "That I stumbled down and curled up in. I remember sleeping there."

"Do you remember anyone else being here?" I finally ask after it's clear he's finished.

He shakes his head and scrunches up his nose as he closes his eyes. "I can hear shoes hitting the floor. I think they gave me a toy. Maybe that's why I don't remember fully. I was too distracted."

He takes large, shuddering breaths. His hand lies on top of his thigh and I grab hold of it. He doesn't move and his breathing pattern doesn't change, but he squeezes my hand.

"I'm sorry," I whisper. "I come here to feel close to her too. I obviously didn't know her while she was alive, but I've come to know her now and you were lucky to have her while you did. She really loves you, Sam. She loves you so much that she didn't want me getting you involved in this."

He looks down at our entwined hands, then up at my face. There's something so disarming about his gaze. The way he closed up moments before has vanished. His eyes are glassy and I feel like I'm staring into an ocean. He sniffs and smiles, transforming into that man I first met almost a week ago.

"Thank you," Sam says. "What are you getting me involved in?"

"I'm trying to find out who killed your mom," I say and notice the split second of surprise in his eyes. "She told me she didn't do it."

He shakes his head. "No, I never thought she did. Everyone I know accepted that narrative so it makes it kind of... challenging to say otherwise."

"Will you help me, then?" I ask and then backtrack, realizing how forward it is to ask someone that about their mother. But then again, I did do that with Lottie. "At the very least, maybe we could figure out if you and Lottie and Denver are related. But you don't have to if you don't want to."

"No, I want to," he says. "I can show you some stuff I have of hers at my apartment."

"Yeah, sure. Just let me grab my keys."

Chapter Twenty-Five

SAM'S APARTMENT IS BY the waterfront. From the twelfth floor, he has a beautiful view of the harbour. I make a beeline for the window as soon as he opens his door even though that's not the most socially acceptable thing to do. A cold front blows in over the water. Clouds dark and blue trail snow in their tendrils. A boat chugs its way down the narrows, adorned with tiny lights along its sails. The waves crash against the side of the boat, but I can see them building further out as well. If I wasn't here for a reason, I could sit and watch the storm blow in. Instead, I turn and find Sam, leaning against a wall, watching me. I blush.

"Sorry," I say.

He shakes his head and rights himself. "No, don't apologize. The view was part of the reason why I picked this place. You can sit there until I find the albums."

I shrug out of my coat and hang it on a wooden chair with a plaid cushion in his little kitchen. The round table surrounded by four chairs sits right in front of the sliding glass door I've been looking out. His place isn't big, but it's only him so it doesn't have to be. The door opens into a living area which he's decorated with a long, plush couch and another one of Penny's landscape paintings above. On the opposite wall, a flat screen TV balances in the centre of a giant wooden bookcase, all the cubbies filled with vinyl albums.

"Whoa," I breathe.

Sam returns from the small hallway I've yet to investigate, cradling a stack of photo albums in his arms. He catches me mid snoop, bending to check out the records at the bottom of the shelving unit. He smirks.

"See anything you like?" he asks.

"A lot of musical theatre." I state. "Where's your record player?"

"It's in my studio," he answers easily and offloads the photo albums onto the coffee table in the centre of the room.

"*Annie*?" I ask with a smirk.

He joins me by his records, stretching his legs out in front of him. He studies me for a moment, then shakes his head.

"You've never been to a play," he says. Not a question, a statement.

I raise my eyebrows and pause, my hand about to pull out another soundtrack. A spark appears in his eyes as he sizes me up. How does he know he's right? I don't give anything away, though, and reach for another record.

"I'll have to take you to one, then," he says.

I laugh. "No, I'm good. Something about people randomly bursting into song doesn't do it for me."

He places a hand on his chin, thoughtfully. "You could start with something like *Rock of Ages* or *Sweeney Todd*." He snaps his fingers. "Or *Book of Mormon*!"

"What got you started on them?"

"My mom." Sam smiles and points to the record I pulled out. "She took me to *Joseph and the Technicolor Dreamcoat* right before she died."

I inspect the record. It's well worn, old, with a peeling photo of Donny Osmond on the cover. The inside flap has a note to Penny. It was a gift from her mother. I look up at Sam.

"I'm sorry," I say. "I didn't realize it meant something to you."

He shrugs. "I get it. It's not the first time someone's commented on my love of musical theatre."

"I don't want to be that person. I'm sorry. I made a really rude judgement." I run my fingers over the inscription on the inside of the album. "It brings you closer to her, doesn't it?"

He looks skyward, at his popcorn ceiling, and I slide the record back into its place. I take a breath and study him. I've underestimated how hard this must be for him. I don't think I understood the oddity of someone coming into your life and telling you that they have all your missing pieces.

"A lot of things bring me closer to her. I think my life's work has been about feeling close to her. You know she was an artist, right?" I nod, my eyes slipping to the painting above his couch. He follows my gaze. "Yeah, that's hers."

I shake my head. "Everything she did was gorgeous. I could never."

"*I* could never," he laughs, then moves to stand. "Can I show you my studio? I'll bring the photo albums and we can look at them there. I'd love to show you some of my work."

I stand, feeling zero murder vibes from him. I know what happens in a movie when you follow someone deeper into their house, but this isn't a movie, and I am curious. I follow him down the hall I couldn't explore without him earlier. It's narrow, with a bathroom to the right, another door to the left, and what I assume must be his bedroom straight ahead. He takes the door on the left and opens it to the only colourful room in his apartment.

Beautifully intricate designs fill every free space of wall in the room. They haven't been drawn directly on the wall, and instead, are all tacked up overtop of each other. I catch the original design for his kraken tattoo next to a large window that pours light into the room. It's surrounded by other sea creatures—sharks, whales, a winding version of Nessie or possibly Ogopogo. The sea creatures bleed into other animals, a ferocious lion, a flock of birds, a paw print with flowers woven around it. Each section of the wall is divided into a category that bleeds into another, somehow creating a cohesive, almost mural-like appearance in the room. I feel like I've stepped into a piece of his mind. And I love it. I can feel my heart breaking and mending while looking at his illustrations, something I'm not familiar with on any level.

It takes me a while to realize I haven't said anything. I circle the whole room before noticing his intense, yet amused gaze on me.

"Sorry," I say when I finally find my voice. "Just, wow. You're your mother's son."

He breaks into a grin. He walks further into the room, which invites me to further embarrass myself. The room is not large, but it feels like another world. A beige love seat sits under the window. A strip of LED lights line the edges of the ceiling that Sam shifts to different colours. I note the colours dancing off an old record player sitting next to the couch. He turns on a lamp next to his drafting desk. It illuminates his latest work—a mermaid. I glance down at my tattoo and step closer.

He laughs awkwardly, a hand going to the back of his neck. "I was inspired by your tattoo... And you, I guess."

I meet his eyes for a moment, then shift back to the mermaid. I hadn't noticed at first glance, but her features are unmistakably mine. The upturned nose, the pixie-like shape of my chin and cheeks, my thick arched brows. The eyes are closed, but the head is looking toward the surface, hair that I wish I had flowing behind. It's unfinished. Only the head has colour while the body and tail lay bare.

"You told me about your tattoo and I figured you might want to see what you'd look like as your own mermaid. I also, kind of, wanted to see that in case I never saw you again."

"Why would you never see me again?" I ask before thinking better and adding, "This is beautiful."

"Thank you," Sam says. "Wasn't sure if you'd want to speak to me again after I bailed on you."

"I get why you did," I say and eye the photo albums he dumped on the couch. "This is a lot."

He sits next to the albums. I stand and wait, not wanting to be overbearing, but wanting more than anything to see what's inside. I take one last look at the mermaid, then plop down beside him. He opens the first book and sets his hands over it.

"When I moved out of my grandpa's house last year, he gave me all the photo albums. I don't know if he didn't want them or if he thought they'd make me feel closer to Mom. I didn't ask. I just took them with me." He looks down at the album, then back up at me. "This one is all her childhood."

We flip through pages of Penny growing up. A few times, he stops to tell me a story. I get a clear picture of Penny's life through the pages. She's so carefree. So ready to take life by the balls and go for what she wanted. Even as a kid, her spark is evident. Her eyes are pools that seem to see straight through to my soul in every picture. It's the same way I feel when I look at her paintings. The next album is entirely devoted to her progression as an artist. She was gifted right from the start.

"Grandpa did the same for me," Sam explains. He gestures to the deep green album at the bottom of the pile. "That one has all of my art."

My eyes light up at the thought. "Can I see?"

"Yeah, of course," he says. "I want to show you something first."

He reaches for the thickest album. 1993–2001 is scrawled across the front. Her time at university up until her death. He doesn't explain, seeming to sense I already know how important these photos are. Penny's effervescence shines through the shots from a disposable camera. There are countless photos of her at different parties, art shows, and everyday life. There's also one of her in front of Shirreff Hall. I put my hand on top of Sam's for a moment and pause, shocked to see her where I live, in the flesh and not as I see her now.

"It's so weird to see her alive," I say.

Sam stays silent, then deeply exhales. "I guess it would be weird for you."

"I'm sorry. That's insensitive. It's definitely weirder for you."

He smiles and shakes his head as I straighten up and shift marginally away from him. In my haste to stare at her photo, I've nearly jumped into his lap. He doesn't seem to mind, though, as if he's somehow at ease with the girl who's uprooted his life.

"Stop saying you're sorry," Sam says. "You have nothing to be sorry for. If anything, you're doing me a favour."

"I am?"

"I've spent my life wondering what happened to her. This may be absolutely wild and I may not have expected you to walk into the tattoo shop and tell me you see dead people, but you seem to know what you're doing. Or, rather, you seem to be committed to what you're doing enough that you're eventually going to do it well."

I stare at him. Some form of disbelief floats through my mind. I've known him for a little less than a week and he already has faith in me.

"Thank you," I say and we lapse into silence again for a few pages.

Five pages later, he pauses on a photo and I immediately know why. Penny's a little older here. From what I know of her story, this must be the end of her second year. The rigidity of her features, just behind her smile, tells me that she already knows she's pregnant. But that's not why he paused. It's because next to Penny is Denver. It looks like an end of semester party. They're in the creative writing lecture hall, brightly lit, with a table full of food in the background. Other students mull around the edges of the photo, but the focus is clearly on Penny and Denver. I pull the photo from its plastic casing and turn it over. *Leah's Creative Writing Summer Semester Party 1995*, is scrawled on the back in loopy printing. I place it back in the album.

"What?" Sam asks.

"What does that one mean to you?"

He shrugs, his eyes flicker between mine and the photo. "I don't know."

"That's Denver Keyes. I'm almost certain he's your father."

This doesn't surprise him. He merely nods, but keeps his eyes trained on the photograph. Minutes pass before he turns the page again, which is fine because I need a moment to process too. Penny wasn't in Denver's class in summer semester and Leah was one of the only people who knew about the two of them. So that must mean Leah encouraged Penny to come to the party and take this picture, if only for a memory.

The swish of crinkling plastic jars me from my thoughts and the photos switch from university, to Penny's growing stomach. Her whole pregnancy is documented in a matter of pages, then jumps to her living life as a mom.

"I have a baby book too," Sam says. "In case you were wondering where the copious amounts of me were. These books are mainly about her. I think it was something cathartic for Grandpa after she died."

I nod and watch Penny age in pictures. From new mom, to artist, to bridesmaid, to mom again. Penny has never mentioned Lottie's father. Denver is fair game; old news. Lottie's father is a mystery.

"Sam," I say, breaking the silence. "Weird question but, do you know who Lottie's dad is?"

He makes a face as if expecting the question, then shakes his head. "No one ever spoke about it. And if I've learned anything from my own paternal experience, it's that if no one talks about it, that means there's a secret."

"Do you think the secret is big enough to kill over?"

He turns the page. "Maybe."

I glance down and zero in on a photo of Penny, holding a newborn Lottie and grinning while standing next to a scowling woman also holding a baby. I've seen her face before too and it takes a moment for me to place her in my brain.

"Elle," I say.

"What?"

"That woman. Her name's Elora. She was on the swim team with your mom. I don't think she knows how to make another face. Do you know her?"

"I think she was my mom's best friend. She always seemed to be around when I was little, but I haven't seen her since Mom died. I can't remember the funeral so I don't know if she was there."

"Do you know who the baby is?"

"Yeah," he says and nods. "My mom and her friend were pregnant at the same time. They gave birth a few days apart and always talked about how their babies would grow up and get married." He pauses for a moment. "I don't know why I remember that."

I wonder what Elora knows. Sam turns the page and I focus on a photo of his grandpa with a laughing Lottie. She looks maybe four months old. Penny doesn't have much time left. I'm about to ask if Sam's grandpa might know anything more when the lights suddenly go out and the album clatters onto the floor. Time has slipped away and dull sunlight no longer filters through the window, leaving us surrounded by swirling, indistinguishable lines on the wall, seeming to creep closer in the dark.

Sam stands. "The power must have gone out. Come on."

He holds out a hand and guides me down the hall and into the main room of his apartment. The darkness is less encroaching here, saved by the larger sliding doors that bank in light from the harbourfront. The storm moved in while we talked in his studio. Small specks of generator created light emanate from below, but apartments and buildings around are shadowed. Misty gales of snow blow against the sliding doors, making it impossible to see clearly. A few inches of snow have already accumulated on the balcony.

"Wow," Sam says, and I realize how close he is next to me up against the window. "I haven't seen a storm this quick in years."

I slip my phone out of my pocket and glance at the time. 7:02 p.m. We've been in the studio for a few hours.

"I know this is a lot to ask, but would you mind staying here tonight? It's nasty out there. I'd feel better if I knew you were safe and not out in the storm."

"Very 'Baby It's Cold Outside' of you."

He laughs. "I promise I'm not trying anything."

I stare into his eyes. I've never seen ones so honest before. For some reason, I can't imagine a mean bone in his body. So I nod and tell him I believe him.

Later that night, I lie on his couch and he lounges on the floor, sketching in one of his books. Sam had offered me his bed and volunteered to sleep on the couch, but I refused. I didn't want to inconvenience him more, so he found me blankets and I'm pretty sure he gave me his own pillow and I made a bed on the couch. I changed into one of his gigantic shirts and curled up, using the remaining data on my phone to sift through Instagram. But I feel his gaze on me, so I meet it.

"What?" I whisper.

"Do you think you'll be able to do it?"

"Do what?

"Do you think we'll find who killed her?"

My heart skips a beat. *We.* The more people I get on my team, the more I believe I—no, we—actually can do it.

I smile. "I think we might."

Chapter Twenty-Six

FRIDAY MORNING LIGHT JOLTS me awake. Stormy skies and blankets of white-walled snow give way to sun shining through the clearest sky into the apartment. We didn't close the drapes last night, too entranced by the worsening storm until we fell asleep. I run a hand through the newly formed tangles of my hair and take in the apartment in natural morning light.

Sam lies on the floor, a blanket haphazardly tucked to his chin, covering only his upper body. His sketchbook is open, a fairly detailed portrait of my face taking shape. I asked him what he was drawing last night after I realized he kept glancing up at me. A camp lantern illuminated his living space, casting shadows on both of us, and apparently highlighting my face enough that he took interest. I threw a blanket on him when midnight came and the storm hadn't stopped. Even though he's on hardwood floor, he looks at peace. The sharp plains of his jaw relax. A lightness settles in my stomach as I register this change in him from last night. Going through the photo albums, talking about his fractured family, his jaw was set, working, uncomfortable.

I sit up and stretch, peeling back the blanket. Cool air hits my bare legs and makes me shiver as I walk over to the windows. The sun beats down on the crystal snow and I shade my eyes. The cloak of snow and ice over the world soothes me. I unlock the sliding door, open it a crack, and breathe in the crisp air. The wind blows loose snow on the railing up into my face. I close my eyes and sigh.

"You act like you've never seen snow before," Sam says.

I startle and turn around. He's so close and I kind of want to touch his shoulders and grab hold of him. Why is this somehow intimate? What's wrong with me? I swallow and shake my head.

"I'm from Montréal," I say, emphasizing the French pronunciation. "I'm hardly a stranger to snow. I just love the world like this. Cloaked in this pure, crystallized blanket, washing away everything and starting anew."

His eyes bore into mine and his lips quirk up. "I love that. I've always seen it as more of an inconvenience, but I can see the appeal from up here." He walks away and into the kitchen. I close the door. "Besides, can't be too much of an inconvenience if I get to wake up with you."

Heat creeps up my neck and onto my cheeks. "That was extremely forward." I laugh.

He shrugs, but keeps eye contact, judging whether I'm feeling the same way. And though I have no idea, I find myself entertaining the thought. I think he senses this as he breaks, looks down at the marble countertop, and smiles.

"What's the plan today?" Sam asks, opening the fridge and staring at the meagre contents inside.

I pull out one of the stools, sit, and lean my head in my hands. "Nothing murder related. I have a creative writing assignment due tonight, so that. Though, I guess that's vaguely murder related, by extension."

He glances over his shoulder. "By extension?"

"Denver Keyes is my professor. That's kind of what started this whole thing. I may have thought he killed Penny at first."

Sam turns around, carton of eggs in hand. He kicks the fridge door shut and nods. "I guess that's a fair assumption. It's always the husband, right?"

"Or jilted lover."

"Something to do with love," he says and cracks an egg into a frying pan. "Enough to drive a person mad, one way or another."

I raise an eyebrow. "Do you really believe that?"

Another shrug. "In some ways. I think there's good and bad kinds of *mad*, though. There's the mad where you kill someone and then there's the mad that's, like, I will do anything for you, take a bullet for you, kind of love."

"Those are both quite extreme," I say.

"Love is, don't you think?"

I've only ever loved one man. Though to be fair, it was just high school first love. But I see his point. I remember the very highs and the very lows of being in love at sixteen. I remember feeling out of my mind and also wanting to set my brother on him when he dumped me.

"You're not wrong," I admit.

He laughs. "Do you like eggs?"

Campus is dead when I get back. I expected people to start coming back around now. I guess Friday evening is the slightest bit early. We still have two more days of break.

And then there's me.

I don't really know if I got any further on the cold case thing, but I know my next steps. I have to talk to Lottie, convince her, Sam, and probably Denver to take DNA tests. I have to talk to Leah about Penny and Denver and Jason and Elora. And then I have to convince Sam to let me talk to his grandpa. I guess it's a multifaceted sort of plan.

Sam dropped me off in front of Shirreff Hall. I had every intention of going in, but campus looks so nice right now so I kept walking. The snow blankets the grass and walkways, pure and untouched since no one's back. In the glow of twilight, the snow glistens in white tinged shades of lilac, ultramarine, violet, and sapphire. The lamp-posts illuminate my way, making me feel as though I've stepped into Narnia.

I smile and pull my hat the tiniest bit further down. Am I dressed for a walk? Maybe not. I didn't expect snow when I left for Sam's yesterday, so even though I have a warm coat and hat, I'm wearing ankle booties and forgot my gloves. I shove my hands into my pockets and jump as someone crosses my path.

"Maryl?" they ask in confusion.

I look up into the face of Lewis Pickering, the last person I want to see right now. I'm torn between telling him to fuck off and just rage screaming. But he takes this hesitation and runs with it, bridging the distance between us and latching onto my elbow.

"Do you have a thing for elbows?" I ask, stupidly. It's the first thing that pops into my mind at the touch, along with the notion that I want to throw up.

He laughs, an overindulgent noise that borders on being fake. His grip tightens as I try to squirm away.

"We didn't get to finish our conversation the other day," he says.

I mentally go through how long ago it was that I literally ran away from him. Another unhelpful part of my brain wonders if he's complained about this on the internet, then stops, because even though I don't want to admit it, I think he's dangerous.

"There wasn't much of a conversation."

I finally dislodge myself from his grip and take a step back. I scan the barren pathways and curse myself for walking away from the residence hall. No one is around. At all.

"Well, I guess I wasn't really interested in the conversation part," he says and shoots me a grin that sets my teeth on edge.

What would he do if I puked on his shoes?

"I'm not interested in any other part."

He rolls his eyes and advances on me again, tilting his head down and bringing his mouth to my ear. "It didn't seem that way a month ago."

I push against his chest, wanting nothing more than to run away, but not trusting myself to stay upright in the snow. Shock registers on his face at the force. He almost loses his footing, but makes up for it by invading my personal space and grabbing hold of my wrist. An image of Penny's bruised wrist flashes in my mind and I involuntarily shudder. Lewis smiles and his arms come around me, one hand resting at the back of my neck.

I freeze. I know he doesn't take no for an answer so anything I say won't matter. I register sound somewhere but can't waste thought on it. I wrack my brain for everything Stephen's taught me about self-defence, but all that comes to mind is that scene in *Miss Congeniality.* With my arms pinned between my body and his, I don't have the swing room to use them. His hands roam my body. His lips come down on my neck. I take a deep breath, throw my leg back, and thrust my knee up into his groin.

Lewis Pickering drops instantly, crying out and buckling at the knees. Because of his tight grip on me, I fall with him. Pain and ice jolts through my left arm as I slam it into the ground. Tears form in my eyes, but I blink them away and push myself up, knowing he won't stay down for long. I pivot on my heel back to Shirreff, needing enough ground for a slight gap between us. When I turn, I run into a human-sized wall and scream.

"Hey!" Sam says as his strong arms steady me. "What's going on here?"

Samuel Walsh has come to my rescue. I close my eyes and sigh. Objectively, I would have been fine. I would have run away from Lewis and called campus security. I would have reported him and tried my damnedest to get him fired. I would have told Denver Keyes what a piece of shit his teaching assistant was and hoped he believed me. But I can't deny power in numbers.

Sam looks down on Lewis, literally and figuratively. Disgust creeps over his features as I realize how much he must have seen and that he must have been the one I heard.

"Here's what's going to happen," Sam says confidently. His arms tighten around me. "You're going to get up and you're going to walk away. You're never going to touch or talk to Maryl again. I assume she's told you the same, right? I'm telling you again because I think you'll listen now that two people know what kind of scum you are. And if you ever come near her again..." A laugh. "I don't think you'll like what happens"

He lets his words sit in the silence. I don't dare look at Lewis, but I can hear scuttling as he lifts himself off the wet cobblestones and breaks into a run.

"Fucker," Sam mutters. He doesn't say anything for a few moments and I assume he's watching Lewis leave. I stay where I am and listen to the rapid thumping of his heart steady. "Maryl, are you okay? Did he hurt you?"

I pull back from him and look up into his wide eyes, sparked with concern. I bring my hands up to my face and notice they're shaking, but I'm not sure if that's from cold or shock.

"Come on. Let's get somewhere warm and figure this out." Sam pulls me to his side and we walk back to Shirreff Hall.

In the comfort of my dorm room, I tell him about my history with Lewis and what happened tonight. It all comes tumbling out of me in a way that makes me aware of how much I needed this. I study him as I speak. How he shrugs as I admit how Lewis and I first met. The way his fists clench when I tell him about Lewis harassing me at the pub. How his eyes widen and narrow with concern when I talk about tonight.

"I'm okay, I think," I say.

I inspect my body as Sam does the same. He reaches out and touches my wrist, already bruising. He draws his hand up my arm to my elbow and I wince at the touch.

"You were holding it when you ran into me," he explains. He examines my arm further, touching different places and waiting for a reaction. His hands are large and skilled, but soft. "My grandpa taught me the basics on injuries. He was a fisherman and an outdoorsman, so he knows all about first aid. I'm no doctor, but I don't think anything's broken. You can bend it and it's not extraordinarily painful. I prescribe ice and rest."

"Thank you," I say. "For everything."

He drops my arm, runs his hands along his jeans, and smiles. "No problem. You looked like you had it covered anyway, but backup never hurts."

I nod. "You're definitely my backup in more ways than one."

"Yeah, you're lead investigator and I'm second in command," he says with a laugh. "You know, if you'll let me. I know we just met."

"Your mom's going to be mad at me."

"What do you mean?"

"She wanted me to keep you out of this. If she finds out you're second in command, then she'll be pissed."

He shrugs. "Moms get that way." A grin. "You know, I think it's really cool you can talk to her."

"I don't know how all that works," I say with an awkward laugh. "I didn't even believe in it until last month. It's weird."

"It's awesome. I'd give anything to have that sort of power."

"Well, you've got me. If you ever want to know if a ghost's around, I'll tell you. I guess... If I even know."

Sam laughs again, the most musical sound, then something catches his eye. He gets up and walks toward Lottie's desk. The bulletin board above it is full of photos. Sam's focus on my well-being left blinders up on the rest of the room. My room is as much my own as it is his sister's. He pulls one of the pictures away from the wall. It's a selfie of her and Grayson, one that features more of her face than his. It's crystal-clear, taken on portrait mode with the background a blur. It takes me a moment to realize what he's focusing on in the photo.

"I've looked for this since the day my mom died," he says and distractedly sits down next to me on my bed. I glance down where his finger is pointing. The necklace.

"She says that's all she has of her mom. Her parents were given it when they adopted her."

Jade. Blessing. Eyes. Moth.

The words all fall into place.

"I have to talk to her. Can we make that happen?"

I nod and pull out my phone. I'll tell her when she gets back on Sunday. This week has slipped away from me as I've learned more about their world. I don't know if she's still mad at me. I text her anyway.

Maryl

Do you have any of your baby pictures? If you do can you bring some back here with you?

Chapter Twenty-Seven

I HAVEN'T SPOKEN TO Lottie since the Friday before break and it makes me more anxious than I'd like to admit. She didn't return on Sunday. She texted me saying she'd be back in the dorm on Monday morning instead, and yes, she'd bring some baby pictures. But I couldn't sleep, so I wasn't in the dorm, and instead I sat downstairs in the Shirreff Hall cafeteria and sipped stale coffee. I didn't know what to say to Lottie or Penny, so I avoided them both. When Leah came in to work, I shrunk away from my seat and left.

Why am I avoiding people? This is the most important part of the mystery. I have to bring everyone together to fully get information, but I also can't force people into doing what I want.

So I'm here. Sitting next to Hale in Creative Writing, not loving him or my life; not loving my choices; not loving the fact that I can't find Lewis Pickering and that flicker of unreliability furthers adds to my brewing anxiety.

"You good?" Hale asks when class ends.

The truth is no, I'm not good. But I don't want to tell him anything because my last conversation with him is still bright in my mind. He was so weird when we had dinner. He kept talking about Lottie and how she's a bad roommate. He kept comparing her to Blake, who is apparently the best roommate ever.

"Yeah, I'm fine. Why?"

He shrugs. "Why do you think Keyes doesn't have our assignments ready? He's usually so on top of things."

"Maybe reading week got to him too," I say and slip into my coat. I scan the front row of seats in the lecture hall and find Lottie's eyes. She raises an arm and nods to the door. *Thank god.* "I'll see you later, okay?"

I don't wait for Hale's response, but register his grunt of annoyance. When I've finally made my way to the front of the lecture hall, my name is called. For a split second, I think it's Lewis, and for whatever reason reach for my phone, intent on calling Sam. But then my eyes lock on Denver.

"Professor Keyes," I say. I almost feel ridiculous and ballsy enough to curtsy, but I don't.

"I wanted to talk to you about your assignment, if that's all right?"

I make eye contact with Lottie and hold up a finger. She nods and pulls out her phone. A moment later, I feel mine vibrate in my pocket. Denver leads me back to his office like he did two weeks ago. I sit down in the same chair and stare at the same painting.

"I read your story," Denver says as he settles into his chair. "And having read all of your previous stories, I know that it's biographical fiction."

I flush. "You only read mine?"

"I went through A to L as I normally do, but couldn't get through the full stack. My TA quit on me and he usually covers the second half of the alphabet."

I can't help the gasp I let out. He quit. Because of *me.* I nod as if I understand his struggle, and truthfully, I do. He has double the amount of work he usually does because of Lewis.

"But I read yours," Denver continues. "And I want you to talk to me about it because I think you've found out something important. Or rather, you've found someone."

I freeze and stare straight ahead. Maybe it was a mistake to write about a woman finding her friend's long-lost family. I don't know who to tell first. I know Sam wants to talk to Lottie, but he seemed hesitant to meet his father. Well, presumed father. Denver breathes in my hesitation, a furrow forming between his brows. It's in this inquisitive gaze that I see Sam. I recall his patience as I told him about Lewis and his anxiety as he ran out of that coffee shop at our first meeting outside of his work. Denver exudes calm, but his legs twitch. His eyes dart to the door momentarily, then come back to me.

"I found someone," I say when he catches my eye again. He relaxes instantly, shoulders slumping, creases flattening. "I don't know what my place is in all of this. I'm juggling three, technically four, people reacting to each other and I don't know whose emotions I should prioritize. I hate being the middleman, but that seems like my role in all of this and I don't know how to deal with—"

"Breathe," Denver instructs.

I close my eyes and do. When I open them again and see the concern and care softening his, his body leaned toward mine, I'm hit with déjà vu so hard that I almost start crying. There's no doubt in my mind that Sam is Denver's son.

"I'm almost certain I found your son," I whisper.

He leans back in his chair and sighs. He takes his glasses off and runs his hands over his face. "Thank you. That is enough for today. I appreciate you doing this and I know where you're coming from. Just knowing I'm so much closer than I've ever been is quite a feeling, so thank you, Maryl."

"You're welcome," I say and I truly mean it. I hope beyond all hope that it works out well for the both of them. "I'll let you know when I know more."

Lottie's rearranging her bulletin board when I walk into our room.

"Oh, sorry," I say, "if I messed up your photos. I thought I had it in the right spot."

She looks at me and raises an eyebrow. "Did it fall?"

I shake my head, take a deep breath, and ease myself down onto my bed. "I have something to tell you."

"You're not pregnant, are you?"

I laugh. "God, no."

"Okay, good." Lottie plops down on her own bed. The springs creak under her as she reaches into her nightstand and pulls out an envelope. "So what's up?"

"I think I may have found your brother," I blurt because I don't know how to make the news any less dramatic.

"What?"

I tell her about the week I've had. She stays completely still and silent as I let her know how close she was to a piece of her family. By the time I've finished my story, she's wiping tears from her eyes and trying to pretend that she isn't a heartbeat away from a sob.

"So what do we do? What's next?" she asks through shuddery breaths.

"I took a picture from one of Sam's albums. That's why I asked you to bring baby photos. I wanted to see if they looked similar."

Lottie stands and rushes over to my bed. She opens the envelope and pours the contents out into her hands. It's a small stack of photos. A few Polaroids, but mostly glossy photo prints. She lays ten photos across my comforter. I glance over each of them until one stops me in my tracks. An infant Lottie stares back at me, all bright green eyes and chubby cheeks. She's lying on a knitted blanket in a backyard, grass visible around the edges. I reach into my backpack and pull out the folder where I've stored the stolen photograph. I lay it down next to the one on the grass.

One where she's laughing with her grandpa. Next to each other, there's no denying that this is the same baby, on the same day. She looks around four months old and has the exact same daisy printed onesie on in both.

Lottie picks up the two photos and stares. Her mouth slowly drops open. The tears come to her eyes but she doesn't wipe them away this time.

"You're going to roll your eyes or something, but my horoscope said someone from my past would reappear and I would have to embrace them. That's me in both of those photos. And he knew my necklace too. There's too many coincidences for it to be a coincidence."

"I know."

"So what do we do now?"

"He wants to meet you," I say. Lottie resurfaces from the photos. Her eyes widen, a trace of fear in them. "I guess that's the first step. You guys could talk and then do a DNA test. I looked it up and a lab here can get results within 24–48 hours."

"You'll come with me, right?"

"Of course I will."

Chapter Twenty-Eight

"Do you approve of me introducing Sam and Lottie to each other?" I ask Penny.

She's mad at me. I totally get it, but at the same time, I just... don't. I'm trying to help her but I can't help her without a full picture. The more people I meet lead me closer to the truth.

Penny shakes her head. She stands with her arms crossed, looking down at me from my place on the floor. I rest my head on my hands and watch her begin to pace. Like mother, like daughter.

"I can't stop it, can I?" she asks.

"Why would you want to?"

She lets out an exaggerated sigh and closes her eyes. "I don't know. I feel like such a terrible mother for not having them know each other already. What if they meet and they're angry at me?"

"Trust me, they're not." I smile and hope it's reassuring. "They're excited to finally connect."

Or, at least, they're both open to the idea. I just need to make it happen. Penny stops pacing and stares at me. I feel like I'm being read. Some sort of internal judging is happening and Penny will eventually tell me what won in her mind. But for now, her seafoam eyes bore into me. I stay completely still and let them.

"I think you have some planning to do," she relents. "Go get them together. Denver too."

The heavily tattooed receptionist at Inked in Sin openly laughs when I walk into the shop. I roll my eyes. I came here once before, when Sam wasn't speaking to me, to see if he was in. He wasn't. But the receptionist had no problem telling me that I wasn't Sam's type. Unfortunately for her, I think she's wrong.

Sam told me to meet him here when I asked if we could talk. I said we could talk by phone, but he suggested in person. That way, he'd get to see me. I don't know how Penny will feel about her son flirting with me, but I can't say I mind.

"Guess who I'm here to see," I say, getting the slightest rise out of the receptionist.

She raises her eyebrows and gets up from her office chair without saying a word to me. She loudly enunciates when she gets to the back of the shop, "Sam, this is getting ridiculous. That girl is here to see you again."

I don't hear his response, but I do hear the silence in the wake of it. Whatever he's said has left her speechless. She scoffs, then reappears at the front of the shop. Not for the first time ever, or even today, she gives me a once over, then waves me back.

It doesn't take me long to find Sam. His station is at the middle of the shop. A few designs similar to the ones on the walls of his studio hang on the walls here. He smiles as I walk back into his space and take a seat on the black leather stool. His hands work quickly as he cleans the area. He picks up a leather-bound scrapbook and hands it to me, letting me know I can look at it while he cleans up.

I open the book and am once more entranced by his work. He creates beautiful worlds in ink. The first few additions in the book are the original designs for his tattoos. After that are a series of pictures showing finished tattoos next to the drawing. As I flip the pages, I realize that Sam's specialty is watercolour tattoos, the ones that are mostly linework, but look as though they've been painted onto your skin with watercolour. I've seen thousands of tattoos like this ever since the trend began, but there's something about his work that almost has a magical quality. His birds come alive, his fireworks look like they could jump off the page and into the sky. I'm so enthralled by his work that I don't realize he's ready to go until I reach the final page and look up to find him staring.

"That's me," I gasp.

The last page in the book is the sketch he made of me last Thursday. Sometime between then and now, he finished it. I'm struck by how lifelike it is; how perfectly he captured the odd way the light was hitting my face that night; how accurate he represented the question in my eyes. I glance up at him then back down at the portrait.

"That's a copy," he explains, rubbing a hand along the back of his neck. "I have the original if you want it."

"I do," I say. I'm momentarily caught off guard. So much so, that I completely forget why I'm here and that Lottie's waiting outside. "Lottie."

"What?"

"You wanted to meet Lottie. I'm about to spring something on you and I don't blame you if you say no, but I brought Lottie here. You said you wanted to meet her and I talked to her yesterday and she said she wanted to meet you too, so she's here."

"She's here?" His face lights up as he grins, showing off the cute gap in his teeth. "Where? Is she in the shop?"

"I was trying to get her to come in—she's actually been in here twice for a tattoo with McKenna—but she's outside."

Sam stands in a flash and starts walking to the front of the shop. I shake my head, bewildered, then place the book down on the black countertop. I quickly follow and get to the front to find him bundled in his winter coat, shoving a hat down over his tight curls.

"Sorry, reacted without thinking. Got excited. But it's freezing out and I don't want to keep her waiting," he says when I catch up to him, then louder, "See you tomorrow, everyone!"

There are several shouted and muffled goodbyes. Sam grabs hold of my hand and pulls me out of the shop and into the blistering cold with him. He scans the street. He quickly lands on Lottie, who's standing underneath the awning of a store next to the parlour, under layers of a turtleneck, scarf, and knitted toque. All that's visible are her eyes and even from here, I can see the brightness of them.

It's as though they notice each other at the same time. Lottie looks up when the door opens and steps forward. Her eyes slide over me and find Sam. She appraises him, then begins walking toward us. Sam's tense shoulders lower when she stops at the bottom of the steps. A hesitant smile appears on Lottie's face.

"Hi," Sam says as he descends the stairs. He drops my hand and holds it out to her. "You won't have any memory of me, but I know you."

Lottie laughs awkwardly and takes his hand. "Hi, I'm Lottie. I think you probably know that, though."

"I'm Sam. Samuel Walsh."

"Very James Bond," I joke.

They both look back at me and I blush, thankful for the cold's ability to disguise the pink on my cheeks.

"Do you mind... Can I hug you?" Lottie asks.

Sam opens his arms and Lottie slips into them, where she immediately starts crying. Sam remains unfazed and pulls her closer.

"Let's go somewhere warm, okay? I know a place if you'd like to get some food. Or we can go to my apartment if you're comfortable."

"He's a good chef," I supply. "You should go."

"You'll come, right?" she pulls away from him and wipes at her eyes.

I nod. And that's how I get sucked further into a family reunion. When we get to his apartment, I sneak away to the bathroom, giving them some time alone to figure things out. I run my hands through my hair in the bathroom mirror, admire a watercolour painting of cliffs and wild waves hanging overtop of the toilet, skim through the medicine cabinet, pull back his clear, bubble printed shower curtain and read some shampoo bottles, then grab my phone. I've killed fifteen minutes. That's definitely not enough time, but there's only so long I can pretend to be in the bathroom without raising eyebrows.

I exit to the sounds of laughter and smile.

Lottie sits at the table, attentively listening to Sam's story. I stand in the hallway on the outskirts of the room, watching them, feeling as though I'm intruding on something. Sam cuts open a package of peppers and catches my eyes from across the room when he looks up again. He cocks his head to the side and waves me in. A subtle gesture that Lottie doesn't catch.

"Grandpa's a bit of a wild card," Sam explains. "But he's the best man I know. He's taught me everything. Made me feel loved despite missing half my family."

I sit next to Lottie and she grabs my knee and squeezes. I pat her hand in return, then we both pull away.

"What're we having?" I ask, the smell of chili powder, garlic, and onions filling the air.

"Fajitas," Sam says and nods toward Lottie. "Vegetarian."

Lottie blushes this time, but looks pleased. In the six months I've known her, I've seen more than my fair share of people get weird about her vegetarianism. I guess not eating meat in the seafood capital of Canada gets people a little riled up. I should know, I don't eat anything from the sea.

"Sounds perfect," I say. "Are you guys okay with me here? I feel like I'm intruding."

"You're our buffer," Lottie says.

"You're always welcome here," Sam says at the same time.

"Such raving reviews." I laugh.

As Sam cooks, he talks about his childhood. He grew up in Halifax, always trying to find a connection to his mother, which is how he got into art. When Sam's grandma died and then his mom a few months later, his grandpa had a little break from reality. Depression hit hard. Even at five years old, Sam could tell something wasn't right. Sam views being allowed to stay with his grandpa as something of a miracle.

Art stayed a constant in Sam's life. He painted his way through elementary and high school. He won awards for his work. Everyone saw the promise in him and people that knew likened him to Penny. Sam went to Nova Scotia College of Art and Design (NSCAD) for Fine Art. During his degree, he started apprenticing at the tattoo shop and walked into a full-time job after graduation.

"So I guess it's been a decent life. I found my way eventually."

Sam plates the fixings for fajitas in front of me and Lottie, then comes and sits with us. I try not to flatter myself when he chooses the seat next to me. We eat in contented silence for a few minutes.

"I was going to take you to Mom's favourite restaurant originally," Sam mumbles through a mouth of food. Lottie's eyes light up. "Another day?"

She nods vehemently, swallows, then smiles. "Yes, please. And I'd like to meet Elliot too, if that's alright."

"Of course it is," Sam says. "You don't even have to ask."

"Well, I don't know how you feel about me. You could be like who is this random girl in my apartment pretending to be my sister?"

Sam looks at her like she's grown an extra head. He wipes a string of cheese away from the corner of his mouth. "Tell you what," he says and lays his hands flat on the table. "How about we do the DNA test that Maryl suggested tomorrow. Hopefully we'll have results by Friday. We can reconvene then and I'll take you to meet Grandpa Elliot."

"That's Maryl's birth—"

I shove Lottie's shoulder. "We're doing it. I honestly don't think we need it. He has your birthday on his arm and you both have those eyes. You're related."

Sam literally knocks on wood, then continues to eat. He and Lottie smile at each other. I glance down at my food.

"By the way, you're not mad at Penny, right?"

Chapter Twenty-Nine

I DECIDED TO SKIP classes and sleep in for my birthday, only to be rudely awakened by a series of texts from Sam and Lottie. My annoyance quickly slipped away as I realized how cute and frantic they both were at the prospect of their DNA results. Which is why, three hours later, I'm standing in front of a Hydrostone house in the north end of Halifax. Penny and Sam grew up here. Lottie would have spent the first few months of her life here as well. The grey clapboard siding covers the whole house. A porch spans the entirety of the front, the white frame of an awning sheltering it. The front door and shudders are painted a deep red, almost burgundy. It's the kind of house you could use for a Hallmark Christmas movie.

Sam's beat up Toyota is parked in the driveway behind a black pickup truck. He leans against the rusty bumper of his car, shifting from foot to foot. He straightens when he sees us step out of the cab.

"So are we doing this outside or are we going to Maury it up inside? Your grandpa could be Maury. I'm clearly not as old. Or a man," I say once we reach him.

Sam's eyes crinkle at the joke. "Let's do it here. Just in case, you know?"

"Are you worried it's going to say you're not related?"

Sam shrugs and looks at Lottie. "I don't know what it'll say. I don't want to shock Grandpa without there being concrete proof."

I narrow my eyes and glance at Lottie. She seems subdued, but not surprised. She shuffles her feet, though I'm not sure if it's from cold or nerves.

"Someone give me a phone," I say and hold out my hand.

Sam's the first one to grab his. I take it. It's open to his email app. I scroll until I find a little blue dot next to the email from the lab. I open it, but don't read, and instead look at the two people in front of me.

"You ready?" They nod. I skim the email until I find what I need. "Your DNA has a 25% match, which suggests a potential link on the maternal side." I pause and watch them both let out dramatic, audible sighs. "Congratulations, you are siblings!"

"Half-siblings," Lottie says. She blinks, then scrunches up her nose. "What does that mean, though? Why's the percentage so low?"

"Do you want the super technical answer or the simple one?"

"Simple," they both say.

"We only have so much of our parents in us. 25% is actually pretty high for one person. It's not 50% because fifty would mean that you have the same mother and the same father."

"What's the other 50%, then?" Sam asks. I raise my eyebrows. "Yeah, you're right. I don't really want to know. Should we go in?"

Lottie nods and Sam gets off his bumper. He takes his phone back from me and slips it into his back pocket. We follow him up the driveway and chipping white stairs. They creak as we step on them, so I jump up quickly, paranoid that I might fall through. Sam eyes me, a smirk on his lips. He's trying hard not to laugh. I sidle up next to him on the porch, nudge his hip with my own, and then remember Lottie's here, probably watching, and we're also about to talk to her grandpa about death... So...

I sit on the edge of a Muskoka chair as Sam rings the doorbell and waits. I'm about to question why he can't use a key when the door opens.

An extremely tall man, taller than Sam, with broad shoulders, a mess of grey stubble and greying sideburns, and a lined face, tanned from years of work in the sun appears on the other side of the door. On any other person, this would be intimidating, but on Elliot Walsh, it's endearing. His face breaks into a grin, creasing the lines at the corners of his eyes and disarming his imposing stature through joy. His large hands clap Sam on the back and draw him into a big bear hug. Sam melts into him, looking equally elated. When he pulls back, Elliot's dark eyes framed behind equally dark rimmed glasses scan me and Lottie. Confusion creases his straight browline, but his smile remains plastered on his face.

"You going to introduce your friends, Sam?" Elliot asks. His voice is calm, but the colour has drained from his face and his eyes have skimmed over me and zeroed in on Lottie.

"Let's go inside," Sam suggests.

Elliot steps back and opens his arms. Lottie and I pass through. I turn just in time to see a silent conversation between Sam and his grandpa.

They size each other up, as Elliot points skyward and Sam closes his eyes then nods. He walks over the threshold. The door closes. The house is bright and inviting, but the air is uncertain.

"Come, make yourselves at home," Elliot says. "Take off all the winter gear and come to the kitchen. I'll make some coffee."

He passes by. I stand still on the cool tiles, watching Lottie. Her shoulders shake and she grips the front table as though her legs may give out if she doesn't. I rush over to her and grab her hands.

"Are you okay? What do you need?" I whisper.

Her eyes are glassy with unshed tears. She blinks them away and shakes her hair out of her collar. "I'm okay. It's just a lot."

"If it makes you feel any better," Sam says, bending to join our hushed conversation, "I reacted the same way when Maryl told me about everything."

"Yeah, you're doing better than him. He actually got up and left."

Lottie laughs. "Don't tempt me. I'm halfway there."

"Big week," I mumble. "You know we're here for you."

She takes both of our hands and squeezes. "Yes, thank you. I'm glad I met both of you."

Pep talk completed, we shed our winter clothes. I slide along the entryway floor in my socks, like I used to do at my grandparents' house. Sam laughs and I challenge him to do the same with a simple raised eyebrow.

"Later," he says and nudges my shoulder with his.

Lottie is first to enter the kitchen, but not the first to sit down. She hesitates next to a bright yellow chair. I brush past her and sit down in a lilac chair opposite hers. Sam sits in an emerald green one between me and Lottie, which leaves the deep red one for Elliot. On Sam's encouragement, Lottie finally sits.

Elliot turns around, holding two steaming cups of coffee. He carries them over to us and places them on lace coasters on top of the wooden blue table. There's so much colour inside the kitchen. Every appliance has a bright, shiny finish in varying vibrant colours. It's as though a rainbow exploded in here and painted the world technicolour. It strikes me that maybe this is true. Maybe Penny's hand was also at work in here. Elliot avoids looking at the three of us as he brings over the last two coffees, but when he notices Lottie in the yellow chair he freezes. Sam smiles behind his mug.

"Of all the chairs you could pick," Sam whispers, but in the silent kitchen, we all hear it.

Elliot scrapes his chair along the soft light wood of the floor. He eases his large body down and stares at Sam, waiting for an explanation.

"This is my friend, Maryl," Sam says, gesturing at me. Elliot's eyes stray to mine only for a moment. "I met her a few weeks ago. Uh, she's kind of changed my life. And I think she's about to change all of ours."

I blush as Elliot studies me. He smiles warmly and full with all of his teeth showing. He reaches a hand out to me and covers mine with his.

"It's very nice to meet you, Maryl," he says. "It's not often someone comes along and changes my Sammy's life."

I smile back. "It's nice to meet you too. Your house is amazing. So much colour. It's nothing like my parents' house."

He looks around the kitchen and covers his mouth with the hand that had been on top of mine moments before. His eyes glaze over and for a moment, I feel he's very far away. But he resurfaces with a sigh and another one of his smiles that make me feel like I did when Mamie was proud of me.

"Mom redid the kitchen," Sam says, "when she was pregnant and doing that whole nesting thing. We never changed it."

Elliot gasps and a crease forms between his eyebrows. Before he has a chance to ask the question, Sam continues.

"Maryl put some things together that I've never been able to. She saw my tattoo." He runs a hand down his arm with the dates. "And my eyes. That's how it started, I think. Two innocuous details that got her thinking and it kind of exploded from there. I wanted to come here today and introduce you to someone... Or, I guess I'd be reintroducing her."

"Charlotte," Elliot breathes.

Lottie sits ramrod straight in the sunflower chair. Her face is a mask of indecision, anxiety, and on top of all that, happiness. She lets the tears flow freely as she reaches toward her grandfather.

"Hi," she says. It's all she says before a sob bubbles out. Then she laughs. "I'm Lottie. I'm your granddaughter."

Elliot's face drops, a brief flicker of fear flashes in his eyes, but then, like Lottie, it's replaced with joy. The grin reappears and he's out of his chair in half a second. His arms encircle Lottie. It's the closest, tightest, most emotional hug I've ever seen. They both shake, enveloped in something that's far too powerful to name. I find myself reaching for Sam at the same moment he reaches for me. We squeeze each other's hands as Lottie and Elliot mumble words of reassurance amongst themselves. They pull away after a few minutes, Elliot going back to his chair, but still holding Lottie's hand.

I look between the three of them, then push my chair back. "Do you mind if I excuse myself while you guys catch up with each other?"

"Oh, yes," Elliot says. "Make yourself at home. Go on your own personal house tour and come back if you have any questions."

I smile and leave. I put as much distance between myself and the family as I can by heading upstairs. The stairs and upper level of the house are lined with an olive-green shag carpet that probably hasn't been changed since the 70s. It's quiet up here. I half expect Penny to pop up and talk to me, which is why I'm so surprised when I turn the corner from the stairs and into the hallway to find a middle-aged woman cloaked in shadows and a waterlogged dress. I jump, but stop myself before I let out a shriek.

"Hello," I whisper and without thinking, take a few steps toward her.

She smiles and juts her chin out to one side, pointing to the room at the end of the hall on her right. She disappears into it and I follow.

"Maryl, right?" she asks when I walk into another room full of colour. I nod. "I'm Christine."

Christine sits in the centre of a four-poster bed with an ornate iron headboard. A bassinet lies in the space between the bed and the wall. This must have been Penny's room. The room is like a time capsule of

Penny's life. Another detailed landscape, this time of a fishing village with colourful houses along the shoreline, hangs above her bed. An upright desk is covered in paints and a half finished canvas, as if Penny was taking a break. Photographs of friends, but mostly young Sam and Lottie decorate her walls along with a bookshelf next to her art space. Toys and clothes scatter the floor.

"Wow," I breathe.

"It's been like this since the day she died," Christine says. "My husband couldn't bear to change anything in here. I think it's why he still lives in this house. I think he feels close to the both of us here."

"Your husband?"

"Elliot is my husband, yes," she says with a smile. "He had a few years of bad luck back then. I died shortly before Penny did."

"You did?" I say and then cringe. Of course she did. "I mean, how? How did the two of you die so close together? Do you know who killed her?"

She laughs and it's magical, just like Sam's. Lilting and singsong. "You have a lot of questions, darling. My husband was a fisherman—Sam may have told you—but I've never been a fan of water. That's a funny thing growing up in a coastal town, not so funny when you're on a boat during a freak storm."

"So you drowned?"

"Unfortunately. Can't you tell?" She holds up her arms, sleeves dripping with water that disappears once it hits the bedsheets. "I fell off the boat and got tangled in a net. By the time I was freed, it was too late. It's purely a coincidence that Penny and I died so close together, but nonetheless tragic. It did a number on my husband and I can't say I'm surprised. Had things been reversed and I was the one still living, I don't know how I would've survived."

I digest this, then walk over to the bed. I run my hands along the floral comforter. Christine watches me as I take a moment to drink her in. I can see pieces of Penny, Sam, and Lottie in her. She doesn't have exactly the same eyes, but they're still a deep shade of blue. She has a gap in her smile like Sam. She's tiny like Penny and Lottie. Her wet dark blonde hair hangs to her shoulders in curls that frame her face like a halo. She rubs a hand against the back of her neck, like I've seen Sam do when he's uncertain.

I sit down on the bed.

"Why are you still here?" I ask.

She shrugs. "I could leave if I want. I've no unfinished business like Penny does. I stay here for Elliot. He may not be able to see or talk to me like you can, but he can feel me and it brings him comfort."

"That's really sweet of you," I say with a smile. I notice a picture of her and Penny together on the bedside table. They both look wispy and young, not knowing what was coming for them, enjoying a day by the harbour. "What's Penny's unfinished business?"

"I think you know," she says. "It's why you're here, isn't it?"

"Do you know who did it?"

She shakes her head slowly and opens her mouth to speak when a clatter rises from downstairs. Loud voices travel through the floor. I push myself off Penny's bed and walk to her bedroom door. Sam's voice booms above them all, vehement *noes* above the din. I turn back to Christine to gauge her reaction, but she's gone. I run down the stairs and listen from the front hallway.

"Grandpa, no! We've talked about this. You have to stop," Sam says.

"I can't stop. That means putting Lottie in danger and I cannot allow that. I got her to safety once and I'll do it again if I have to."

"No!" Sam yells.

"What is it?" Lottie asks hesitantly. "What do you not want him to tell me? If I'm in danger, shouldn't I know?"

"You're not in danger. It's not real." Sam breathes out.

"Like hell, it isn't!" Elliot shoots back. He slams his hands on the table, upturning a mug. "She has a right to know what I did, Samuel. All these years I didn't pursue an investigation because of her. She has to know."

"An investigation into what?" Lottie half-shrieks.

"Into Penny's death," Elliot says, the wind in his sails draining. "I knew she was murdered, but no one believed me. I dropped it and found a home to keep you safe. They couldn't get you."

"They?"

"Here we go," Sam mumbles. It sounds like he falls into a chair.

"There's a curse on our family," Elliot says. It reminds me of the wise old man in a horror movie. "None of the women live past sixty. If our matriarchs live past that age, the family who cursed ours will be wiped out. Their entire lineage will die."

Alarm bells ring in my head. Sam told me his grandpa has some outlandish ideas, but this? I've stretched my beliefs enough to admit that I'm actually seeing dead people, but I can't for a curse.

"I don't follow," Lottie says.

"That's because it's all bullshit," Sam mutters.

"Samuel," Elliot admonishes. "Everything I'm saying is true. If they can't find you, we win. This is why I gave you away. I needed you to get to sixty. I needed you to break the curse that killed your mother and my wife and her mother. It goes back hundreds of years. I cannot lose you to this too."

"I think it's time we leave," Sam says. The chair scrapes against the floor and moments later, he's in the hallway, face pinched. "I see you heard all that." I nod. "Good."

Lottie scurries after him. Her eyes are wide and the joy I saw in her has disappeared. Her breath comes quick and all I want to do is hold her, tell her it's not true, tell her I agree with Sam. It's all bullshit because there's no other explanation. But she slips into her boots and right past me out the door. I look between my frazzled friends and Elliot.

"It was nice meeting you," I say.

I grab my coat off the rack next to the door and step into my boots, not bothering to zip them up. I hurry outside. Sam slams the door behind me.

Chapter Thirty

LOTTIE STARES STRAIGHT AHEAD in the passenger seat. Her hands firmly clasp the sides of the grey leather. Her breath comes out uneven and I'm almost certain she's about to cry. I sit in silence and wait, trying to make sense of my own thoughts before I say anything. Sam's eyes, sparkling with concern, meet mine in the rearview mirror. I shrug in response. There's many things I could say to Lottie, but she has to be the first to speak. I feel like I've overstepped enough as it is.

Sam drives, seemingly aimless. The light wanes and we pass Dalhousie. I don't know where we're going. Intuitively, he's picked up that going back to Dal is probably the last place Lottie would want to go right now and I can't say I blame her. All of her family dreams are crashing down around her and if it weren't for Dal and me and my ghost ability, we wouldn't be in this mess.

"I'm sorry," Sam says, finally.

"For what?" I ask before realizing the apology wasn't directed at me.

Our eyes meet in the mirror again and he smiles before briefly turning to Lottie.

"For Grandpa," Sam replies. He sighs and taps his fingers against the steering wheel. "I should've warned you."

"He seemed so... so convinced. So adamant about it all," Lottie says. Her eyes don't stray from the winding hills of the seaside road, waves lapping the shore, illuminated by headlights.

Sam continues to tap the steering wheel to some unknown tune. Lottie switched off the radio almost as soon as we got in the car. Sam raised an eyebrow, but didn't complain since she was noticeably frazzled.

"I don't know what to say about this," Sam says, scratching the stubble along his chin. "I should have said something before we went in. I didn't think he'd say anything. Obviously, I was wrong."

"Is this something he does a lot?" I ask.

Sam sighs. "He knows how it sounds. This is something he's said since Mom died," he turns to Lottie and nods. "You're right. He's convinced. He always has been. I've heard about the curse my whole life. When I first started dating in high school, he sat me down and told me that if I ever got someone pregnant, I better hope she has a boy. Not exactly the conversation I expected to have for *the talk*, that's for sure."

I snort out a laugh, but Lottie stays silent. Her hair acts like a curtain, shielding her face. I can only read her from her white-knuckled hold on her seat. I undo my belt and peek my head into the front, reaching forward and grabbing hold of her hand, unclenching it. Lottie squeezes.

"You don't believe it, though, right?" I ask. Lottie whips her head toward me, the first time I've seen her face since we left the house.

A mixture of fear and bewilderment turn her features. Her wide eyes narrow at my suggestion.

"Personally? No, I don't. I don't live in a world where witches and curses and evil families exist. I live in the real world," Sam says.

"How can you be so confident?" Lottie's voice borders on hysterics. "It's not your life on the line. That's where the confidence comes from, isn't it?"

"Your life is not on the line, either. I promise. Grandpa has no business saying any of that."

"Is dementia a factor?" I ask the question that's been on my lips since I overheard his raving at the house. "Do you think it's possible that maybe..."

Sam shrugs. "I think there'd be a lot more issues than this if it were dementia. When everything first happened, he started making claims, but he stopped once he realized how people were seeing him. Years later one of our neighbours told me that Grandpa was acting like a raving lunatic after Mom and Grandma died. I was, like, nineteen, so they thought they could just casually tell me they thought my grandpa was nuts. They also casually told me they were so concerned back then that if anything went wrong, they were going to take me in. I guess that's nice? I don't know. It was an odd conversation, but it matters contextually. Grandpa's been saying this for years. I think it's how he copes with the two tragedies back to back."

Lottie sits back in her seat and closes her eyes. I turn to Sam, silently begging him to do something to make this better. He puts a hand on my forehead, shocking me with what I think is a nice gesture, then pushes me. I fall into the backseat again.

"Seatbelt on," Sam mumbles. I roll my eyes and buckle up. Sam's thumb absently drums the steering wheel once more, then he switches lanes, and makes a U-turn.

"You can't yell at me to put on my belt and then do something illegal," I say.

Sam smirks. "Seatbelt on so I can *do* something illegal, then."

"Where are we going?" Lottie asks, snapping to attention after her phone buzzes.

"I thought we could get something to eat. Food usually calms me down. Thought it might work for you too."

"That's really nice of you. We could go to the pub on campus," she suggests.

"You really want to go there?" I ask.

She nods and directs Sam. Sam shrugs it off and heads back to campus. Silence lapses between us again as we move away from ocean inlets and the city comes into focus again. This time, the silence is more comfortable, but the wheels are still turning in my head, wondering how Elliot Walsh and the curse fits into this mess. Though the pieces don't quite fit together, a theory builds and I glance toward Sam. It's fleeting, but he catches it.

Sam parks on the street a few blocks away from Dalhousie, so he doesn't have to pay for parking. Lottie gets out first and starts walking, bridging a distance several feet in front us.

"What?" Sam whispers, almost there.

I stare at Lottie's back and bite my lip. "It's nothing."

Sam laughs. "Oh, it's not nothing."

"How do you know?"

"I knew when you looked at me that last time in the car and then refused to make eye contact again. You're not even doing it now."

I stop walking and stare into his eyes. A playful glint lights them up and I know I'm about to extinguish it.

"I think it's a very real possibility that your grandfather killed Penny and doesn't even know it. I think he may have had a psychotic break and making up the curse is either part of the delusion or as you said, a trauma response to tragedy."

As expected, the playfulness drops. He makes a small noise of recognition, then continues walking. I stand and watch both siblings walk away from me, one totally oblivious and the other understandably annoyed. He turns and beckons me to follow him once he realizes he left me behind.

"Don't you think I've thought of that? He never pursued an investigation even though he was convinced she was killed. I always thought that was suspicious as hell. It may be stupid, but every single piece of me knows he would never do something like that. He wouldn't kill his own daughter."

"You're certain?"

"As certain as I can be."

"Will you be mad if I look into that? To know for sure."

Sam shakes his head and comes to a stop next to Lottie. "I promise I won't be."

"Promise you won't be what?" Lottie asks and opens the door to the pub.

I step through and open my mouth to respond, but that's as far as I get. The pub is eerily silent and empty at first glance, but a moment later it comes to life as everyone from the swim team jumps out. In spite of myself, I startle and laugh. I should have known they'd do this. Every time someone on the team celebrates a birthday, we throw a "surprise" party. It's hardly a surprise at this point in the year, but with everything going on today, I honestly kind of forgot it *was* my birthday.

I turn to Lottie and grab her hands. "Thank you for being a part of this, even today." She nods and smiles back, but I can tell she's on autopilot. "Thanks so much, guys! I completely forgot we did this, so I am genuinely surprised."

I weave through groups of my teammates and other friends who joined in on the party. My mind stays with Lottie as she silently slips away. How long is long enough for me to stay here? Probably at least until they bring out the cake, but that's usually not for a few hours. I bite my lip as I pretend to be engaged in conversation. Sadie and Riley talk animatedly about our fun meet in Toronto. Only half the team is going, and the three of us happen to be a part of that group. My eyes slide around the room, trying to find Lottie, but land on Sam instead. Sam who is standing with a beer in his hand and Hale right next to him.

"Shit," I mutter, and since it's the first thing I've said in a while, both Sadie and Riley stop and stare at me.

Sadie looks at Sam appreciatively. "Who did you bring?"

"Just a friend."

"Oh, yeah, he totally looks like one. Not like the two of you were clearly checking each other out outside or anything. Clearly nothing going on between the two of you."

"There is nothing going on between us. Yet."

"He's a good-looking dude," Riley adds. "If he has a personality to match the looks, then I say go for it. Better than the Orlando Bloom wannabe next to him."

I laugh. I've never heard someone describe Hale like that but it is the exact look he has down pat.

"That's Hale, right? Your other would-be suitor?" Sadie asks and I nod. She wrinkles her nose. "He's the jackass who yelled at you for a bad grade. Get rid of him and pick Mr. Mystery."

"Sam," I say.

"Much better name," Riley approves.

"That's a real name."

"You think they're gonna fight?" Riley asks.

"God, I hope not. I really don't need that kind of entertainment today," I say and down the rest of my drink.

Sadie takes my empty glass and levels me with her gaze. "Be careful. I don't trust Orlandon't."

Riley snickers and shoves her shoulder. I walk away as they start to come up with a nickname for Sam. Sam sees me right away and his eyes light up, but only for a moment as he turns back to Hale who appears to be mumbling something.

"Hey!" I say once I reach them. "Thank you for coming!"

"Yeah, no problem," Hale mutters. "Happy birthday!"

"I had no idea it was your birthday," Sam says and reaches out to my shoulder to pull me closer. The noise level in the pub is louder than I've ever heard it. "I wouldn't have made you come out if I knew."

I nod, then shrug, trying to let him know it was no big deal without letting Hale in on it. But Hale notices the subtle language; the way we've figured out how to talk without actually talking. He bristles and I can see how right I was about the two of them standing together. It might be fine for Sam, but Hale is angry. I've been stupid with him. I hadn't made it clear post-reading week that friendship was all I wanted from him, but I can tell from his face that he's expected more and Sam showing up, touching me, having an unspoken code, is the catalyst.

"Do you know where Lottie went?" I ask the two of them, which I hope he can realize is code for 'can you go find her while I neutralize a goddamn bomb?'

"I think I might know where she is," Sam says and hands me his drink. He grabs his coat from the back of a chair and covers his muscular arms. "I'll text when I find her, okay?"

I smile as he walks away, then turn back to Hale. A storm brews behind his dark eyes. His hair has fallen over them and he doesn't bother to brush it away like he usually does. I glance down at the drink in my hand and tip it to my lips. His eyes follow every last one of my movements, the only part of him that isn't completely frozen, but he doesn't say anything until I've swallowed the ice-cold beer.

"So, you're the kind of girl that brings a new guy to every party," Hale says.

I breathe out instead of making any sound. Somehow that wasn't what I was expecting him to say. My thoughts scramble.

"Excuse me?"

He snorts. "'Excuse me' isn't an apology."

"And what is it that I have to apologize for? For being my own person and not wanting to hop on your dick? For having more than one friend? Oh! I know! I should totally apologize for ruining your birthday, right? Oh wait..."

"Please, I'm not the one ruining your birthday. Your supposed friends already did that."

I cock my head and put down the mug of beer. Hale watches me intently once more. I roll my eyes and pull my phone out of my back pocket. Sam hasn't texted yet, but I'm also pretty sure I know where Lottie went.

"Look at you, Nancy Drew."

I shove my phone in my pocket again and grab my jacket off the same chair where Sam's once was. "I don't need this," I say and shrug into the coat. "If you see Riley, tell him I'll be back for cake."

"Yeah, sure, just need a quickie." Hale says, eyebrows lifted along with a corner of his mouth. So clever.

I raise an important finger. "I'm that kind of girl, right?"

His face falls and his eyebrows draw together in confusion. To even think I could be ruined by immature words clearly says how little he knows about me after two months. I laugh and leave him staring at my back. Not confident that he'll actually talk to Riley, I pull out my phone and send a quick text to Sadie.

As I open the door to the fourth floor of Shirreff Hall and run into Sam, I realize I'm right. The door bumps into his hip and he gasps, but doesn't say anything more. He puts a finger to his lips.

Lottie stands at the end of the hall, staring out the window. I can tell she's talking from her hand gestures, but can't hear anything she's saying. Penny stands next to her, hands reaching out, but hesitating. Penny's eyes are closed as she listens to her daughter's cries. Her lips move and I get the chilling sense that she's mumbling *I love you* over and over again. I can almost hear it in my head.

I turn to Sam and whisper, "Can you see her?"

He jumps, not expecting my voice in the echoing quiet. His eyes narrow. "Mom? She's here?"

"She's here a lot. Especially when people she cares about are as well."

Sam stares at the space next to Lottie. The space where Penny isn't. I reach up and guide his face toward Penny. He places his hand over mine on his cheek. Penny does the same to Lottie. As if I'm some kind of conduit, both Sam and Lottie gasp. They both lean into the touch and breathe deeply. The declarations of motherly love swirl around my mind, getting louder and louder until I'm sure they're screaming off the walls in the empty corridor. I close my eyes as my head feels like it'll burst. Then, it stops. I take my hand off Sam's cheek and he and Lottie snap to reality.

"When did you guys get here?" Lottie asks. "What happened?"

Behind Lottie's shoulder, Penny has disappeared. I know how much energy it must take for her to comfort her children in this form, especially because I'm also suddenly wiped. I grip Sam's coat to steady myself and his arms come around me.

"Penny was here," I whisper.

Lottie runs her hand along her jawline. "I felt her."

"I heard her," Sam says with a disbelieving laugh. "That was her voice. I haven't heard it in almost twenty years."

I beam at both of them before the world goes black.

Chapter Thirty-One

Headaches plague me from Friday on. Lottie and Sam were adamant that I should see a doctor, but what would a doctor do to combat what was clearly not of this world? I convinced them to go back to the party, to eat cake and smile for pictures, and then I went to bed. In the morning, Lottie hovered over me and Sam kept texting. I wrote my assignment for Denver underneath my blankets, trying to make sense of Elliot's curse claim, Penny's murder, and my ghosts. In the end, I solved nothing.

"You good?" Lottie asks during the creative writing lecture break.

I'm not. For the first time since the beginning of the semester, I'm sitting in the front row with Lottie and Hancssicole. I didn't want to be near Hale, so even though I saw him, I walked past. Disappointment lingered on his face and I felt the tiniest bit of satisfaction, but that was soon replaced by pain in my skull. And because I'm so close to the front of class, I couldn't put my head down without it being obvious.

I nod. "Yeah, I'm fine." But my voice betrays me.

"I still say that you should see a doctor. No one faints for no reason."

"You can't tell me you didn't want to faint after the day we had."

"But I didn't. You did. And that's not healthy, especially not all the headaches after."

I sigh and blow hair out of my face. I try not to notice Lottie's intense gaze. "You try dealing with a ghost in your head, then," I mutter.

"Do you think that had something to do with the curse?" Lottie whispers, leaning in close to me.

"No, I don't think it had something to do with the curse. I think it had to do with channeling a damn ghost and not actually knowing how to do that."

"What curse?" I look up too fast, causing pain to shoot through my skull, and wince. Hale stands in front of us. Hanessicole smiles while I grimace.

"What do you want?" I demand.

"You didn't sit in your spot."

"I don't have a spot. And I'm perfectly content here."

"Really? Cause you look like you're dying."

"Flattering," I deadpan.

He takes a step back, almost as if he's about to leave, but he stops himself. He drums his fingers on the white wood, sighs, then stares me straight in the eyes. I hold his gaze and raise an eyebrow.

"Look, I wanted to apologize," Hale says.

"So do it. Apologize. But you can't keep doing dumb things, calling me offensive names, then apologizing like it fixes everything. Sometimes you have to think about your actions before you do them."

Hale stares. For a moment, I think he's going to walk away, but the hesitation turns into confidence. He nods, acknowledging what I said, not doing anything about it.

"Is this about Penelope? The curse?" Hale says.

Lottie perks up and I groan. *Do not entertain the devil.*

"What do you know?" I ask.

"Nothing. Just that I grew up here and there's different folklore. There's the curse on the MacDonald Bridge. Sea monsters in the Basin. The explosion ghosts. You hear it all. Maybe it's some sort of revenge curse? I don't know. It's probably bullshit, but you're kind of obsessed with this so I could help with, like, local legends."

I try to smile pleasantly. "Thanks, Hale. I'm not going to be *obsessively* looking into anything until I get back from Toronto. I leave on Thursday. So maybe after that?"

He opens his mouth, reaches a hand forward, and then freezes. He nods and walks away. I nearly laugh as he retreats, but the sound doesn't quite make it out of me. Lottie purses her lips. Denver walks back to the front podium and class begins again. Lottie nudges my elbow with hers and I glance down at her notebook.

Revenge?

I eye Denver while my head remains down, then write in my own notebook: *idk. Maybe he knows something.*

Lottie raises her eyebrows and scrawls another note: *But who would want revenge? Do you think he knows that?*

The thought struck me as he walked away. He knows more but he isn't letting on. And that might be my fault. I turn in my seat and find Hale's eyes in the crowd easily. He's watching me. I face the front once more and flip my hair over my shoulders, as if this hides the fact that I was staring at him.

Denver talks about the benefits of free writing. Writing without thinking or planning; without worrying about rhetoric or mechanics. Just writing. In the last twenty minutes of class, he lets us roam in the world of free writing. We clear our minds and go.

When all is said and done, I look down at my paper and see, in a different hand than my own: *Trust your instincts, Maryl. This will get you farther than trusting unworthy people, especially those who steer you away from truth.*

I read it over until I'm aware of people moving around me. The front of the lecture hall crowds with students. Lottie remains seated, staring down at the words that appeared on my page. Soon, it's just the two of us among the chaos of our peers sorting through their papers.

"What does that mean?" Lottie whispers.

"Who am I not supposed to trust?" I ask, then note the pain in my head has subsided, almost as if that message was waiting to come out.

Footsteps approach us and I slam the notebook shut. Denver stands in front of me and Lottie. He chuckles at my sudden movement, but he must be used to it at this point.

"Miss Laine, can we speak?" he asks.

I slowly turn to Lottie, rest my hand on top of hers, then nod. "Sure, we can talk," I say. Lottie squeezes my hand. She smiles up at Denver and for the first time, he truly takes note of her. "This is my friend Lottie."

His eyes widen and he takes a step back. A shuddering breath comes deep from his chest. He pops his glasses up and rubs a hand over his eyes. "Goodness," he says. "It's like seeing a ghost."

I laugh, the same hysterical, nervous one that's bubbled several times throughout this period. Neither person questions it. They both stare at each other, sizing the other person up.

"Lottie was adopted just after she was born. She's never known her family until recently when she met her biological half-brother," I say.

"And grandfather," Lottie adds.

Denver takes this in and nods. His lips stay pressed in a firm line.

"They have a maternal link according to their DNA test," I explain.

He lets out another deep breath that turns into a whistle. "Well, of course. You can't look that much like Penny and not... But that means... Does that mean you've found my son?"

"I believe so."

"And in your story this week," he continues. He brings his hands together in front of him, grasping for something in his mind. "Can I assume the Larissa character was, in fact, Lottie?"

Lottie whips her head toward me with a gasp. "You're still writing about this?"

"Is it true?" Denver asks. A smirk plays on his lips, but his eyebrows furrow. Like me, he's caught somewhere between disbelief and fear that it might actually be real. "The curse?"

"I don't know," I admit. It's the first time I've said out loud that I have no idea if the impossible is possible, especially if I've already been proven wrong once before. "I want to say no. I don't believe you can be cursed and it all fits a little too perfectly. But I also didn't believe in ghosts two months ago and now," I open my notebook and show him the exercise from today, "Now they're writing in my journal."

He turns the journal toward himself and clucks. "I've heard that outside of the academic sense that some, uh, psychically inclined persons use free writing to channel with the dead."

"Do you believe that's possible?" I ask.

He shakes his head. "Like you, I'm firmly in the things I thought impossible have become possible within the last few weeks camp. You've opened my mind. Though I should probably give Penelope some credit there too. I hope you still trust me."

"I think I do, somehow," I say and trace the letters. "Is this Penny's printing?"

"It's been years since I've seen it, but no, I don't believe so. It's a hand I'm unfamiliar with. Do you recognize it?"

I run a hand through my hair and gather it back into a small ponytail. "I do. I just don't know where I recognize it from."

"Another mystery," Lottie mumbles.

"Everything's a mystery these days," I mutter. I close my eyes and sigh. Luckily the world doesn't go dark. Instead, it brightens for a moment. There's one thing I can do before I leave for the weekend. "You should take a paternity test. I'm sure Sam would love to meet you."

"My father's name was Samuel," Denver says, his voice light. "I would love nothing more than that."

Chapter Thirty-Two

I LEAD SAM THROUGH the halls of the Life Sciences building on Wednesday afternoon between my lecture and lab. He texted this morning with the results. To no one's surprise, Denver is his father. So I'm leading not quite an ambush, but certainly not a planned meeting. I assume Denver also knows the results by now, especially given the email from him sitting in my inbox with the subject line: *Good News!*

We climb another set of stairs, a choice I made after realizing Sam was too antsy to stand in an elevator for four floors. I'm in shape, obviously, but these stairs always get me. While I wind myself, Sam continues to babble on. I smile and turn to him at the top of the stairs.

"What?" he asks.

"Nothing." I shake my head. "You're so flustered. It's kind of cute."

"You're only saying that because you haven't had your life overturned twice in the past week."

"Uh, hello," I say and gesture around my head. "I can see dead people, remember? That shit kind of flips your life around."

"You've had longer than a week to get used to that."

"Have I? Cause I saw my second full on ghost and then channeled another and passed out, so I'm pretty sure this was also a big week for me."

Sam laughs, hesitant but musical. "Okay, fine. You win on the paranormal scale of life overturned-ness."

"Thank you," I say and begin walking away. Sam's hand closes around my wrist and pulls me back to the windows by the stairs.

"Before we go in, I have something for you." I raise an eyebrow as he hands me an envelope. "I didn't know that last Friday was your birthday. When I found out, I wanted to get you something."

I smile and feel my cheeks warm, my fair skin betraying me. I run my finger along the seam of the envelope and rip it open. A card painted with a watercolour humpback whale slides out. Waves swirl around the whale who is wearing a party hat and singing happy birthday in bubbles. I laugh at the absurdity. This is the cutest thing anyone has ever made for me.

Inside is a sheet of paper and tinier versions of the party whale, swimming around with their hats and birthday bubbles. I can't hide the grin. I unfold the piece of paper and come face to face with a breaching humpback whale, a real one; large, majestic, and devoid of a party hat. I meet Sam's eyes, which are wide and eager.

"There's this thing through the Whale and Dolphin Conservation where you can adopt a whale and get updates on them. This is Midnight. She's an adult whale and she's actually quite petite for a humpback. I chose her because she's small, but mighty like you, and she frequents the waters around here a lot."

"So, this is me but as a whale?" I ask. He studies my face and panic suddenly enters his eyes. I laugh at him, but mostly at myself. "Oh my God, no, I know it's not an insult. This is probably the nicest birthday gift anyone's given me. I can't even begin to tell you how much this means."

I launch myself into him and he lets out a long sigh as his arms come around me. I wrap my hands around his neck and hold him close to me. I pull back and beam. And then I kiss him.

I stand on my tiptoes and lean in. He stiffens in my arms for a moment, then flattens his hand against my back and pulls me closer. His lips respond to mine before my mind clicks in and I pull back.

Sam shakes his head and licks his lip. "Maryl Laine, what have you done to my life?"

I laugh shakily, pivot on my heel, and grab his hand. My heart pounds in my ears and I don't trust myself to speak as I lead him to his father.

My feet take me back to Shirreff Hall, because apparently I want to tell Sam's mother that I just kissed her son. My lips quirk up at the thought.

A few students mull around the halls on my way up, but no one is actually there once I settle in. Not even Penny. As I begin to wonder why I can't always see her, she appears.

"Sometimes I go for a mosey," Penny says.

A smile plays on her features. She crinkles her nose, something I've seen Lottie do countless times when she knows something I don't.

"I thought you had to stay up here," I say, but I know exactly where she's been.

"I do if I want to be seen. Even for you, I don't have enough energy for that."

I nod and slide down the wall. I pull a leg to my chest and hold onto it, waiting for her to continue. If she wants the dirt, she has to admit it.

Penny rolls her eyes. "I swear you're insufferable sometimes," she says and plops down next to me. A rush of cold air has me rubbing away the goosebumps on my arms. "But I approve."

"You approve?"

"You like my son."

"I do."

"Well, I approve of that over the other two guys you've been involved with this semester. One was an asshole and the other, I can't quite put my finger on, but he made me uncomfortable."

I don't ask which one is which.

"I'm glad he and Denver are finally meeting. I was stupid to think that Denver would be anything but a supportive father figure when I was alive. But maybe this is better. Maybe they can appreciate each other more now that they're older."

"Maybe."

"Though, in a perfect world, I wish we were all together. Including you. I wish I could have met you in my forties instead of eternally twenty-six."

"We met now. That's all that counts."

"You're right," she says and reaches out to touch my hand. A chill shoots up my arm, but I hold on. "It's because of you that all this is happening. I'm so happy my children finally know each other and they're forming their own little family connections."

She's comfortably silent before I ask what I've been thinking about for forever. "Penny, if you're so happy they're all connecting, why won't you tell me who Lottie's father is? I'm sure you know. Is it someone you're concerned about? Do you think he would have killed you?"

Penny shakes her head and looks off into the distance. I wait. When she doesn't speak, I close my eyes and rest my head against the wall. My head hasn't hurt since Monday, but being here next to Penny makes me think about my headaches and what happened on my birthday. Leah told me I had to learn how to use my gifts in a way that didn't overwhelm me and I felt like I was some stupid teenager in a CW show. In theory, what she said makes sense. But when you place it against the real world, it starts getting weird. I don't know why that still surprises me.

Lost in my own thoughts, I forget about Penny and the question I asked. I open my eyes, almost shocked to find her still sitting next to me. Penny stares at me, then sighs.

"I made a mistake being with her father. He knew he was wrong, sleeping with me, and he never owned up to it. I can say the same for myself too. I don't think he had anything to do with my death. He wouldn't have any reason to want me dead."

I study her. Though she's staring at me, she won't meet my eyes. Almost as if I'll find some sort of untruth there if I concentrate hard enough. I'm forced to take her words at face value like I have for every other misleading thing she's said.

"Are you sure?" I ask and her lip twitches. "What's his name?"

"Graham."

"And that's all you're going to give me?"

Penny nods and I hold back a groan. At least it's something, I guess. Something I can give to Lottie. A name that will probably mean more to her in a very personal sense than it will to me on a murder level.

The door to the fourth floor clatters open. Penny jumps, but melts back against the wall almost instantly. Sam steps through and immediately breaks into a grin when he sees me.

"Thought I'd find you here," he says.

I pull out my phone and glance at the time. An hour has passed and my lab begins soon. I push myself off the floor and walk over to him. Penny smiles, waves, then walks off into nothingness. I continue to walk and Sam follows.

"How'd it go?" I ask.

"It was wild. It's a moment I never thought I would ever have." Sam shakes his head and runs a hand along the folded rim of his toque. He clears his throat. "Thank you."

"You don't have to thank me," I say with a giggle.

"I do," he says. Our hands brush. His thumb catches the back of my palm. "You made this happen. He's in my life because of you and I really appreciate what you did."

"What did you guys talk about?" I ask, changing the subject.

"He spent the first little while apologizing for not being there for me, then we talked about Mom. He has so many memories of her. He showed me some sketches she made for him and I showed him some of my work, too. I showed him the moth tattoo. It was a lot. Tears were involved."

He laughs awkwardly and I grab his hand. He squeezes mine and keeps hold of it.

"I'm so glad it worked out for you guys," I say and genuinely mean it. No one deserves this more than Sam. "Are you meeting up again?"

"I think we might this weekend. You're away then, right?"

"Yeah, I leave tomorrow. Which means it's a pause on the investigation. Although, I might do some research in between the meets."

Sam shakes his head. "No, just relax and focus on you. That's what I'm going to do."

I nod. We return to the Life Sciences building and I realize I should have met him here. But then again, I did get more time with him this way.

"Hey, Sam," I say and he cocks his head, his crystal-clear eyes boring into mine. "Have you thought anymore about the curse?"

"Denver showed me your story so I thought—"

"Wait, what?"

"I wasn't going to read it, but he wanted my opinion. I guess you've been writing vaguely true stories for class? He was confused by that one. I kind of laughed it off. You're thinking it might be real?"

"I don't know," I say. "I wrote that on Saturday because I had no other ideas and I felt like shit. But I've been thinking about it lately. Like, I think it's bullshit, but I also think, what if? You know, like ghosts did not exist to me before this year and now I'm talking to them. So if ghosts exist, then why not curses?"

"I feel like one's a bit more out there. But maybe I'm jaded because I've grown up with it."

I look down at my phone again. I'm officially late for class. Sam brings my hand up to his lips and kisses it gently. I smile and pull my hand back.

"I have to go to class. But I need to know everything about this curse. Write it all down and text me, okay? It's important. It's either real and that's our answer, something your grandpa made up during a psychotic break and used to kill his daughter, or it's not true and someone made it up to cover their tracks."

Sam's face goes blank as he takes this in, but he pulls out his phone. He backs away from the classroom door a few paces. "I think you may be right," he whispers and laughs because it's all so wrong. So unbelievable. "I don't like any of those options, but you're right. There's something here. I'll text you."

Chapter Thirty-Three

SAM TOLD ME TO take a break, but I can't. My mind swirls around possibilities as his texts come in. My fingers frantically type theories into the Notes app on my phone, and frenzied searches into the ether. Sadie looks at me like I have two heads, but doesn't say anything, just pushes her earbuds in and stares out the window.

Sam

> Grandpa got super paranoid before Mom died. I didn't have a word to describe his behaviour back then, but I realize it now. I remember him talking about the curse after she died. Again, I didn't really understand. Every year on the anniversary of her death, he'd go off about it.

The bus full of swimmers travels through Eastern Québec, past forests of barren trees and winding, hilly roads. I'd already been thinking of Penny, but this put my mind into overdrive.

Sam

> There's a curse on the Walsh family that involves another family. Something about killing the lineage of each. It's completely bonkers to even consider. I didn't think anyone else knew, but maybe Grandpa's blabbed

I chew on my lip. The line where this thing is fictional or unbelievably, actually true blurs between texts.

"Sadie, you ever heard about curses here?" I ask.

"In Toronto?" she replies.

I shake my head. "No, in Halifax."

"Oh," she says and pulls an earbud out. She flips her fading, but still glossy red waves to her other shoulder. "Well, yeah, there's the MacDonald Bridge one. I think there's, like, a cursed statue at the Maritime Museum. And then, not Halifax, but there's the whole Oak Island thing."

"Do you believe them?"

She shrugs. "Maybe. It's within the realm of possibility. My father would say yes. Generational curses are a thing in Hinduism and my father was convinced there was one on our family for years."

"Do you think a curse can involve death?"

"Why?"

I don't have an answer that makes sense, so I drop it.

Sam

Apparently the curse only kills the female line in the family. It's related to another family, but I've never heard Grandpa say who and I don't know if he actually knows, either. If a woman in the Walsh family stays alive past sixty, then something bad happens to this other family. I've heard him say that it goes back hundreds of years but I find that hard to believe. Why would he be the only one to know about it?

Why, indeed?

In the time before the swim meet on Saturday, I sneak away to Robarts Library on the University of Toronto campus. It's an odd-looking building: all ugly beige concrete with a section that juts out diagonally on the top floors. It's free range to walk around for everyone. But I flirt my way to floors 9–13 where all the off-limits books and resources are.

I find stacks of books on curses, the paranormal, dementia, family history, familial killings, ancestry, insanity pleas, and gruesome murders, and make a wall of them at an open table a few floors below. I skim through sections and jot down anything I think might be important. Anything that might help me understand better. But eventually I come to one conclusion:

I don't know what I'm looking for.

I sigh and close the book in front of me. The page outlines statistics about family members being the most likely suspects in many criminal cases. What does that do for me if I already know that? Everyone knows the victim usually has some relation to their killer. I place the book back on top of my wall and move to close my notebook, but something catches my attention. Another phrase written in someone else's printing.

Give yourself grace, Maryl. The answers won't come all at once. Take a break and come back fresh. Don't give up.

I exhale and look around. It's the same handwriting as before, but this time I wasn't even aimlessly writing. I didn't even realize it was happening. Pain traces the line of my sinuses. I close my eyes and run my fingers along my brow bone. My phone buzzes loud against the tabletop.

Sadie

Where tf are you?? We're starting now and your race is third, remember??

"Shit," I mumble.

I immediately become the worst person ever as I shove my notebook back into my bag and leave all my books on the table. A split second of guilt seats itself in my stomach, but I don't have time to waste on the emotion because I'm pretty sure my teammates and Coach Jaffee are going to kill me.

I run through the library, unfazed by the glares. I don't stop running until I reach the Athletic Centre, which is luckily only about two minutes away. Cheers emanate from the Varsity Pool, flanked by completely full bleachers on both sides. I slip into the empty change room and find one of the last remaining lockers. I swap out street clothes for my sleek, black, supposedly lucky Speedo bathing suit. I feel around my bag for my goggles and swim cap, and cringe when I come up empty. *Come on.*

I slam the locker shut and mentally curse myself as I walk out of the change room and locate the rest of my team. My feet carry me over while my mind floats somewhere above the pool. Sadie catches my eyes and widens hers. I plop down next to her and shake my head.

"What is wrong with you?" Sadie asks.

"Nothing," I hiss. "Aside from the fact that I'm an idiot. Can I borrow your cap and goggles for my race?"

Sadie's face drops and I get it. This isn't like me. "Yeah, sure. How did you forget?"

"I don't know," I mumble.

She hands me the items balled in her lap. I slap the cap on over my bun. She nods, but doesn't say anything more. I can see the wheels turning in her mind as much as they are in my own. I don't like what she's probably thinking about me.

"Laine!" Coach Jaffee yells. His hulking form appears in front of me as the swimmers in the pool finish up. I glance up expectantly, but his glare sends my gaze back to my knees. "It's so nice of you to finally join us. May I ask what pleasure brought you here?"

"Sorry I'm late," I say and genuinely mean it. I feel like I could barf.

"Are you ready to go?"

"Of course," I say and dare myself to look at him once more. His eyes soften.

"Good," he says. "If you can't race, you can't race. But if you can, show up and show out."

"Yes, Coach!"

A loud speaker breaks up the celebration in the pool. My race is announced. I push myself off the bench and walk on unsteady legs to my spot. People I've never seen before take their places beside me on the diving boards. I lower Sadie's bright pink goggles over my eyes and step up on the board. My breath comes out shaky as I realize how stupid I am to race right now. I haven't done any warm-up, I haven't eaten since breakfast, I haven't given myself the foresight to have my own swimming supplies with me.

Another shaky breath.

The swimmers around me get on their marks. Noise swirls. I bend and brace my foot against the slanted incline of the board. I grab the front, look at the competition on either side of me. I'm dead centre; my favourite place to be. Confidence begins to brew inside of me.

A breath.

And we're off.

I hit the water with a force and feel an immediate sense of comfort. The world falls away as I slice through the pool over and over with my breaststrokes. The noise and anxiety of the arena disappear as my legs kick. The wall is in my sights. A 100m swim is quick when you're in the zone. Barely a blip on your radar; you pretend no one else is around, only focus on your speed and your movements. Nothing else matters. It's you and the water.

But much like I did earlier this semester and very much for the same reason, after I flip, after I'm well on my way back to finish, I falter.

Why would he be the only one to know about it?

He wouldn't have had any reason to want me dead.

Give yourself grace, Maryl. The answers won't all come at once.

My speed evaporates. My arms and legs stop carrying me and for a moment, I sink. I breathe in water and sputter. The world comes to a grinding halt and all the noise that I drowned out seconds before, comes flooding into my ears. Blackness tinges the edges of my vision. I reach out and grab onto one of the rings dividing the lanes.

The race ends.

The swimmer from the next lane appears beside mine. "Are you okay?" she asks.

I can't find my voice, but I nod. I'm only about ten feet away from the edge of the pool and somehow that's worse than having this happen in the middle or all the way on the other side. I almost had it.

My opponent, the winner of the race, guides me the last few feet along the divider. I grab hold of the edge of the pool and hands reach out to lift me. I sit on the wet tile, right on top of the blue line that surrounds the entire pool. A towel comes down over my shoulders. I rip off the goggles and cap, and shake out my hair from its bun. Voices swarm around me and I sit, trying to catch my breath.

Fingers snap in front of my face and I jump, then focus. Coach Jaffee. "Laine," he sighs. "You said you were good."

"I was," I say. Tears threaten to bubble over.

A hand touches my shoulder, light, caring. Motherly. I look at my arm and see the perfectly manicured French tips first, then the ring. My mother's engagement ring is a solid rock of a diamond, framed by even more diamonds. I follow the hand up to her face and catch the faintest edge of disappointment tracing the concern in her dark eyes.

"Mom," I say and throw myself at her, but not before noting both my dad and Stephen beside her. "I'm sorry."

"Hush," she says. "Of course, I'm disappointed, but you have no reason to apologize. Tu vas bien?"

"Oui."

She helps me stand and the pool erupts in applause. A much different applause than I received at my last competition.

My weekend ends here. Mom assures Coach she'll get me back to Halifax, and she does with a neat little plane ticket. I'm back before the rest of the team with the weight of my mother's disappointment.

"Chérie," Mom says when I call her once the plane lands, "don't let this hold you back. It was only one race. Whatever stupid mistake you made doesn't define your swimming career."

"I didn't think it did," I mutter as I hoist my backpack onto my shoulder and get in line behind the businessman who occupied the seat beside me.

"Bien! This means you have to work harder!"

"The season is over. It doesn't matter how hard I work now."

"You have to keep your spot. Prove to your coach that you still belong on the team after *that* performance."

I wince and sniff back another bout of tears. I refused to cry in front of my mother and I refuse to do it on a plane. The thing is, though she may have an aggressive way of saying it, she's right. I said I could do something I knew I couldn't and I paid for it.

The phone line crackles and I check to make sure the call wasn't dropped. Mom's name is still on the screen, but it's not her voice that comes out of the speaker.

"Maryl, listen to me," Stephen says, out of breath and slightly frantic. "I didn't get to talk to you because the Orchestrator of Everything monopolized you all yesterday and this morning." I laugh. "But I wanted to tell you something."

"Okay, shoot," I say. I smile at the flight attendant who waves and wishes me a nice day.

"Mom's wrong. I'm sure you've figured this out on a number of things she's so adamant about in life. I don't know if you've got this one yet."

"What do you mean?"

"Swimming isn't everything, kid. What you did isn't nearly as bad as what I did when my swimming career ended. I figure I should tell you this now because Mom laid on the guilt pretty hard. When I had my shoulder issues, she was so devastated and I felt like the worst son ever. Until I realized I wasn't living for her. I didn't care if I never swam again. It wasn't my dream."

I sigh and follow the arrows that lead me to the exit. I pass the tank of lobsters and feel a sense of home I never felt so acutely until last fall. "You're forgetting I'm not you. You never liked swimming. You letting go of it isn't as hard as me letting go."

"You're not even letting go!" Stephen groans. "You had a medical emergency. You almost passed out in a pool. If your coach doesn't understand that then he's an asshole."

"I told him I could race when I knew I shouldn't have."

"We all make mistakes. Doesn't mean our lives are over or we give up."

I step through the sliding doors of the airport, cool air hitting my face. I stand in the wind for a few moments, weighing the opinions of my family over my own. A horn honks. I head over to the nearest taxi and give the driver directions to Shirreff Hall.

I've made so many mistakes this year.

Chapter Thirty-Four

"HEY, YOU'RE BACK!" HALE says as I step out of the taxi in front of Shirreff Hall. "I thought you took a bus there."

I chuff and roll my eyes. "Yeah, I did. But that was before."

"Before what?"

It's at this moment that all the tears I refused to shed choose to fall. I don't make an effort to stop, because at this point, I know I can't. I can't hold back any longer. Not now that I don't have a side of mother's judgement.

Hale stands on the front steps, frozen in place for about a minute before he rushes toward me. He takes my bag from my shoulder and replaces it with his arm. I'm drawn to his side. He mumbles words that I'm sure are encouragement, but my mind isn't present enough to listen. My mind also isn't present enough to realize I'm moving, though my feet scrape along. By the time we get to the door of his dorm, I've come to my senses. I untangle myself from his side as he opens the door and steps in. A soft *smush* sounds as he drops my bag onto the floor.

I step inside and easily fold myself in the space next to my bag. Hale stares at me with wide eyes, the rest of his face absolutely blank.

"Sorry," I say, then drop his gaze.

I focus, instead, on what I assume is a family photo on his desk. Both the desk and the photo are tucked away into a little corner. Something draws me to the gold frame. I recognize Hale and his messy hair immediately. The other people seem vaguely familiar too, but it's probably because I've been in this room, in this exact spot a few months ago. In the photo, a man stands behind him with an identical mop of curls but lighter, plus a full reddish beard. Three women stand to their right, two clearly young teenagers who gracefully skipped their awkward stage and one dark-haired woman glaring at the camera in a sleek power suit who I assume is his mother. If he notices me staring, he doesn't say. He comes and sits next to me.

"What's going on?" Hale asks.

I sigh. "Remember when you were angry at me because you got too involved in all the murder stuff and failed that test? You were right. I did the equivalent of that, but in the pool."

"So, you lost a race?"

I nod and wipe at the corner of my eye. I explain my weekend to him. He says nothing, just breathes next to me. I don't know why I'm telling him this apart from him just being here.

"My teammates keep texting, but aside from saying I'm okay, I haven't answered. I guess someone must have told Lottie because she's texting me too, asking me if I'm all right and—"

"Has she apologized?"

I stop babbling. My mind short circuits. "What?"

"Lottie," Hale says slowly. "Has she apologized?"

"For what?"

"For dragging you into all of this. I mean, it's her issue, right? That guy at your birthday party is her brother and then there's Professor Keyes who is somehow related to that situation... Lot of people in your life and taking up your time because of someone else."

I take a shaky breath. I don't want to admit I've been thinking the same thing. If I never knew Lottie, I wouldn't be in this mess. I wouldn't have lost the race. I wouldn't have taken my focus off swimming and my studies. I wouldn't be crying on the floor with some guy I don't even like. I'd be blissfully ignorant to all the stupid ghosts of the world. I'd be plain old Maryl, the future marine biologist and current college swimmer.

Instead, I'm that girl who passed out in a pool because she was thinking about dead people.

"Some people are kind of toxic," he says and waves his hands as if that'll help me grasp his point. "There are people that aren't meant to be in our lives. I think Lottie might be one of those people for you." I laugh because I don't know what else to do. Hale's eyes drip with pity and part of me wants to slug him. He sighs and slings an arm around my shoulder. I slip away. "Think of everything you could have done this semester if you weren't trying to solve a murder, which, by the way, is probably a suicide."

"I want it all to stop," I breathe. "I don't want to do it anymore."

"Do what?"

I shake my head and another laugh comes out. I'm bordering hysterical at this point. "All of this. All the ghosts. All of the bullshit that's taking up space in my mind." I run a hand through my messy plane hair. "I'm done. I can't do it anymore."

"Maybe you should get a new roommate."

I swallow and take a look at Hale. My heart aches that he's not Sam. It aches as I wish I could be looking into the pools of his eyes. I hate the heartache and force myself to not want Sam. To not even think about him, because like it or not, he's part of the problem too.

"It's fine. Only a few weeks left and then I never have to deal with this ever again."

Hale nods. He grabs my hand and squeezes it. My first instinct is to jerk away, but I force myself to stay within his grasp. "Don't get involved. Just shut her out."

I want to tell him that's stupid and defend the roommate I've come to love, but every rational bone in my body has gone to sleep. All that's left is emptiness, disappointment, and failure. My phone buzzes and I pull it out of the pocket of my sweatshirt. I almost cry.

Lottie

Are you on your way back?? Honestly, freaking out here. I have something to show you

Hale peers over my shoulder and lets out a low snort. I quickly stuff it back in my sweater. I push myself off his floor. He stands and hands me my bag.

"Thanks for the talk," I say. "See you in class tomorrow."

I make the short trek back to my dorm and stand in front of our door for far too long. The dry erase board reads our real names today and I don't have any urge to change it. Once I feel ridiculous enough for hesitating outside my own room, I pull out my key and open the door. Lottie sits cross-legged on her bed, hair pulled up into a messy bun with tendrils falling on either side of her face. Her eyes are red-rimmed, cat eye smudged, resembling more of a raccoon. For a moment, my anger melts into concern, but concern is quickly replaced by annoyance.

What has she gotten into now?

"Thank God, you're back!" Lottie says. She throws her computer off her lap and onto her bedspread. I shift out of my coat and plop down on my bed, saying nothing and avoiding her gaze. "You're not going to believe what happened today."

"Oh, yeah?" I mutter and slip underneath my covers.

"But first, how are you? Sadie told me everything, are you okay? Are you sick? What's going on with you? I tried texting and calling but you never answered."

Once more, I almost cave to her frantic energy. But my anger at myself has transformed everything I might have felt and now I'm angry at her. I'm not okay. But I would be if it wasn't for her and her stupid ghost mother. The first twinges of a headache sting around my sinuses. I yank off my glasses and place them on the bedside table.

"Do you need a moment? Have you seen a doctor?"

"Lottie, please shut up for, like, half a second," I say and she freezes. I can't see her, but I know her too well now. I know what she does when she's insulted. "I can't do this."

"Okay, I'll leave you alone for now and let you rest."

I sit up fast and stare at her. Her eyes shift between me and anywhere else in the room.

"No," I say. "I don't just want to rest. I want out."

"You want out," she repeats, slowly. "What the hell does that mean?"

"I want out of this. I don't want to play ghost hunter anymore. I don't want some cold case to take my focus away. If that's something you want to do, then that's on you. I'm out."

Lottie doesn't move, so I slip down and turn my back on her. I listen to her uneven breathing and try to steady my own.

"So that's it then?" she finally says. "All this work and you're done. Okay, cool. But don't try to pin this on me. I was not the one who saw a damn ghost or started a murder investigation. That was. All. You. So you can have your pity party and whenever you're done feeling sorry for yourself, I'll be here."

"I'm not having a pity party. I'm done. I don't care anymore. Let me live my life."

She laughs, dry and unfunny. "Okay."

We exist in uncomfortable silence. I stare at a blank spot below the photographs on my wall. I let my eyes unfocus and blur. Anger envelops me as Lottie incessantly types on her laptop. I want to tell her to shut up as much as I want to tell her I didn't mean anything I just said. But my own self-pity stops me from doing either. My phone buzzes again. There is no one I want to talk to right now, but still, I reach into my sweater and pull it out.

Sam

You're done with everything now? Thanks, Maryl. I'm glad you have the luxury of forgetting about all of this and dropping off the face of the earth.

The laugh that escapes me is so deep and mean, so like an evil queen from a Disney movie, that it surprises me. "You told on me."

Lottie doesn't respond so I decide to ruin my life further.

Maryl

I'm glad you're disappointed in me. Join the fucking club.

My fingers hover over the send button. Three dots appear as he starts typing. I hesitate. The dots disappear. I exhale and delete everything.

Maryl

K

Chapter Thirty-Five

Denver Keyes makes an uncomfortable amount of eye contact with me as he addresses the full lecture hall about not submitting work on time. I missed the deadline for the last assignment while I was away. I didn't submit anything over the weekend either. It felt pointless.

"Is he looking at you?" Hale hisses.

"I am part of the problem, yes," I say.

"What?"

I wave him off and he goes silent. I stare down at the white tabletop until Denver finishes and consider leaving out the back exit since I have no paper to pick up, when he calls my name.

"Miss Laine!" his voice booms over the chatter. "May I speak with you, please?"

There's part of me that considers still walking out the door, but that part of me is weighed out by logic. Logic tells me I can't run out because he knows me too well at this point. So I make my way down the incline of the lecture hall, past the line of students waiting to pick up their graded assignments, to Denver, leaning against the back corner of the blackboard.

He studies me for a moment, then his eyes shift to my left. Hale has appeared beside me, uninvited. I silently plead with him to leave, but he doesn't get the message.

"You can wait for me outside," I tell him under my breath, and when he doesn't move, "Leave."

Hale's eyes widen for a fraction of a second. He nods solemnly, turns, and walks away. I follow him through the crowd as he weaves his way toward his paper, narrows his eyes at the grade, then rushes out the open door.

"You were harsh on him this time?" I ask, turning my attention back to my professor.

Denver's eyebrows raise, clearly not what he expected me to say. He shakes his head and waits for the mass of people to thin. Once half the alphabet has cleared, Denver gestures to two chairs at the front of the lecture hall, pulled into the table where his papers are scattered, along with a coffee cup and his briefcase. I sit and wait for him to take the seat next to me, but instead he looms overtop of me from the other side of the table.

"So let's talk," he says.

"Sure," I say and cross my arms on the desk. "What should we talk about today? Me or the past?"

He looks as though he could laugh, the sort that comes from exasperation. Instead, he shakes his head and conceals an eye roll. "This is about you, Miss Laine."

"So I'm Miss Laine now. After everything I've done for you?" I ask. The slightly spiteful, completely done part of me takes my voice up a level. But I've forgotten that Denver is not one to care about what other people think.

"You didn't turn in your assignment this week."

"I was at a swimming competition and had an accident. I didn't have time. But now that you've got me here, did you pull all the other students who didn't submit a piece aside, or just me? Just the ones who your family members snitched on?"

He turns his face away from me, but I catch the split second moment of surprise register on his features. I've embarrassed him, which means that like Lottie told Sam about my behaviour, Sam probably told Denver.

"Look, Maryl," Denver says and I nearly snort at him suddenly switching to my first name. "I know you had a meet. I know lots of students involved in university sports try and use the sport as their excuse. However, you have never done that which leads me to believe that excuse is not correct."

"That's bullshit," I say. The brash and offensive Maryl he first met comes out. "The only reason you know it's an excuse is because your son told you."

He sighs, long and profound. "You started something and you have to finish it."

"It's not my job to solve a murder from twenty years ago!"

"No," he agrees and leans closer to me once more. I shrink back in the chair, our easy camaraderie gone. "But it is your job to pass this class, isn't it?"

"Are you threatening me?"

His eyes widen and he takes two steps backward. I've misinterpreted him, but I won't give him the satisfaction of my mistake. I push myself up from the chair, nearly tipping it over, then storm out. Hale waits on the other side and a keen sense of déjà vu hits me as I remember that first time I stormed out of this lecture hall. Hale follows as I stalk away. I angrily zip up my coat and nearly catch my finger in my haste.

"I take it that didn't go well," Hale says.

"Don't pretend like you weren't listening."

"Okay, I was," he says and jogs to catch up to me as I hold the door open. "I think you should report him."

"He didn't do anything wrong."

"He threatened you," Hale states as if this is the most offensive thing in the world. His voice rises into a slight screech and I roll my eyes so hard it hurts.

"He didn't, really."

Hale grunts. I continue walking and he continues telling me why Denver is a piece of shit. I nod at the appropriate moments, but I'm really making my game plan for the rest of the day. I have to start training again if I want to keep my spot on the team. Which also means I have to formally talk to Coach Jaffee. I haven't said a word to him since the meet and he hasn't reached out to me, aside from making sure my mother got me home.

Hale follows as I bypass the more scenic route to Shirreff and turn down South Street. I run my hand along the rock wall that separates the fenced off tennis court from the road. A car speeds by and obscures Hale's words further. The cobbled brick of New Eddy comes into view. It's always impressed me how well the brick in New Eddy and Newcombe matches to the rest of the building. You can hardly tell where the original building ends and the extension begins, apart from Newcombe having a fifth floor while the others end at the fourth.

I turn up the driveway and note Hale's switched topics to one that requires my attention.

"Are you still not speaking with your roommate?" he asks.

I purse my lips and pull on the rust-coloured door. "It's not that we're not speaking." It is. "We just have nothing to say to each other right now." And also Sam didn't want me speaking to him so I took that one step further and extended that to Lottie.

"You're not really friends anymore, right?" he asks as we tromp up the stairs.

I clamp my hand against the railing and let out an extended sigh. "I don't know. I think I hurt her, but I meant everything I said. I just want to stop all the nonsense."

Clarity brought me that conclusion. With clarity came guilt. I felt like a horrible person for wanting to separate myself from the drama. But why should I feel guilty if that's what I want?

"I think it's the best choice," he says.

He stands in front of my room as I unlock the door. I step inside and feel guilty at the relief that washes over me. Hale may be onto something. But I'm not sure who is and isn't good for me right now.

"Maybe," I say and throw my backpack onto the floor, only to pick up my swimming bag.

"I mean, I don't know everything about you guys, but you seem to fight a lot. This is the third time, right? She seems to really drag you down. So maybe it is best you go your separate ways."

I root around my swim bag, making sure I have everything I need. Once more, my goggles are missing. When I come up empty, I scan the room, then head into the closet. Lottie needs everything clean. She hates my side of the room and will clean up my mess if it's especially bad. My goggles sit on top of a pile of towels in the closet, clearly Lottie's doing. Instead of being grateful like usual, heat creeps up my cheeks and annoyance settles over me. I pull down a new towel along with the goggles.

When I step back into the room, Hale stands next to my bedside table. He jumps and flushes when I catch him. I raise my eyebrows.

"Sorry," he says. "I was just... Maybe I shouldn't have been snooping, though I wasn't really snooping..."

I follow his gaze to the framed photograph on the table. "That's my grandma."

"I thought it might be," he says and picks it up as if my voice is permission. He studies my grandma with five-year-old me. "You look like her. Same nose, lips, and face shape. Even kind of the same hair."

I reach up to my hair, just touching my collarbones now. I cut it a few weeks after she died and kept it that length. Subconsciously, I must have gone for the same style.

"Thank you," I say and clear my throat. "She's my favourite person ever. I wouldn't want to look like anybody else."

Hale places the frame on the table, gingerly. He turns back to me, gaze falling on the items in my hands, then trailing back up to my coat. "Oh. You're leaving."

"I'm going to the pool, yeah."

He grimaces, but lets himself out. I follow him and lock the door again. I wave and watch him walk down the long corridor. I half expect something to jump out at me when it empties, but no one appears, not even a living, breathing human.

I cross campus back to the Dalplex, feeling confident... which slips away once I stand in front of Coach's office. Though, as luck would have it, I don't have to wait long because the door swings open. Coach Jaffee's face opens up in surprise when he sees me. I smile.

"Maryl! How are you?" he asks and gestures for me to come in.

I deflate into a chair on the other side of his desk. "I'm doing well," I say, only a little bit of timidity creeping into my voice. "I wanted to apologize."

"For what?" he asks with genuine curiosity. He slips into his rolling chair and folds his hands on the desk.

"For—for losing. For not finishing the race. For going in when I knew I couldn't and shouldn't have."

He chuckles. "Well, apparently you don't know, but you did finish the race. The girl in the lane next to yours allowed you to finish."

"She was the one who helped me?"

He nods. "Exceptional sportsmanship. So you did finish that race. Maybe you shouldn't have raced it, but we live and we learn."

"That's it?" I ask, shocked. "You're not angry?"

"We all have off days, Maryl. Generally I like to know about them before I put my team into the pool, but sometimes we can't control that. I'd be a big old asshole if I held this against you. You were clearly sick. I'm not going to get angry at someone for having something potentially dangerous happen in the water."

"I was certain you were going to kick me off the team."

Another laugh. "Not that easily. And quite frankly, you beat a record when it counted. I wouldn't dream of getting rid of you. We need you next year if we're going to pull off another winning season. Let me know if you can't swim next time."

I smile and the world balances on its axis once more. Until...

Sam

Something important happened so your BS doesn't matter right now. Call me back.

I delete the message.

Chapter Thirty-Six

I SWIPE ON A wine-coloured lipstick in our full length mirror. I push a stray artificial daisy out of the way and accidentally pull it out of the flower border lining the mirror. Lottie sits on her bed with a compact, huffing in frustration at my clumsiness.

Lottie and I avoided each other all week. If she was in our dorm, I stayed away. If I was in the dorm, she stayed away. We were only together to sleep and only spoke, begrudgingly, if we needed the other to turn off a light.

I miss her chatter. I miss her voice and eccentricities. All I have to do is admit I'm wrong; that I was stressed out and I don't hate her or Sam. I was just scared and reactionary and wanted a minute of normalcy. But even if I apologize for being a dick, I'm not sure I want to go back to the way things were.

I run my hands along the sides of my gauzy ivory shift dress, the hem finishing asymmetrically at mid-thigh. I'd ordered the dress impulsively and finally found a reason to wear it. The Athletic Banquet always happens a few weeks before the semester ends. One night to let go and have fun before final projects and exams begin.

Lottie eyes me as I pull my short hair into a low bun. I leave a few tendrils hanging, framing my face. I bend, pick the fallen pink daisy up off the floor, and fasten it to the back of my bun with several bobby pins. Lottie nods appreciatively.

"Good choice," she says.

I smile, warmth filling me up over the innocent comment. My phone buzzes off my bedside table. I walk over and pick it up. Three new messages from Sam. I roll my eyes.

"Why does Sam keep texting me if he doesn't want to speak to me anymore?"

Lottie returns my eye roll, but says nothing. I delete the messages. They're more of the same. He keeps telling me this is important. Lottie is afraid. I glance at Lottie, casually applying pink and purple shades of makeup that complement her flowery, off-the-shoulder dress. She seems unbothered and anything but fearful. I don't push it or ask. I open the drawer of my bedside table and rummage.

Something is missing. I know it immediately and feel inappropriate, immediate tears prickle. The velvet box holding Mamie's earrings is gone. She willed them to me and I knew they had to come with me to university. I wore them on my first day here and they've sat in that box in that drawer ever since. Now I can't remember the last time I saw them next to my glasses case. Guilt washes over me, then anger.

"Did you take my grandma's earrings?" I accuse Lottie.

"What?" she asks, eyeliner pencil freezing mid-swipe.

"The earrings. The ones always in my bedside table. I was going to wear them tonight."

She screws up her features and shakes her head. "I haven't taken anything, but I'll help you look. What do they look like?"

"You've seen them," I insist and slam the drawer shut. "I wore them on the first day of school."

"That was six months ago."

I sigh. "Okay, fine."

I gather up my makeup and shove it into my overflowing makeup bag, then throw the bag onto my desk. Lottie jumps, but says nothing as I grab my sparkly clutch, place my phone inside, and wrestle with my dress coat until I'm finally cozy inside it. I further avoid her gaze as I slip my feet into little lace peep toe heels.

As I walk toward the door, she finally speaks. "I didn't take them, Maryl."

The sincerity in her voice shakes me and I pause with my hand on the doorknob. "I know."

I lean against the wall outside our dorm and text Sadie.

Maryl

Are you ready to go? Meet you downstairs?

Sadie

Look to your left

I look up and catch a glimpse of someone walking down the empty corridor. For a moment, I think it may be Sadie, but whoever's walking toward me is primarily made up of shadows. Goosebumps form on my skin and I close my eyes. My phone buzzes in my hand. The figure is gone when I look again.

Sadie

Wrong left

I laugh at my stupidity and this time, actually look to my left. Sadie stands next to me in a gorgeous emerald dress that works perfectly with her russet skin and bright red hair.

"I see you've freshened up the mermaid hair," I say.

"Of course," she says and fluffs up her beach waves. "I don't have to be in a pool for a while now. It was time for some spice."

We walk away from the dorm room, Sadie talking about anything and everything. I feel guilty leaving Lottie alone, even though I know she's coming with her journalism friends to take photos for the *Dalhousie Gazette*. But I also feel, with sinking certainty, that I'm being watched.

When I feel eyes on me again, it's dinner. Trays of miniature roasted potatoes, steamed rainbow vegetables, saucy chicken Parmesan, a variety of salads, and a steaming pasta with scallops make their way around each banquet table. Tables are divided by sports, most having multiple to accommodate their large teams. The Athletic Banquet is always held at a hotel near campus, this year it happens to be The Westin Nova Scotian. Sadie sits next to me, picking scallops out of her pasta. I absently move my fork around my plate, trying to find the source of the eyes. Everyone is eating or piling food on their plates. There is no one directly looking at me. Except...

Riley. But he's only staring at me because I zoned out staring at his face.

I smile and mouth a sorry his way. He shoots me a goofy grin and a thumbs up. I stare down at my food and still can't shake it. The back of my neck prickles, baby hairs standing on end. I slyly glance behind me and spy a figure that makes me pause. Not because there's someone actually there, but because the someone seems familiar. At first, my brain connects the dots and I assume it must be Penny. But it can't be Penny.

"You good?" Sadie asks.

I nod and shove food in my mouth. A soggy piece of lettuce. I crunch it around as I search the banquet hall. I itch my neck and look behind me again. No one. I feel like I'm losing a weird game of hide-and-seek I didn't sign up to play.

Across the hall, I see a flash of silky, grey hair, out of place in a room full of twenty somethings and coaches unwilling to admit they've aged. The moment I see it is the moment it vanishes. I scan tables and the little nooks and crannies where hotel staff brought out food and drinks. All odds point to it being a staff member; someone I obviously wouldn't recognize because I don't know them.

The next table over, just behind Riley, I catch a glimpse of a woman. Grey hair, draping dress, cloaked in shadows. I jump and she's gone. My heart pounds and my stomach knots. It's impossible.

I push my chair away from the table and excuse myself. Sadie protests for a moment, but I move too fast for any real conversation. She doesn't follow. I weave my way through white clothed tables and chairs tied with purple and gold ribbons. Whoever I saw is gone now, but I still leave through the Grecian archways of the hall. Outside, I lean against an archway and try to get a hold of myself. The exact thing I've been trying to avoid is happening. The din of conversation and celebration inside the banquet hall fades away as I rub at my temple and attempt to ignore my instincts.

"Oh, cherie," says a voice inside my head. I physically recoil as the familiarity fully hits me.

"No," I whisper, pressing my palms against my eyes, likely messing up the makeup I worked so hard on. "That's impossible."

I open my eyes to an empty hallway. My focus strays to the wall of windows lining the entryway of the banquet hall. The last remaining bits of light stream through them. I steady my breathing while watching foliage blow in the wind outside, then look down at my hands which, while shaky, thankfully only have the briefest hint of makeup on them. I turn to go back into the banquet hall, the conversations coming to a hush as someone official makes an announcement, but I stop at the voice once more.

"Maryl, ma belle," she says.

I turn around again and come face to face with Mamie.

She takes tentative, gliding steps toward me as I stay completely frozen. Her silky, chic hair that she wore in a bob is perfectly poised, framing her face. Her chocolate eyes study me with the same intensity they have all my life. Her favourite moss green caftan, the one we buried her in, hangs loosely around her petite body. She's deathly pale, almost translucent. An oddly comforting factor considering I've only known her skin this way. She looks alive. The vibrant colour still in her cheeks, sparkling her eyes.

"How?" I whisper. It's all I can muster.

"I'm always here, cherie," she says and hesitates before she reaches out to grab my hand. Cold shoots through my arm. "I came here with you."

"Where have you been? Why haven't I seen you until now?"

"You didn't need me until now," she says and laughs when I attempt to interrupt her. "I'm not here to comfort you, Maryl. I'm here because I think—no, I know you're making a mistake. I want to scream, but I've never done that in my lifetime with you, so I'm not going to do it in my death."

"I needed you before now," I whisper.

I want to be angry with her too. I want to yell about how unfair it is to send me into the wild with this thing when she knew all along. But instead, I'm filled with such a profound sadness about all I missed because I was so closed-minded to her beliefs.

"Maybe. But would you have accepted the help then?" I don't say anything and she tsks. "I know you too well. I could talk to Stephen about these things, but never you. I've tried to piece together why that is, but I see now that part of your story needed to be this acceptance of what you can do. I'm only here now because of how stubborn you are."

"What am I supposed to do?"

"Care. You're supposed to care," she says, simply. Her hands encircle my arms, holding on, anchoring me. "That's the most important part in all of this. Care is what drives us."

Her voice is so earnest, it strikes me. It's a double layered message.

"Us?"

"Those of us who see. There's so much we can do to help. But the key to helping is actually giving a damn. You have to care about people. You can't give up when things get hard. I know you had a loss and you feel as if your gift made that loss happen, but it didn't. You cared too much and then not enough. You have to find a balance and give yourself grace."

I gasp. "You've been trying to contact me."

"Oui, ma belle. You weren't ready to see me yet, so I did it the only way I could."

"I love you, Mamie. I'm always ready to see you."

Her lips quirk into one of her wild, conspiratorial grins. "I have so much I want to help you with. But you have to promise me you'll go back and help your friend. She's in danger."

My heart skips a beat, then sinks. I'm a horrible person. Sam told me that Lottie was scared, threatened, and didn't know what to do. I should have said something.

"Maryl?" a voice comes from behind me, this time one of the living. I turn to find Lottie. "Are you okay?"

"I should be asking you that," I say. I note the chill in the air has dissipated. Mamie's gone and I have to hold back a sob.

Lottie raises her eyebrows, but doesn't ask. "I saw you come out here. They're doing swimming awards now and I'm fairly certain you won one. You should come back in."

I mumble a thank you and stumble my way back into the banquet hall. I have so much apologizing to do, but first I have to get through tonight. Give myself some damn grace.

Chapter Thirty-Seven

I LEAVE THE DANCE as soon as I'm able. Lottie took my picture up on stage for my Rookie of the Year win. I smiled for the camera, then excused myself immediately after to murmured concerns. I guess it makes sense that my teammates would be worried about me skipping out sick a week after I basically almost drowned.

The first thing I do when I get back to the dorm is rip out hundreds of bobby pins fastened into my hair. It comes loose in limp strands, until the daisy falls to the floor again. I consider removing my makeup as I stare at my deflated reflection in the mirror, but decide it's not worth the effort. Instead, I take out my contacts and replace them with glasses. I change out of the dress that got way less screen time than I wanted and slip beneath my covers in sweats and a tank top.

My fingers hover over Sam's name on my phone screen. I want to apologize so badly, but Lottie deserves that before he gets one.

Too lazy, or maybe out of any useful energy, to crawl to the bottom of my bed and grab my laptop, I binge *The Office* on my phone. As much as I want to care about Michael Scott and Dwight and Jim, it doesn't fully satisfy me. My mind keeps straying to Mamie. Everything she told me, and the fact that she finally appeared, weighs on me. The only consolation is maybe now she'll continue to be in my life.

I pause *The Office*, the episode where the Scranton and Stamford offices of Dunder Mifflin merge, and push myself off the bed. I have to see Penny.

I rush upstairs with zero thought. It takes me standing in front of the window on the fourth floor to realize I didn't put on any shoes. I catch my breath and slide down the wall.

Penny isn't here. But I'm certain she can hear me.

"I'm sorry," I say. I search the nooks and crannies of the hallway, knowing she's not showing herself to me. I rub my hands over my bare arms, wiping away goosebumps. "I know you're here, but you don't have to come out if you don't want to. I'm sorry. I wasn't thinking. Or maybe I was thinking too much. I don't know. Whatever I was doing, I'm sorry. I'm back and I want you to know I care and I'm going to figure this out."

Penny materializes in a haze and walks toward me. She stops in front of me and I stare at her shoes.

"Look at me." I do. She looks down at me with a wry smile. "Thank you. Now go and tell my children before you do anything else."

Something in the way her voice stays steady and harsh makes me certain she means business. I scramble to my feet and scurry back downstairs. When I get back to our room, Lottie is already at the door. Her eyes widen when she sees me.

"I went to see Penny," I explain.

Lottie opens the door. "You forgot shoes."

"I know," I say and follow her inside.

"That urgent, eh?" Her voice drips with sarcasm, but when she turns to me, her eyes soften. "Are you okay?"

I nod. "Yeah, I'm okay. Just had a day."

She waits. There's about a million things I want to say to her but I don't know where to begin. When I don't say anything, she turns away, throws her camera case onto her bed, and takes off her coat and sky-high heels.

"I'm sorry," I say to her back. "Like, really, genuinely sorry. I don't think I've ever been so stupid. This is the dumbest thing I've ever done and I don't know why I did it. I could blame my mom and say she got in my head, but I'm the one making the decisions. I'm so sorry I made you feel like everything we've done this semester hasn't been worth it. I'm sorry I blamed my failure on everyone else but myself. You all told me to take a break last weekend and I didn't. I ignored advice because I was too obsessed with getting answers. That's on me."

Lottie turns to me, then sits down on her bed. Those damn green eyes bore into me as she struggles to find words.

"I want to forgive you, but you have to listen to your own advice, too. You told Hale that he can't keep trashing you and apologize later. You can't do that to me either."

"I never trashed you," I say and propel myself forward. I sit down next to her. "I would never. I've worked so hard my whole life with swimming and I felt like I was losing that over something I just started figuring out."

"Maryl, this is my whole life. You have to understand that. I've spent my whole life looking for answers and these people and now that I've found them... It's like you thought that was your out. I would never ask you to drop swimming. I never did. I just never expected you to come home and stop talking to me."

Fuck. The guilt I've been holding at bay all this time comes crashing over me so hard I almost start crying. I hold it together, solely because I know this isn't about me. Me getting upset over the stupidity of my own actions isn't going to help anybody.

"I am so sorry. I understand. It's like we both went through the same thing last week for different reasons. I hope I didn't derail anything."

"You didn't, exactly," she says, but she chews on her lip as she says it. "Things have been happening that I haven't been able to tell you about."

"You're being threatened?" I ask.

She blinks. "Did your ghost friends tell you that?"

"Only partially," I say with a little laugh. "My grandma told me and—"

"Your grandma?!"

"That's who I was talking to at the dance. She was mad at me for being a dick too. She's also the one who's been writing through me."

"Whoa," Lottie whispers. "I'm glad she finally showed up for you."

This time, I finally do cry. Emotions I've kept locked away overwhelm me. All the new grief that resurfaced once I found out I could see dead people and the one dead person I wanted to see wasn't showing up crashes into me like a tsunami. I've barely let myself dwell on it, but it was bound to burst at some point. Lottie, because she's the best person I've ever known in my life, throws her arms around me and squeezes until I can stop. She cries with me. We pull back with streaky faces and laugh at each other.

"I really am sorry," I tell her.

"I know."

"Sam told me you were afraid and I ignored him. I'm so sorry."

"It's okay. Really, I promise. But don't ever do it again." She mimes cutting my throat. "I'll set my ghost mom on you."

"Yeah, no worries, she already got on my case today."

Lottie laughs, then grows somber. She freezes mid-laugh and looks me in the eye. "Some really creepy things have been happening." She gets up and walks over to her desk. A stack of papers lie inside the file folder she keeps in one of the plastic drawers underneath. I take the paper on top of the pile. "This is the latest one."

I raise an eyebrow. "Latest?"

It's a letter addressed to Lottie in a boxy typewriter font.

Lottie Walsh,

You must think you're an angel on Earth. But angels fall too. I'd watch myself if I were you.

"Arguably, not the worst one I've gotten." She hands me another piece of paper. "Found this one on my pillow on Monday."

Lottie Walsh,

You're so cute with your tattoos. You flounce around here in little booty shorts when it's winter. I guess you're forgetting that your mom's whoring around is what got her killed. Who's to say you're not next?

A shiver goes down my spine and I immediately hate myself. I was here when she got this and I didn't even ask if she was okay.

"You got one before this, didn't you?" I say, remembering her words when I came back from Toronto.

"There was one my desk Saturday. The first one."

She hands me the pile. One for each day this week. I sift through, each letter saying something about her, her mom, or what we've been investigating. The creepier ones detail something Lottie was doing that particular day. She tells me where she found each of them; all in various places around our room.

"So someone's been breaking in?" I ask. She shrugs. "Have you told anyone about this? Other than Sam, I mean. Like the police?"

"I went to campus police on Monday. I wanted to wait until you were back in case we needed to do something. They asked me a bunch of questions and eventually thought that because you and I were fighting that you could be doing it. Apparently they get a lot of roommate drama."

"Well," I say slowly. "That's unhelpful."

"Tell me about it!" She flops facedown on her bed, then pushes herself up again. She reaches underneath her covers and pulls out the copy of *Dracula* she's been making her way through. A folded piece of paper sticks out of it. We both freeze. "This wasn't here when I left."

Lottie plucks the paper from the book and unfolds it with shaking hands. I lean over to read it with her.

Hope you had fun tonight, Lottie Walsh. Did you see me?

"I want to vomit," I say.

"Someone's been in here, touching our things and watching us. What if they have a camera in here? Maryl! This is probably where your earrings went. They're taking things too!"

"How are they even getting in here? What do they want from us?"

"Maybe it's part of the curse."

I instinctively snort in disbelief, but it's half-assed. It's marred by fear invading my bones. I observe our room. Nothing else looks disturbed, nothing else seems missing. The window between our beds is locked shut, not broken. Our door has no evidence of being tampered with.

"Does anyone else have a key to our room?"

"Grayson has one, but he's nowhere near here and also wouldn't do this," she says. She closes her eyes, as if hurt and mutters something under her breath. "I gave one to Sam. It can't be him, right?"

I stay silent as my mind pieces things together. What if Sam is putting an end to his grandfather's mess? What if we've gotten too close to the truth and the only option is to scare us away?

Without a plan, I dial Sam's number. It rings twice before he picks up.

"What are you playing at?" I ask when he answers. I regret the words immediately. We're not in a detective movie. I don't need bold, bad cop phrases.

"What are you talking about?" He sounds almost amused.

"You're the only other person with a key to our room and Lottie's getting threatening notes. Catch the drift?"

"You think...?" he trails off and laughs. "You're joking, right? It's past midnight and you're calling to accuse me of what? Stalking my sister?"

"Did you do it?"

He laughs again, then the line goes dead.

Chapter Thirty-Eight

Saturday afternoon, Lottie heads to Pier 21 to check out her family's records while I tackle her brother. Lottie didn't want to admit it, even after I made my ballsy call to Sam, but it's a hunch I have to follow. Albeit, a hunch based on the tiniest bit of evidence, but still a hunch.

I bang my fists against Sam's door, praying he's not at work. A neighbour peeks her head out across the hall. I smile politely and the door opens. Sam appears in the doorway in a pair of jeans, a half buttoned light blue shirt that's bunched at the elbows, and a towel slung over his arm. He looks me over, then tilts his head skyward with a groan.

I snort. "Good to see you too. Let me in."

"Why would I let you in?" he asks, holding onto the baseboard around the door. A muscle flexes in his forearm.

"Because we need to talk," I say, then glance behind me and note the woman still there. "And I'm annoying your neighbours."

Sam sighs. "That sounds like your problem," he says, but steps aside.

I stroll into the apartment feeling vaguely triumphant. Sam closes the door and leans against it. He draws the towel through his damp hair and eyes me warily. I sink slowly onto the couch and meet his eyes. I try to think of something to say, but falter under his gaze.

"You know," he says, saving me the trouble of starting, "you have a lot of nerve showing up here after saying nothing to us for a week and then calling me out of the blue at midnight to accuse me of whatever the hell you think I'm doing."

"Lottie's being threatened. You're the only other person who has a key."

"Are you sure? Or are you so tired of looking that you're going to settle on the easiest target?" He throws his towel onto the couch, just beside me, and I jump.

Am I sure? Something itches at the back of my mind. Something about the day I lost my keys... and yet, "I resent that. I'm not tired."

He laughs, but not the friendly sort. "Yeah, you're something else."

I push myself off the couch, angry energy coursing through my body. I stalk toward him until I feel like I've backed him into the door, and not that he's resting there. "Okay, fine, I did it all wrong and I suck. Happy? You're still not telling me what you did."

"Because I haven't done anything." His voice is level and his eyes are steady. The only ounce of emotion I see in him is a smirk he can't quite hide.

"Do I amuse you?" I ask.

"It amuses me when people jump to conclusions they can't back up. You dropped off the face of the earth and now you're coming back and claiming that I'm fucking you over. So yes, I find that amusing."

"Rich," I hiss and poke him in the chest. "You think you would have gotten this far without me? Without me you wouldn't know your own father."

"Would you like a thank you?" He swats my arm away. "I wasn't talking about that. You gave up. You dropped this as fast as you took this on."

"Well now I'm back and I want a damn answer!"

"What's the question? Did I threaten my own sister? You really must know me less than I thought if that's your assumption."

I take a step back to gather my thoughts. He's right. I don't know him that well, but it works both ways. He may be capable of hurting Lottie and his grandpa may have been capable of hurting Penny. His eyes stay trained on me and part of me still melts in those blue rimmed pools. I'm inexplicably drawn to him even though I want to stay mad and keep fighting.

I lick my lips and meet his gaze. My voice comes out strong and confident. "Did you?"

"No, I didn't." A chuckle bubbles out of him once more. "God, the nerve. How do you have the balls to come here and barge into my place, but you don't have the balls to finish this thing?"

"I'm finishing it right now."

"With me?" His eyebrows raise, playing. "Weird strategy, but okay."

I let out an exasperated sigh, bordering on a scream. "Here's the thing. I think your grandpa killed your mother. You only make up a curse if you need an excuse. I don't know how you fit into all this, but I think you do."

"Some mighty confident words for a theory you're not actually confident in."

"How is someone getting into our dorm? There's no sign of forced entry so it's someone with a key. You have one."

He shrugs. "I don't, actually."

"What?"

"Lottie said she'd give me a key but she never did. I don't want to assume anything because I've known her for, like, a month, but she's kind of flighty sometimes."

My face falls. Fuck. I've lived with her for six months and I know this. It's not an assumption. Sometimes Lottie does forget to do things she said she would. I recover quickly and shake my head.

"How do I know that's true?"

"Your face answered that one," he says and mimics the smug assuredness that fell away from my face in an instant.

And in my moment of resignation and probably confirmation that someone else, someone more insidious, is breaking into our safe space, I say the one and only thing that comes to my mind. "Oh, fuck me."

A laugh, and then he's on the move. He bridges the two-step distance I created between us. "Gladly."

I gasp and his lips are on mine. I wrap my arms around his neck, knitting my fingers in the hair that brushes his collar. *Holy shit.* This kiss is different and far more intense than the innocent one we shared a few weeks ago. His hands find my waist and work their way up, slipping under my unzipped coat and pushing it off. It falls to the floor with a swish.

I break off from the kiss to his bewildered, yet mischievous face, and kick off my boots. He leads me to the couch and pulls me down onto his lap. I straddle him and shake my hair out of its ponytail. He grins, takes my face in his hands, and leads it back to his lips. I bunch my hands in his shirt. They busy themselves on the few buttons that Sam had done up, easily popping open and revealing his toned chest. I pull back, solely because I'm a thirsty bitch and want to bask in his sculpted body.

I run my fingers along the outline of a secret tattoo. A sparrow with splashes of blue, red, and yellow sits on his left peck. I make a mental note to ask him the story behind it when I'm not on top of him.

"You never showed me this one," I say.

"People don't really like when you take your shirt off the moment you meet them."

I laugh and trail kisses from the bird, to his clavicle. He arches so I can nuzzle him. He groans as I kiss along the planes of his neck, paying special attention to the dip below his Adam's apple. As I find my way back to his lips, his hands weave their way under the hem on my Dalhousie sweater. He rips it off my body a second before our lips connect once more. A fleeting thought passes through my brain. *I'm not wearing a bra today.*

I don't care.

His hands relish this fact and cup my breasts. God was not generous when He made my swimmer's body, but Sam is unfazed. Sam is *aroused*.

I can feel the press of him between my legs. My breathing comes out fast and I bunch my hands at his collar. Heat radiates off his chest. I grip his shoulders and push his shirt off to even the score.

He breaks away for a moment to toss his shirt away. When his eyes meet mine again, there's a playful glint in them. I smile and lean into him, a blush creeping across my chest and up my neck. His hand lightly traces my jawline.

He opens his mouth to say something, but we both jump at the loud bleat of my phone. I fall off his lap and nearly off the couch. My legs wind up in his lap, my bare back against the sticky leather. I pull my phone out of the back pocket of my jeans.

"It's Lottie," I say, breathless. "Hello?"

"Okay, so I found something weird," Lottie says.

I turn on speaker phone and rearrange myself into a sitting position. Sam throws a blanket at me and I clutch it to my clearly cold upper body. The phone rests on my knee and Sam focuses on it too intently, making an effort to diffuse our situation.

"You're on speaker," I say.

"You're still at Sam's?"

"Uh, yeah," I say. "He proved me wrong."

Sam chuckles. "You never gave me a key, Lottie."

"I didn't?" she asks, then pauses. We hear rummaging from Lottie's end of the call. "Oh my God, I didn't. It's still in my bag. Remind me to give it to you. I made you a personalized keychain."

"Lottie! What's weird?" I snap.

"So I found the Walsh family lineage and I'm literally the only living female."

"You're joking," Sam says at the same time I exclaim, "What?"

"And all before they turned sixty," she says. She shuffles papers as she speaks. "We know how Penny and our grandma died, then great grandma died in a car accident, great-great grandma died in the Halifax Explosion, and three times great grandma died in childbirth. It goes on. But the point is, they all died young."

A sinking feeling knots my stomach. I glance at Sam who's gone similarly still. I chew my bottom lip. "We have to talk to Elliot again, don't we?"

Chapter Thirty-Nine

Back in my Dalhousie sweater, I sit in Sam's car and redo my ponytail. We don't speak about what happened. I try to start the conversation a few times and fail. Where do I begin to talk about my feelings for this man I've only known for a month? What even are my feelings? And where do those feelings fit in with what we're about to go and do?

"I'll grab Lottie," I say when Sam stops the car in the loop outside Shirreff Hall. We were going to meet her at Pier 21, but she took photos of the records and high tailed it back to campus to pick up her other research.

Sam nods and smiles. I can see him internally freaking out, a disingenuous hint to the smile. I don't know which part of today bugs him. I pause with my hand on the door handle.

"Sam, are you...We're okay, right?"

He blinks in confusion, then his eyes widen. "Oh no. No, it's not about you. You were a nice break. Wait, no, I mean..." he groans and I smirk. "There's so much going on right now and you are the least of my worries. You make more sense to me than my sister being threatened and my grandpa possibly being involved somehow."

"So it doesn't bug you that we probably would have gone further if Lottie hadn't interrupted?"

"Does it bother you?"

I flush. "I don't think so."

The contagious grin returns to his face. "Go get Lottie."

I slip out of the car and into Shirreff. I half expect Lottie to be waiting outside our dorm, which is why it's even more of a shock when I find Hale standing there. He jumps when I tap his shoulder.

"What's up?" I ask.

"I was waiting for you," he says. "No one's home."

"Lottie's not there?"

Hale shrugs. "If she is, she's not answering."

I purse my lips and pull out my key. Sure enough, Lottie isn't home. I move to pull out my phone and realize I've left it either in Sam's car or apartment.

"Can I use your phone?" I ask and Hale hands it over. I dial Lottie's number. "Hey, it's Maryl."

"Did you lose your phone?" Lottie asks.

"I temporarily misplaced it. Where are you?"

"I'm chatting with Leah. She doesn't know much about Elliot but she had some info on Graham."

Graham. I'd almost forgotten the name. Of course Leah would know.

"Shit. You'll have to tell me everything in the car. Sam's waiting outside."

"Okay. I'll head out."

I hang up and give the phone back to Hale. I mumble a thank you. His eyes are wide as he rubs the stubble along his chin.

"Where are you headed?" he asks. He follows as I quickly descend the stairs.

"We're figuring out this curse."

Hale freezes mid-step. I don't stop with him.

"I thought you were done with that," he says, overlooking me from the railing above.

"I'm back now. Things changed."

I saunter down the final flight of stairs. Once I'm at the bottom, I hear, "Can I come?"

Fifteen minutes later, we're sitting in front of Elliot's house in Sam's car. Though everyone tentatively said it was okay for Hale to join, no one really wanted him here which resulted in a very silent car ride. Lottie shifts in the front seat, bursting with whatever information Leah told her. Sam's eyes warily pass over Hale in the backseat. Hale shrinks against the door, seemingly regretting his decisions.

"So," I say and draw everyone's attention to me. "Should we go in?"

Sam pops his door open in response. I slide out of the backseat and stand next to him. "Did he invite himself?" he leans into me and whispers.

"He asked. We could have said no."

"We probably should have. I don't trust this guy and I don't think my grandpa will."

I shrug and look overtop of the car to see Hale finally exiting. "Then he can sit out in the cold."

Sam laughs and walks up the drive. I follow. As I pass Lottie, she grabs my arm. She's practically bouncing with anticipation. She glances over her shoulder and watches Hale fall in line behind Sam.

"I hate him," Lottie says and I snort. "But I think we have a new suspect."

"Graham?"

Lottie nods vigorously, then frowns. "I probably shouldn't be excited that my father potentially killed my mother, but I am."

"Why do you think that?"

"Leah told me the only Graham she knows was married to another one of their friends. If that Graham is my father, then Penny had an affair with him and he cheated on his wife. That's motive, isn't it?"

"You mean he killed her because he didn't want his wife finding out?"

Again, a vigorous nod. "It's that or I'm cursed."

"Hey!" Sam calls from the porch. "Are you guys coming?"

We scurry up the driveway, hopping around patches of ice. Sam pulls out a key once Lottie and I stand next to him. Hale falls to the back of the pack, standing on one of the first steps. He wrings his hands together and stares up at the sky. I turn when I hear the door click and swing open. The bright colours of the old house assault me once more. I hesitantly step inside behind Lottie. Hale stays on the threshold.

"Do you need to be invited in?" I ask. "That's a vampire thing, isn't it?"

Hale smirks and enters. It's quiet, aside from the drone of a television somewhere at the back of the house. Sam calls out to his grandpa, then carries on further. The three of us stand and wait in the front foyer. I scuff my foot along the ugly patterned linoleum tile. Lottie hangs her peacoat on the back of the desk chair. She bends to take off her shoes. I wonder how long she thinks we're staying here.

Sam reappears from around the corner with a grimace. "You'll have to wait here, Hale. Grandpa doesn't feel comfortable talking about this with outsiders."

Hale takes a step back, affronted. "What about Maryl?"

"I've been here before."

A flicker of anger passes through his eyes and his brows crease. But he relaxes his shoulders and glances toward the sitting room outfitted with shag carpet and paisley couches. He settles in while Lottie and Sam head back to Elliot. I quickly kick off my boots and hurry to catch up.

Elliot sits in a green armchair at the back of the room. A large screen TV is set up in front of him on the opposite wall. Sliding glass doors lead out into a spacious backyard, full of browned grass and what must have been a garden, but is now a mess of overgrown weeds. I catch Sam's eye, also staring longingly at the garden. Lottie gracefully sits down on the plaid couch and smooths her hands along her jean skirt and tights.

"I'll be out here to fix the garden when the weather gets nicer," Sam says. "Maybe Lottie could help too?"

Lottie smiles and nods politely. I move to sit down next to her at the same time Sam does. He catches my hip and guides me to sit in between the two of them. It's a quick, simple touch, but it makes my entire body tingle. I blush and pray no one noticed.

"So you finally believe me, do you?" Elliot says, his gaze directly on Sam.

"I'm not sure yet. I believe you know something. I do think it's important."

"I found some records," Lottie says, pulling a notebook out of her bag. "There's been a lot of early deaths in the family."

"You're correct," Elliot muses. He picks up his glasses from his end table and places them gently on the bridge of his nose. He reaches down once more and I realize there's a stack of papers sitting next to him. Sam walks over to his grandpa and takes them when he offers. Sam returns and hands me two newspaper articles. I pass the second to Lottie. "I showed these to Penny before her death. I wish I'd done it sooner."

The articles are from *The Chronicle Herald*, one of Halifax's newspapers. The one I'm holding is dated from 1999. It's a profile of a prominent family—The Ebbs. It's a name I've never heard before with accomplishments I've also never heard of. I peek at Lottie and Sam, both engrossed in their articles. Skepticism creeps over me. There's a typo in the headline, and several more grammatical and spelling errors in the article, itself. One, I can excuse, but there's no way this would have been printed with so many issues. I look up and find Elliot's eyes on me.

"Are you sure these are real?" I ask. Lottie and Sam startle.

"Get out," Elliot demands.

I stand, but still feel the need to defend myself. "I don't mean any offence, I—"

"Get. Out."

I purse my lips and turn on my heel. I hand Sam the newspaper and gesture for him to check his phone. He nods. In the kitchen, I pause and text him.

Maryl

Be extra careful with those papers. I think they're faked. Mine was full of spelling mistakes. How about yours?

Hale's eyes widen when I join him in the front room. I hold back a laugh and sink down into an armchair with the same matching paisley pattern as the couch.

"I thought you've been here before."

"I've also been kicked out before."

We fall into silence and I strain to make out what's happening in the other room. But the TV is too loud and they're speaking too quietly. Hale sits there obliviously, earbuds in, and eyes closed. My phone buzzes with a thumbs up from Sam. I sigh and tilt my head back like Hale. Of course, he has the benefit of not seeing what's there. I gasp and sputter out a cough.

Christine peeks through the stair railing. She grins at me. If it was the first time I met her, the grin combined with the long dripping hair on the stairs would have scared the shit out of me. She has major *Grudge* vibes right now. I raise my eyebrows at her, trying to establish a silent conversation.

"You're right to question. No one killed me. We sometimes make mistakes that catch up to us. I've always thought Penny made one of those. My mistake was getting on a boat when I knew I couldn't swim. Elliot's mistake is being too trusting. I think Penny had a bit of that too. Trusted the wrong person, then crossed them," Christine says. Like the first time, she disappears as fast as she appeared.

"You okay?" Hale asks, jarring my thoughts. "Pardon the phrase, but you look like you've seen a ghost. You've lost all colour."

I wave him off. "Oh, no. I'm fine. Been a weird day."

"I'll bet," he mutters.

I lean forward in my seat. "What the hell does that mean?"

Hale pulls his earbuds out and taps his phone. He leans forward as well. "I assume it's your lipstick on his collar."

I blink a few times as my mind races to put things together. I'd thrown on lip gloss earlier today that had a bit of a tint, but it's long gone now.

"Did you not notice?"

In spite of myself, the corners of my lips turn up. "I guess not."

Hale sighs. "So I guess we're friends."

"I guess," I say, though I'm honestly not quite sure we are. I'm a fair-weather friend that only seems to appear when I'm down and he's a fuckboy who really only wanted me in bed. "Look, I'm sorry if I misled you somehow, but I think we're better as friends."

Hale nods and returns to his music. I inwardly groan and wait for Sam and Lottie to be done. I'm not sure how long I sit there, only that I'm sufficiently bored by the time they come back. I immediately stand. Lottie seems shaken, while Sam finds my eyes and shakes his head.

As we leave, Sam leans in and whispers, "You're right. Someone faked the articles."

Chapter Forty

"Apparently the Ebbs are behind this curse on our family. They're supposedly a family of prominence within Nova Scotia, but the prominence and riches that they have came at the expense of our family," Sam explains once we're back at the dorm. "Of course, that is, if you believe it."

"You don't believe it?" Lottie asks, looking up from her laptop.

Sam shakes his head, but says nothing more. His shoulders slump in disappointment and I know why. Of all people, I wanted Lottie to come to the conclusion it was faked on her own.

I watch her furiously type. Once we returned from Elliot's house, Hale left us alone and we headed back to talk. Lottie and Sam filled me in on my gaps in the conversation. The articles were most of the info Elliot had. They were all on the Ebb family. The other papers were collected obituaries of female Walsh family members. Elliot insisted that all of this meant something, especially since the details in the articles claimed the Ebbs had made special deals, quite possibly of the supernatural. An offhand comment like that in a professional newspaper, not on Halloween, makes me even more certain the articles were faked.

I stare at the ceiling and run my hands over my face. We've been back for twenty minutes and I laid down immediately. Sam sits at the end of my bed, my feet in his lap. His hands rest on top of the fuzzy socks I've been wearing all day. Lottie's typing is the only sound in the room outside of the ticking of her alarm clock. I breathe out and blow a chunk of hair out of my face. I meet Sam's eyes and raise an eyebrow. He shrugs.

The typing stops.

"Do you guys have, like, a thing going on?" Lottie asks.

"What?" I say, completely caught off guard, while Sam laughs.

"You seem super close. And I can't complain because I like both of you and think you'd probably balance each other out, but if you're having a silent conversation right now, I'd like to be involved in it."

"I don't take back what I said," I say and glance at Sam. He nods. "Those articles aren't real. Someone falsified them and somehow got Elliot to believe it."

"He said he showed them to Penny before she died and she believed them too," Lottie says with a huff.

"Well I don't."

Lottie keeps my steady, confident gaze for a moment, then looks down. I sigh. Her typing starts up again. Sam runs a hand along his jawline. He squeezes my foot, then moves to pull out his phone. Both siblings begin to type and swipe, both with similar pursed lip focus. I close my eyes and wait for one of them to come up with something. But the week, or the day even, catches up with me and I doze off, only to jump awake when Sam gets up and drops my feet onto my bed.

"Sorry!" he says with a smirk. "Didn't realize you were sleeping."

"I wasn't," I mumble and right my crooked glasses. I push myself into a sitting position and draw my legs up to my chest.

"Look, Lottie. These are *The Chronicle Herald*'s archives from 1999/2000, right around when those articles were supposed to be from. There's nothing here."

He tilts his phone toward her and she bats his hand away. "I know." She shows him her laptop screen, open to the same archives. "I looked up the name too. I can find a lot of old records for Ebb in Halifax, but nothing recent unless it changed into Webb."

"That would have been harder to prove in the early 2000s," I say, almost to myself, but they both catch it.

"You're right," Sam says and sits down on Lottie's bed. He drops his phone in his lap. "But why did someone go to all this trouble? Whoever made these is the killer, right? But why would they even make them? Why not just do it?"

"It's important Elliot believed in the curse so that he wouldn't talk," I say.

"You don't think he did it now?" Lottie asks, shock creeping into her voice.

"Someone put in a lot of effort to do this, but I don't get why Elliot would. It doesn't make sense that he'd create these papers only he would see. Can you drug someone to make them believe what you want?"

"You can probably hypnotize them," Sam suggests.

Lottie closes her laptop and shakes her head. Her breaths come out shaky. We're so close I can feel it in my bones, but there's so many pieces missing.

"What about Graham?" I ask.

"Who's Graham?" Sam replies. I fill him in on what Leah said about Graham. Sam's phone slides off his lap, a brilliant moment of punctuation to the revelation. He makes no move to pick it up. "So Mom had an affair with a married man. Fuck. This guy could be our murderer."

Lottie swipes her hand over her eyes. I want to reach out and hug her, but I know that's not what she wants right now. She pushes off her bed and starts pacing in the bedside table sized space between us.

Her voice is shaky, but full of anger. "How dare I finally find my family and my mom's dead and my dad's a murderer. How dare the universe do that to me!"

I edge to the end of my bed and hang my legs over the side. Sam makes the same half movement, ready to stand and comfort. I nod to him, the remaining, unproblematic member of her family. He stands in her path and she hesitates momentarily, before collapsing in tears in his open arms.

"Hey," Sam says, running his hands up and down her shaking back. "You got me. I'm not gonna die or kill someone. You got me."

A muffled laugh comes from Lottie's mouth, crushed against Sam's chest. I avert my eyes from their family moment. I run my hands along the frayed stitching on my comforter. Sam whispers more words of encouragement, too low for me to hear. Lottie's sobs switch to small sniffles. I glance up the moment she pulls away, her eyes puffy, red-rimmed, and still wet, her nose and cheeks flushed.

She takes my hand and keeps hold of Sam at the same time. "I love you both. Thank you for dealing with my emotions."

"You have every right to be emotional, Lottie. I can't imagine how you're feeling right now," I say. I may have experienced frustration, joy, disappointment, fatigue, and everything in between while investigating, but this is Lottie's life. "For what it's worth, I truly am sorry for how I dealt with this recently." I pause. "And Sam, I'm sorry I accused you of threatening Lottie and being in cahoots with your grandpa when I thought he was the murderer."

Sam simply snorts and rolls his eyes.

"There was another letter here when we got back," Lottie admits. "I wanted to look at the Ebb thing first."

I open my mouth to speak, but I'm too flustered for anything to come out. She reaches for the floating bookshelf above her bed and pulls out an envelope.

"Fancy," I say. "That's the first envelope, isn't it?"

She nods. "It's addressed to both of us."

"Where was it?" Sam asks. His jaw clenches and his eyes throw daggers at the paper in Lottie's hands. It's the first I've seen him react to this situation and I realize how wrong I was to ever suspect him.

"It was on my bedside table. I'm surprised you didn't see it, but I guess I did swipe it first."

I think back to when we first walked in. Though tired, I did catch a flash of blue by Lottie's alarm clock.

"What's it say?" I ask.

Lottie runs her nail through the top of the envelope, then passes its contents to me.

"I feel like I'm in *Pretty Little Liars*," I mutter before I read the note aloud. "Maryl and Lottie, it seems you've joined together again. Pity. I was hoping I could get you to kill each other and put an end to this the easy way. Guess not."

I turn the piece of paper over, making sure nothing is on the back. It's blank. I look up to Lottie's ashen face and Sam's narrowed eyes.

"How long do you think we have before they act?" I ask.

"The closer we get, the more they're going to amp up," Sam says. His fists clench. "Come stay at my apartment."

I sneak into Sam's bed on Sunday night. Neither Lottie nor I were comfortable with him giving up his bed when we barged in on Saturday, so I took the couch in the main room and she took the one in his studio. In the midnight darkness, I can't tell much about him or his decorating choices, but I can see a dark pattern snaking across his bedspread and artwork on the walls. I love that every wall of his space is covered in art.

He turns over in bed as the door creaks open and reaches for something that turns out to be a lamp. I jump and close my eyes as light assaults my vision.

"Couldn't sleep either?" Sam asks.

I shrug and squint. "Surprisingly, I slept fine last night. But it turns out wallowing in uncertainty all day kind of gets to you."

"At least Lottie's getting some rest," he says.

There's something unreadable in his eyes. I take a few steps toward the bed, a double with bookshelves as the headboard. Half the shelves contain books, while the other half is messy with piles of paper and art supplies. Sam pulls back the covers and I climb into his bed.

"Sometimes I create when I can't sleep," he says, following my gaze.

"I talk to ghosts when I can't sleep," I say and lay my head down on his bare chest, right on top of the sparrow. His heart beats steadily beneath me.

"Any here?"

"None that I've seen."

His fingers roam through my hair and pause at the curve of my shoulder. I try to relax into him and fail. I can't place my finger on it, but something is wrong. I push up against him and stare at his face. His eyes are distant, almost a deep green in the yellow light.

"What's the sparrow about?" I ask, trying to reach him.

"Mom always called me sparrow. I guess it's kind of like the moth. A lot of my tattoos are tied to her."

I follow the splotches of watercolour with my finger. He shudders. "I like that," I whisper, then, "What's going on?"

"I think I figured out our missing piece," he says. A breathy laugh escapes him as he reaches for his phone. "And I don't like it for a few reasons. But look."

He navigates through his email app, then clicks on a link. He turns his phone to me when the Ancestry page loads.

"I got an email when I laid down. Lottie added me to her tree on here and convinced me to get it so I could add things about the family she doesn't know."

"She's very convincing," I say.

Another half laugh. "Ancestry emails a lot. I don't know why I opened this one, honestly, it just said there was a new leaf. Fate at work again, probably."

"Probably." I swallow. "Why does it matter?"

"This isn't a leaf that either of us added. Someone did an Ancestry DNA test and their leaf came up as a potential match for Lottie. Their DNA suggests they're half-siblings."

Sam navigates to that specific part of the tree. I freeze. Connected to Lottie's name with a new tree sprouting off is a name I know, followed by several other familiar suspects.

Possible Half-Sibling: Hale Butler

Father: Graham Butler

Mother: Elora Hale

Chapter Forty-One

After much debate with Lottie, I sit beside Hale during class the next day. He could assume I know nothing about the leaf. He also may not have opened his email yet. If Sam and Lottie only got the email late on Sunday, it's quite possible it could still be untouched Monday afternoon.

Denver stands at the front of the lecture hall, droning on about our next steps in the class. We handed in our final assignment and now it's time for fine tuning. We take his advice on our pieces and try to workshop them. Editing, as he says, is a constant process. One we should have been working on all semester. I absently doodle in the margins of my notebook and feel Hale's eyes on me. I nearly look over to him when I see my grandmother's handwriting.

He's not sorry.

I shift and lean on my elbow, obscuring Hale's view of my notebook. I hastily scribble out the words.

"What are you doing?" he whispers.

"I'm tired and doodling."

He seems to accept this for a moment and stays quiet. But then I feel his breath on my neck. I straighten up and inch away from him.

"Tired 'cause you're still solving murders?" he asks.

"Thought you didn't care about that, or me for that matter, after Saturday."

"I care about you," he says and I can't tell how genuine he is. I truly don't know if he ever liked me or if he's been pretending—keeping me close to keep tabs on our progress. "Which is why I wanted you to stop pursuing it. I still think Lottie's a bad friend for continuing this."

I grind my teeth and bite back a snide response. I face the front of the classroom and tune into Denver's words again. He scrawls something on the board and I realize, though I'm physically present, my eyes are unfocused and I've lost the will to refocus. I remember all the times Hale trashed Lottie and tried to keep me angry at her; how he's always seemed to know about Penny and the weirdness surrounding her circumstance more than I have; how he talked about his mom being convinced his dad cheated on her...

"Isn't class more important?" he asks. I shrug. "Fine. If this murder thing means everything to you, who do you think did it now?"

Is he baiting me? I try to judge in his face. There's something behind his eyes, an anger or fear, something darker.

"I think it might be Denver," I say.

"What?!" he screeches. It's a little too loud. A disruption in an otherwise silent room that draws several heads to turn and stare.

I wait for everyone to look away. "Yeah. I think he's tried to get us all on his side and make us think he's safe."

"Seriously?"

No, you idiot.

Hale struggles to keep control of his voice once more and Denver stops his lecture. The already quiet room stiffens. They know what's coming next. Denver narrows in on the sound and stares at Hale, then me. He takes a beat. Of course, it would be me.

"Is there something more important the two of you would like to discuss?" Denver asks.

Hale, angry, bold, and maybe a little confused, throws me under the bus. "She thinks it was you."

Murmurs spread through the lecture hall. Four people in this room know what that means, the rest can only imagine. I make a note to apologize to Denver if I somehow inadvertently ruin his reputation. But he merely nods and continues on with the lecture. Hale says nothing more to me and when class ends, he's the first to get up.

He knows, something screams in my brain. And he has an advantage. Whatever he knows is one step further than us and I can only assume it's dangerous.

"Lottie Arthur, Maryl Laine, may I speak to the two of you?" Denver booms.

I meet Lottie's eyes from across the room. She nods. She knows what I did and why. The next step is telling Denver. Or maybe, telling him a half-truth. I join Lottie at the front and sink down into Hannesicole's empty seat. The three of us wait for the room to clear. Denver leans against the blackboard. There's a stiffness in his posture, a grim set to his features. When the last student leaves, I'm the first to speak.

"I didn't mean it. I don't trust him."

This catches Denver off guard. His confident lean against the board turns into an off balance step forward. His arms uncross as he walks forward.

"Unfortunately because the first year class is so large, I don't know everybody in it. But I assume you mean the boy you always sit beside?"

"Yes," I say. "Hale is his name. Hale Butler."

I wait for any sort of recognition in Denver's eyes, but he just nods. "I've seen him with you all semester."

"I guess we were friends at one point. I don't really know what to say about him. I didn't expect him to be involved in this."

"Why? What's gone on?"

"Lots," I say.

Lottie supplies the details I'm too tired to explain and Denver listens attentively. Mamie's voice in my head tells me to act fast. *Do something.*

"His family tree showed up and his dad's name is Graham. Penny said Graham was my father's name," Lottie finishes.

This is the moment Denver's expression shifts. His eyes darken and shoulders droop. "Oh, Penny," he whispers.

The beginning of a headache pangs against my temple. I meet Lottie's eyes for a fraction of a second.

"I know Graham. I never taught him, but I met him once at a student showcase. He was dating Penny's friend, Elora." He pauses, then shakes his head. "Elora Hale. They married, didn't they? That's where your friend gets his name."

"He told me it was a family name."

"His mother's maiden name." Denver runs two fingers between the bridge of his nose. "Oh, Penny, what did you do?"

Lottie gasps. I whip my head toward her and feel the sting of the building headache. She's staring down at her own notebook, my hand hovers over it at the end of a phrase I didn't consciously write.

"It's her name," Lottie whispers.

Elora Brynn Butler -> Ebb

"Call Sam," I say and stuff Lottie's notebook into my bag while I stand. "Tell him to go to Old Eddy if he's not already there. We have to talk to Penny."

Chapter Forty-Two

A few minutes later, the four of us meet at Penny's spot. Sam had been waiting for me and Lottie there since he dropped us off, absently speaking with thin air. Though my head pounds persistently, Penelope is nowhere to be seen. Denver, Sam, and Lottie look at me expectantly.

"I don't know where she is right now," I mutter, sliding down the wall and rubbing a hand over my forehead.

I close my eyes, aware of some sort of presence. The last time this happened, I passed out, and I definitely don't have time for that today. I feel a hand on my back and jump. But it's large and warm and could only belong to Sam.

"Breathe," he whispers. I do. He rubs the tension from between my shoulder blades. "What's going on?"

I take giant gulps of air and open my eyes. The world seems unsteady around me, darker and hazy somehow. I stare down at my hands. They look nothing like mine. The nails are painted and a bruise rings my wrist.

Penny.

Sam edges away from me and makes me look into his eyes. He opens his mouth, but nothing comes out. He swallows. "You're not yourself, are you?"

"No," a voice comes from me that is distinctly not my own. It's the voice I've been listening to for almost three months. My gaze locks on Denver. Recognition lights up his eyes. "She's let me in. I don't know for how long, but for now, you can speak to me."

All three of them stare at Penny in my body. Why did Penny pick this moment to possess me? That's what this is, isn't it? Questions swirl dizzyingly in my mind, making me feel sick to my stomach. I can hear Penny's thoughts if I try hard enough, but I don't have the focus, nor do I really want to focus that hard and aggravate my head.

"What's happened?" Penny asks.

Lottie is the first to speak. "I have another half-brother. There's Sam and then there's Hale."

Penny's thoughts overwhelm mine with a single word, repeated over and over. *Fuck. Fuck, fuck, fuck.*

Sam shakes his head. "Why didn't you tell us? Why all the half-truths when we could have known everything from the beginning?"

"They weren't half-truths," Penny mumbles. "I didn't know what mattered. I'd spent years believing it was Denver, listening to students parroting my story. I started believing their version. I'm so sorry for that. That was my first mistake."

"Was it?" Sam asks.

I feel my lips tug up, a sad sort of smile. "I guess not. But within the last few months, yes."

"Then let's speak truthfully," Denver says for the first time. He moves gracefully toward us, reaches out a hand, then thinks better of it and drops it to his side. "Tell us everything we need to know."

"I guess that starts with you," Penny says, eyes locking on Denver. "I really did love you. I thought we made a good match. When I got pregnant, I was terrified. I thought you'd leave me, so I left first, before it could hurt. I'm sorry I didn't tell you until it was too late. I wish I'd told you right away. I knew in my heart you'd never leave me over something like that, and yet I let myself be convinced I would. I went back home and told everyone I didn't know who the father was. Then I made the same mistake a few years later. Apparently I never learned my lies hurt me."

Denver shakes his head and sighs. "I think I know the answer already, but who told you I wouldn't care? Who made you afraid?"

Another sad smile. "I think you do. I loved my best friend, but sometimes she was a real bitch."

"I think she felt the same about you," Lottie mutters. Her eyes go wide and she covers her mouth. "I'm sorry. I didn't mean that."

"You did," Penny says with a shrug. Through the hazy din, I see her take in her captive audience. "And you're right. I'm sure Elora had her moments where she hated me, but she was also good to me. I think she assumed things based on her own relationship. Internalized them. Her boyfriend, Graham, didn't want kids. He changed his mind, obviously."

"So what happened?" Sam asks, frustration tinging his voice.

"Well, I had you. Elora was the best during my pregnancy. She cared for me like a child's father should. She took that right away from you, Denver, and I'm sorry. But she loved you, Sam. You were the ring-bearer at her wedding. Then a few years later, I got pregnant again and around the same time Elora did, too. Her husband seemed happy enough, though I had my doubts."

"Of course you did," Sam mutters, low enough that I'm not sure Penny even caught it.

"Elora started thinking her husband was cheating on her when she got pregnant." Sam shifts, Lottie wrinkles her nose, and Denver just sighs. "He did. You all know he did. Graham was a meek person, easily bendable, never really spoke his feelings. He loved Elora's power. He admired her drive and supported her through law school. I don't know when it changed. He did what she wanted when she wanted it. When everything happened, he was a man desperately trying to claw his way out without actually telling his wife he wanted that. And I know that's no excuse. We only slept together once, and I know he was going to tell her he cheated, but then she told him she was pregnant. He stayed for his kids."

Silence falls over the group. I focus on my breathing because it's all I can do. My body desperately tries to push Penny out, while I desperately try to cling to the surface. She has to finish this before I let go.

"But she found out somehow, didn't she?" Denver asks.

My head bobs as Penny nods. "I think so. Maybe not that it was with me... but she knew he hadn't been faithful. So, instead of happily being pregnant together, she almost resented it. The only time I saw flashes of the old her was when she helped my dad."

"When grandpa had his mental breakdown," Sam murmurs.

"Something like that. My mom died a few months into my pregnancy with Lottie. Dad didn't take it well. He would drink at night, go on these hour-long rants, then pass out. He never remembered them in the morning, but then, as time went on, he'd still be a little off when he woke up. He was paranoid, but I think it was mostly because he didn't know what was happening to him. I was so embarrassed. I kept trying to get Elora to stay away from the house. I didn't want her to see him like that and judge him. Which is dumb because she was there the first time it happened and had no problem being there for me too while he was going through it."

I don't like any if this. It all feels so icky. I don't know if I want to vomit from the story or the possession.

"It was after I gave birth that Dad really started going off the deep end. I moved in with Elora and Graham to get away from him. I was depressed and not being a good mom and Dad was floundering. While I was gone, I guess he got his shit together. He came to me one night at the end of March and showed me all this evidence about me being in danger. He had all these articles and showed me these notes threatening my life. I told him to go to the police, but he somehow convinced me to run. I was a scared, single mom of two kids. I guess I didn't need much convincing that I was a danger to my kids, because I already felt like a failure. I talked to Elora. I didn't tell her everything, just that I was going to finally tell Denver, get some money, and go off on my own. I still hadn't decided if I was going to take the two of you at that point. Dad half convinced me you would be safer without me."

I digest her information. Bells ring in my mind. Elliot was getting letters, just like the ones Lottie and I have been getting. It's the same damn tactic. Like mother, like son...

My biology, chemistry, and psychology classes all come together and suddenly I'm certain Elliot was drugged. By Elora. She was there the first time he tripped, it was always after a drink—probably a drug diluted into it—and he'd always trip bad for an hour, pass out, and then never remember.

"Grandpa was never like that with me," Sam says. "The only time he'd talk about the curse was on the anniversary of your death. He had a deep-seated fear about it, but he thought he did everything he could because he got Lottie away."

Denver steps forward and hands Penny my paper from class. My hand, Penny's hand, reaches out to take it.

"This is the name of the family who cursed you. Did you know?" Denver asks.

"Now you're saying we actually are cursed?" Penny asks with a smirk.

"No," Denver says firmly. "I'm asking if you've ever seen this name before."

My shoulders move up as Penny shrugs. I yell at her in my brain, trying to refrain from outright calling her stupid, but brimming with anger at the whole situation. We. Could. Have. Solved. This. Earlier. Penny freezes.

"Oh no," she whispers. "It's Elora's name. I did this."

Lottie crouches down in front of Penny. I stupidly think a door creaking open is Lottie's movement. I don't know how much longer I can last like this.

"So tell us straight this time. What did you do to Elora?" Lottie asks.

Heels click down the hall, followed by rushed, clumsy footfalls.

"Now, that's a story, isn't it?" A voice as smooth as silk says.

My eyes trail upward to find a woman with sleek dark curls and a short pencil skirt. Revulsion shudders through my body. She's the spitting image of the woman on Hale's desk, in Lottie's baby photo, from the coffee shop. Elora and her son saunter up to our group.

I fall against Sam's chest.

Chapter Forty-Three

A HAND FANS MY face. I fight my way to the surface. A woman yells somewhere in the background, coming above the worried murmurs around me. Blurry features form in front of my eyes. Freckles. Warm bronzed skin. Eyes like the Caribbean. Sam.

I blink rapidly until he's fully in focus. His hand against the back of my neck anchors me. A slow smile spreads across his face and I wonder what I looked like when Penny possessed me.

"You good?" Sam asks.

I nod, though I'm uncertain if I can stand and my senses are hardly intact. My temple pounds and my eyes burn. I hastily wipe a hand over them.

"Is she done having a panic attack or whatever it is she's doing?" that prim voice asks.

My eyes slowly narrow in on Elora. I cannot believe I didn't recognize her in Hale's room. She's a tiny woman, short, but still somehow imposing. Her heels add an extra three inches and her voluminous curls add another. Her eyes are dark, hooded, and severe, with no signs of laugh lines. In fact, there's no sign of any wrinkle on her face, only showing that it's likely Botox around her stiff mouth. Her pursed full lips make me feel like she never smiles anyway, certainly not now.

"You can address the question to me," I say with a cough.

Elora arches a brow. "Can I, then? All right." She clicks her way over and leers down at me. I wish I could push myself off the floor. "Are you done yet?"

"Yeah, I'm done," I say. My voice comes out even and strong, and most importantly, as my own.

"Perfect." Elora backs away from me and studies us. She circles back, then narrows in on Denver. She slithers over to him and runs a hand along his arm while he eyes her, warily. "It's nice to see you again, professor."

Denver stiffens, then pries her clawed fingers off his arm. "Hello, Elora."

"I thought I'd get a warmer welcome." Elora shakes her head and cackles. "So, I hear we're all gathered around waiting for a story."

I shift my body weight onto Sam, not trusting my ability to stay upright, and having enough foresight to know what Elora says might be damning. I fumble around with my hand until I find my phone discarded on the floor next to my backpack. It must have fallen out. I swipe to the left and bring up the camera, then swipe on autopilot to switch to video. I press record, never taking my eyes off of Elora.

"Penny and I were supposedly best friends," Elora says with a harsh laugh. "But I'm sure we all know by now how wrong that is."

A flash of blue in my peripheral vision alerts me to Penny's presence. I shift my eyes over to her. She leans casually against a wall, mouth drawn in a thin line.

"Let's make a long story short. Penny slept with my husband." Elora rolls her eyes and rounds on Lottie. Lottie shrinks into herself as Elora places a finger under her chin and tilts her face upward. Elora's nose wrinkles in disgust. "You're a gross mixture of the both of them, aren't you? You're definitely Penelope's kid, but your face shape and mouth is all Graham."

Lottie gasps and I want to reach out to her, but my whole being lacks the energy. She steps back from Elora and they glare at each other. It's a weirdly charged staring contest. One that surprises me when Elora looks away first. The tension between them disperses into the air around us. I glance around the little circle. Though distance spreads between all of us except for me and Sam, everyone seems entranced by Elora, following her every move. My stomach knots.

This is our murderer.

And she hasn't come here to play a game. She's come here to end it.

I force Sam to make eye contact with me. The same wariness is there. He glances at my phone, then nudges me with his. He had the same idea. Elora continues her story.

"I'm sure you all know my son, Hale," Elora says and gestures toward a decidedly disheveled looking Hale. His shoulders slump and eyes remain fixed at a point behind my head. "You made a glaring error, didn't you? That's why we're here today."

She waits for him to respond and when he doesn't, she advances. His eyes grow wide and he opens his mouth to speak in rapid succession. "I did an Ancestry DNA test and ruined your big plan."

Elora smiles, satisfied. "Correct. I knew I shouldn't have trusted you to finish this off, but really, honey, who could have guessed how sidetracked you'd get?" She turns back to face us. "Hale was supposed to be the end of this. Of course, my son is a fucking imbecile who cannot manage to do anything right. I've trusted his progress this whole semester. He claimed he was getting there and the money I gave him was going to good use. Apparently he paid a man to harass you," she says to Lottie, "but I gather that didn't work."

"The notes?" Lottie asks hesitantly and turns to Hale.

He shakes his head and stares at me. "No, I wrote those. Mom stole Maryl's key and had a copy of it made."

Elora's eyebrows knit together for a moment. "So you did some good."

And then it hits me. "You paid Lewis to attack me?"

Choruses of questions fill the air. I'd forgotten I hadn't told Lottie or Denver. Hale flushes and stares at his feet.

"That's the wrong girl," Elora sneers.

"I was following the plan, Mom. You told me to make it look like her roommate killed her. They were fighting when he attacked her and I thought her friend wouldn't believe her. No matter what I did, they acted the opposite way."

Sam's hand clenches against my waist. Heat comes to my cheeks and anger knots my stomach. If I wasn't prone on the floor right now, I'd punch Hale in the face. This goes so much deeper than I thought. She was trying to repeat history.

"All right, Elora, I think you owe us an explanation here," Denver says.

"And if I refuse?"

"Then we'll piece together what we know anyway, along with what you've already said. But I really would like to know why you felt you needed to kill Penny."

"Because friends don't do that to each other!" Elora shrieks, reminding me of someone in high school and not a forty-year-old woman.

"Friends also don't kill each other," Penny mumbles.

I laugh, completely caught off guard. Too late, I cover my mouth to hide it. Elora zeroes in on me.

"What was that?" she asks, over-plucked eyebrow arched.

"Don't mind me. Just having a panic attack, or whatever," I say, borrowing her words.

Elora scoffs. "Look. You have to understand that Penny always wanted what she couldn't have. First, her professor," a sharp hand gesture toward Denver, "and then Graham. I loved Graham until he did that to me. I swore to make their lives living hells, but I knew I couldn't do it with both of them alive. If I made their lives hell, they'd fuck off together. One of them had to die for the other to suffer."

"Jesus," Sam says. His voice cuts through the rant, unleashing a snarl from her. "I've spent my life feeling bad for myself because I lost my mom, but now I feel worse for your son. I can't imagine growing up with you."

Silence, then a sly grin. "I remember you. Little Sammy. So helpless and small. Couldn't save Mommy."

Sam's eyes harden. I squeeze his thigh and he covers my hand with his. Much like Lottie, they stare at each other. No further discussion happens, just a war with their eyes. And much like before, Elora looks away first. I don't understand her brand of cowardice when she literally killed her best friend.

"How did you do it?" I ask. The look of shock on her face leads me to believe she hadn't expected a question so bold, so I pry further. "You drugged Penny's dad, didn't you? Made him believe in a fake curse that you were dumb enough to use your own name for, right?"

"Bold words from a girl who looks like she's about to pass out."

"My appearance has nothing to do with what you did," I say, jutting my chin out proudly. "So what was it? From what Penny said, I'm assuming you slipped something into his drinks. You were there every time he tripped. I'm sure you went back and 'helped' him out when Penny was living with you."

Elora's eyes widen. "What Penny said?" she whispers. "You have the audacity to call me crazy when you're apparently talking to dead people?"

"I didn't call you crazy. I hardly think it matters where I got my information. I can see on your face I'm right. So what was the end goal? Why did you kill her here and not at home?"

"If it was here, there would be no suspicion on me. All that would fall to the professor who fucked his student and knocked her up."

"Yeah, no worries. We got your red herring."

"You think this is a game?" she hisses.

"Clearly you do."

Elora snickers and saunters away from me. Her curls bounce as she shakes her head. "A girl after my own heart. You're correct. I mixed ketamine into Elliot's drinks. It wasn't hard to convince him Penny was in danger. I'm good at fabricating evidence. I needed to bend the truth a little bit. Elliot became paranoid easily and once I threatened Penny, he finally acted. He knew that my bogus curse meant business. I'm more surprised Penny believed it. But then again, she always was a bit of an idiot. Choosing art over an actual profession."

Sam holds back an objection, lips pressing into a thin line like his mother's. Lottie tracks Elora with her eyes as she saunters about the hallway, making use of the space in dramatic flare. My head pounds. This isn't going to end well, and yet, I keep pushing.

"It wasn't hard once I knew where she was going. I led her to her death, strangled her, and hung her up for show. I led little Sammy here down a hallway with a bouncy ball so he wouldn't see me do it. He did get to see her in full swing, though."

I gasp, the pun making me sick. Sam's eyes close and his grip on my waist tightens.

"Poor Elliot wanted to keep his sad orphan grandkids safe, so he went with the suicide story and shipped Lottie off. I've kept track of you over the years. Knew you were coming here and encouraged Hale to pick Dalhousie as well. Then, he finally found you. That was the last part of the plan. Kill Little Orphan Lottie. I told Hale to make it look like it was Lottie's roommate, but honestly, if he screwed up and it pointed to him, I made sure there was no evidence connecting me."

"You were going to let your own son take the fall for your murder?" Denver asks. He turns his back on Elora and braces his hands against the back of his head. When he brings them down, they're shaking. Then, a whisper, "Absolutely unbelievable."

Sam's reaction is much the same. His chest shudders against my back. His hand moves from my waist momentarily, so he can draw it over his watering eyes, but it only takes that moment for me to falter. My body, weaker than I thought, slides against him, nudging my phone out from behind me and underneath Elora's shoe. She stares down at it for a moment before she bends and picks it up.

"Well that was stupid," she drawls.

She slams my phone against the ground, hard enough for it to crack, then reaches into her suit jacket. In one fluid motion, she pulls out a handgun and shoots a hole clear through. The deafening shot echoes through the fourth floor corridor.

Elora shrugs as she looks up at me. "You should have thought that one through. But now you must realize why I'm here. I didn't think there'd be four of you, but no one matches up against a gun very well."

Fear surges through my body. I can't move. I can't run. I can't do anything. I may very well die here today. She can't take us all, but someone is first and I'm the easiest target.

Denver, still facing the wall, moves slowly, almost as if Elora were a raptor that could sense thought based on sound. As predicted, Elora turns her gun on me. Sam acts quickly, forcing me behind him, unintentionally sending my body crashing onto the floor. Pain rushes up and down my right side, but I'm alive. He's alive. And a primal screaming bounces off the walls.

"That's not what you told me!" Hale yells. "You groomed me into this! How dare you do this to me! How can you call yourself a mother when you don't protect your son?"

Unexpectedly, Hale comes to life. He jumps on his mother and her legs buckle. She falls to the ground, the gun clattering next to her. Mother and son scramble for the gun, their limbs tangling together. My heart bangs against my chest.

An unspoken agreement comes between me, Sam, Lottie, and Denver. Penny's voice yells in my mind. This is our chance. We have to get out.

Sam lifts me under my armpits, until I'm standing. My legs give on every step and I shake my head. He hoists me into his arms.

The gun bangs again. Lottie shrieks. We don't turn around to watch.

Chapter Forty-Four

As we make our mad dash down the stairs, I realize something that shouldn't surprise me. We weren't isolated. People could hear and see us, and did. People who have nothing to do with what's going on run past us. Denver dials 911 the second we hit the stairs.

"Hi, yes, there's been a shooting in Shirreff Hall at Dalhousie University." He stays silent for a moment, listening, still running. "I don't know. I ran while they were wrestling." Pause, raised eyebrows. "Yes, I know who they are. Elora and Hale Butler."

I lose track of Denver as Sam runs through the open front doors of Shirreff, blasting me with cool air. Some students continue to run further within campus, while some mull around the front drive. My flight or fight response has decided that flight is a far better option. I want to be as far away from here as possible, especially since I have no idea which Butler managed to get the shot out.

I push against Sam's chest, heaving from the run and having to carry a full-sized woman down the stairs.

"Put me down," I say.

He stares at me like he couldn't imagine a worse suggestion, but I can feel his arms shaking. "Why?"

"Because you ran down three flights of stairs with me. Take a second."

"We have to get out of here."

I open my mouth to protest when I notice Lottie, frozen and panting, leaning against the black iron fence at Shirreff's entrance. Her eyes are wide with fear, hands trembling as she brings them up to her face. Sam follows my gaze and eases my feet to the ground. He loops my arm around him.

"Lottie," he says, reaching out to her and making her jump. "We need to go."

Lottie shakes her head and begins to sob. Loud, noisy, painful sobs that make my chest ache. Sam shifts from Lottie to me and back again. He's overtaxed, weighing which woman he cares about needs his help more. He keeps his hand firmly rooted on Lottie's shoulder and murmurs words of encouragement that are unfortunately laced with frantic energy. I keep my eyes trained on the door, expecting Hale or Elora to run out, gun at the ready. Instead, Denver emerges from the residence, phone in hand. He catches sight of us and hurries over.

"They've been inundated with calls and are on their way. I guess that's one positive to a relatively public meeting," Denver says. He shifts from foot to foot, fists clenched, shoulders tensed, ready to run. "You weren't waiting for me, were you?"

"Lottie's having a panic attack," I say. "A real one."

Denver's face falls immediately. He advances and puts his hands on Lottie's upper arms. Sam backs up, realizing he's not equipped to deal with this, fighting to gain control of his own shot nerves. My body weight goes with him and I can't help but think of Westley flopping around in *The Princess Bride.* I hold back the inappropriate laughter. Blurriness plays at the corners of my vision.

"Don't you quit on me too," Sam says. There's a nervous edge to his voice.

I try to smile. It's unconvincing. I can't tear my eyes away from the door. Sam continues to speak but my intensity drowns out his words. The sinking, dreadful feeling that the worst has not happened yet threatens to consume me. That, and a certainty that he's coming. He's coming. He's going to walk through those doors and—

It's Hale. I know it is and this fact both baffles and scares the shit out of me. Because Hale is more unpredictable. Elora will shoot on sight. I know what she's capable of. I don't know what Hale's endgame is.

"Maryl!" Sam snaps me back to reality and I whip my head away from the door. His concern strikes me first, followed by the realization that I'm standing independently.

My breath comes out with a shocked *oh*. "He's on his way, Sam."

"Who is?"

"Who else would be coming after us right now?" I nearly shriek.

Sam's eyes widen, then narrow in on Lottie who has sunk to the floor with her head in between her legs. Denver sits next to her, rubbing slow circles on her back. I advance toward them, but someone rushes past, pushing me aside. I stumble and lose my balance, my strength not quite as high as I hoped. Sam's arms encircle me before I come crashing to the ground. He rights me and holds on, making sure I'm not going to pass out. Though I'm convinced I only have minutes before I do collapse, I take solace in his arms and the worry creasing his forehead. I incline my neck to kiss him.

"The knight in shining armour strikes again, doesn't he?" comes Hale's voice.

A chill goes down my spine. Lottie's cries become frantic and frightened and I realize why as I turn around to face the barrel of his gun. For the second time today, someone is pointing a gun at me, and I have to say it's not something you get used to. My stomach lurches and, unfortunately, I freeze again.

Hale's blood-covered hands shake, the gun swaying with his nerves. Red soaks through the knees and lower half of his pant legs. A smear swipes its way across his forehead, then further mats itself in a curl falling in front of his eyes.

"I shot her," he says, voice wavering. "I shot my mom. She's bleeding so much, Maryl. I don't know what to do. I think she's going to die. What do I do?"

"You can put the gun down," I say, trying to keep my voice level, but failing. "Don't make this worse for yourself."

"Trust me, this can't get any worse for me. My life has been a lie. She's groomed me all my life to do this and I had no fucking clue. Shouldn't I be happy she's dying?"

"She's your mom, Hale," I say, remembering an article that said shooters sometimes respond better when you say their name, as if it grounds them. "Of course you're going to feel this way even though she did terrible things."

"Does that make me any better than her? She killed a woman."

"I know. I'm so sorry for that. I would feel the same way if I found out my mom had killed someone and covered it up," I say, keeping eye contact, trying to ignore the fact that his gun would kill me at this level, at this range.

"I knew my whole life and I still went along with it. She fed me the story about the curse and I believed it. She flat out told me she killed a woman and I brushed it off because... because of magic? How fucking stupid am I?"

A siren pierces the air and the breath leaves my body in shuddering gasps. Though he doesn't seem to register what's coming, I know this can only end one of two ways.

"Hale, drop the gun. I'll help you. We can go back inside and help your mom, okay? We can wait until paramedics get here. We can call them and they can tell us how to stop the bleeding. I'll help, okay?"

His eyes flicker. I can see him weighing his options. The world turns a little slower for me. Police cars pull up on the road behind him, lights flashing, sirens off. My blood rushes through my body and my heart pounds in my ears. My vision blurs. Fingers tingle. I don't know what's pulling me away from myself, whether fear, underlying exhaustion, or a ghost has taken over.

Just when I think Hale is about to listen to me, lower the gun and take my offer for help, something shifts in him. He notices we're not alone. Students, hiding at a far enough distance away are filming. Sam clings to me, slowly maneuvering his body so that he's the target instead of me. Officers make their way out of their vehicles, creeping toward our group.

I notice these details in quiet succession. I don't know how it works for Hale, but I see him realize how things are slipping away. His gun doesn't falter. Instead, his hands steady.

"Hale, put down the gun," Sam says, more forceful than any of my pleas. "It's over now. You're making it worse for yourself this way. I was recording too. I have her confession. What you did is self-defence and I can prove that. I can't defend what you choose to do now."

The words seem to sway him and he lowers the gun, but only for a moment. The swift and subtle movement between his hesitation is all it takes for the police to make their move. I see them advance in my peripheral vision, but keep my eyes trained on Hale so he doesn't know.

"Hale, please," I say.

I don't know what happens next. Not with any certainty, at least. My world fades in and out of view with a pounding darkness. The officers shout something. Hale's frantic eyes flash in my mind. My body moves without my control. Pain tingles through my left wrist as I fall without catching myself first. A shot rings out. Then another.

Darkness engulfs me.

Chapter Forty-Five

I WAKE TO COMMOTION and blinding lights. My vision is hazy and I fumble around on my bedside table for my glasses before realizing how much it hurts to do this and that the table isn't even there. Because I'm not back in my dorm room. I'm in the emergency room.

My left wrist is wrapped in a tensor bandage. Pain shoots through my arm as I flex my fingers. I wince.

"I wouldn't do that," Sam says.

I turn toward his voice and find him lying in a bed one over from me, green curtain wide open. A thousand questions run through my mind; like why we're here and what happened and where Lottie and Denver are. But concern outweighs my confusion. I squint. The bottom of his right leg is splinted and elevated.

"Are you okay?" I ask, my voice thick and dry. How long have I been out?

"I'm good." He nods. "Just a scrape."

A nurse blocks my view of him. She laughs and hands me my glasses from a rolling white table. "Don't listen to him. He's being brave."

I gasp and appraise him. His jeans lie in a pile beside the bed, now a deep red instead of their original blue. He's wearing a pair of sweatpants, shabby and fraying at the cuff of his left leg. A blanket drapes around his shoulders. He's shirtless, I assume because of the electrodes attached to his chest, connected to different machines monitoring him. An IV drips into his arm.

I think I might cry.

"Oh, honey," the nurse says, realizing her mistake. "I didn't mean anything bad. It's more than a scrape, but he's doing well. He's either very brave or very stupid to jump in front of a gun, but he hasn't complained once."

I nod. She continues to speak as she assesses me, telling me about my injury—a sprained wrist and shock that made me pass out—and how I'll have to make a statement to the police when I'm ready. Sam's already made his. After she's confident I seem to have my bearings, she leaves, promising a doctor will see me soon. I flop back onto the fat pillows and sigh.

"I'm fine, really," Sam says.

I meet his gaze. "You are not fine."

He shrugs. "I'm on the mend. As far as gunshot wounds go, this isn't a terrible one. They're filling me up with fluids and pain meds. Watching for any sign of infection. I'll be fine."

"But what if you're not?" I ask, voice squeaking. "What if something unexpected happens? It would be my fault. I promised Penny I wouldn't let anything happen to you."

"I chose to get involved. I chose to jump when I saw him acting. Hale would have killed you. I pushed you aside and startled him enough that it threw off his aim. My choice. You want to know something that's my fault?" I stay silent. "Your arm."

I flex my fingers again and see him cringe. No one told me outright not to do that, but yeah, it hurts.

"Fate really likes making me hurt this arm," I mumble.

Sam snickers. I drop my arm to my side and push myself into a seated position, something that's slightly challenging one-handed. I sit cross-legged in the centre of the hospital bed and face Sam. Maybe it's the power of suggestion, but he's already starting to look better. Less grey.

"What happened?" I ask.

"What do you mean?"

"I blacked out. I remember asking him to not shoot me and then I don't have a great record of things. I heard gunshots, I think. Was there more than one?"

Sam sighs and raises the back of his bed slightly. "Hale shot me first. The cops were pleading with him to put the gun down as well, I don't know if you heard that." I shake my head. "Well, he shot instead. I would not recommend that, by the way." I laugh, but it's watery. I can't even imagine what would have gone through Sam's mind at that moment. He groans and wipes a hand over his face. "Kind of escalated things. I saw him raise the gun again and I'm not sure what his plan was, but they got him first."

My heart drops. "They got him?!"

"Not like that. To my knowledge, he's still alive. It was his shoulder. Shocked him enough to drop the gun, then they jumped on him."

I let out my held breath. I may not be keen on Hale at the moment, but he doesn't deserve to die.

"What about Lottie and Denver? And Elora. Have you heard anything about her?"

"Lottie and Denver are fine. No injuries. They made their statements. I have Lottie's phone right now and she took mine to give them the confession. She's going to bring it back when she comes in later. They needed to get the confession off, they don't actually need the phone."

I close my eyes and sigh again. I can feel myself becoming lighter with every bit of information he has. But in his pause I know the answer to the last question.

"Elora didn't make it," he confirms. "I don't know the details apart from what an officer told me."

"There was a lot of blood on Hale."

"There was."

"Do you think she died there too?"

Sam pauses. He bites his lip. "I guess that would be a fitting end, wouldn't it?"

Chapter Forty-Six

Denver calls me into his office on the last day of class. So much, and not a lot, has happened over the past two weeks. The investigation into Penelope's death was reopened, then closed with Elora's confession. Hale received treatment for his gunshot wound in hospital, then was promptly sent to a holding cell. He's currently awaiting trial for his mother's murder. Rumour has it, he was also expelled. Sam took me to Penelope's grave, somewhere he and Elliot hadn't been in years. We planted flowers, and though it was very moving for them, I had some mixed emotions. I've avoided Penelope. Mamie keeps pushing me to go see her, sending me notes in class whenever I'm not paying enough attention to what I'm writing.

"I wanted to thank you," Denver says. "I always wondered about Penny's death. This is good closure."

"I'm glad it is for you," I say before I can stop myself.

Denver leans against his desk, crossing one leg over the other. "I thought you might be feeling that way. Your stories are usually quite transparent to your emotions."

"Don't they say write what you know?"

"They do. I'm not saying that's a bad thing. Writing can be very therapeutic. I think you processed a lot of your thoughts this semester through these pieces. You'd make a good memoirist."

"Thanks?" I say, though it comes out as more of a question.

"It is a compliment. I actually wanted to bring you in here to encourage you to keep taking my classes. I think you have talent. This could be a productive minor for you."

I sit and digest his words. I cross my arms over my chest and hold close to myself. That's another change in my plan. From easy coasting with French to creative writing, a subject I've actually put effort into this whole semester. This isn't something that comes easy for me, but he's right, the writing has helped.

"I'll think about it," I say eventually.

"Good," he says with a smile. "I hope you also talk to Penny."

I swallow. "Why?"

"I assume from your story that Sam told you much of the same... There's only so much you can blame on a dead woman, Maryl. I get being upset. I can't say I thought infidelity was one of her finest moments, but we weren't there. I'm not her. I don't know what was going through her mind or Graham's, for that matter. I know I believe she didn't deserve to die for it."

"I know she didn't," I mumble. "It's just hard to place that with everything I've done for her this semester."

He nods and pushes himself off the desk. He walks over to the window and stares out at the sun finally peeking through rain clouds. “But look what she’s done for you.”

“She’s made me more confused.”

“A bit of that,” Denver says, but I can hear the laugh in his voice. “But I think she allowed you to discover yourself. Lord knows she’s not perfect, but she brought people into your life, allowed you to question the world a bit more, opened your mind. I think that’s something.”

I visit Penny after my meeting with Denver. The area recently reopened again after days of being quartered off by police tape. The floor is a little brighter now after its deep cleaning, but the unsettling, crawling feeling that comes along with being here has pervaded my senses. The corruption of this place is another reason why I didn’t want to come back.

“Have you seen her around?” I ask when I find Penny.

“Elora?” Penny asks. “No. You?”

I shake my head. Part of me thought Elora would be stuck here too, some kind of karma for her actions. I don’t know how this ghost business works.

“Maybe she didn’t want to be stuck here.”

"I feel like she's got one last bit of vengeance in her. She's probably haunting Graham," Penny says. I can't tell if it's a joke. "I know you're mad at me. Otherwise you would have come to me sooner."

My head snaps toward her. "Do you know why I am?"

"You think I deserved this."

Her eyes are earnest and sad. Her shoulders slump.

"I don't think you deserved this," I say with a sigh. "I don't think anyone does. I just wish you told me everything sooner."

"I guess I was wrong. I'm trying to figure out my feelings about it as well. They never tell you that you have to do that when you're dead."

I linger by the wall where I sunk down two weeks earlier. I don't want to sit and be reminded of it all. The event itself and all its fallout. My parents threatened to rip me out of school since I was involved in a shooting. They were certain I was unsafe. Stephen somehow convinced them I should stay, at least to finish up the semester.

"I don't know why I'm mad at you," I finally admit. "I think it is because you didn't tell us anything and that wasted a lot of time, but I also think it's about me. I'm still trying to figure out this ghost thing and I think I'm mad I even have to do that. I think part of me blames you for being my first ghost and opening the flood gates."

"You've seen others then?"

I nod. I don't want to get into it. It would be easy to tell her I've also seen her mother and my grandma. It's harder for me to admit that I'm questioning so many interactions I've had in life. There are people I now know were ghosts.

Penny smiles and reaches out to hold my hand. I take it, despite the chill that spreads up my arm. I allow her to comfort me with whispered words and assurances. We have an unspoken conversation as I stand there and take in the new version of our spot. Shining white floors, new yellow painted walls, bright, flowering, fake plants in large pots. They've erased the history here, but I still feel it.

"Has anyone else come to see you?" I ask when I finally have a hold on my emotions.

"Lottie, Sam, and Denver have all been here."

I knew that. Lottie and Sam wanted me to come be their translator. But because of my mixed feelings and the fact that the possession left me completely wiped, I opted out.

"So you know everything, then," I say, relieved I don't have to tell her.

She nods and smiles sadly. "Elora's son is going to jail for something that wasn't his fault. My dad visited my grave for the first time in eighteen years. Lottie's finally meeting her father. You're dating my son."

I flush. "I'm not sure about that. We haven't exactly had time to discuss anything official with, well, with everything going on."

"I know I said not to get him involved, but I'm glad you did. I'm glad I met his future wife."

Flustered, I giggle. "Oh God," I say. "Oh no, no, not yet. We haven't even gone on a proper date yet. Did—Is that what he said?"

"No, just mother's intuition."

We share a look, then something shifts. The air grows cold and a breeze picks up. None of the windows are open and the air conditioning isn't on. I look around for a source of the wind, brushing a strand of hair out of my face. The room takes on a glow, brighter than I've ever seen anything in my life. So bright, I need to shield my eyes.

Penelope closes her eyes and grins. I've never seen her more at peace.

Though I've never seen it, though I've never entertained the idea of belief, I know.

"Tell them I'll be around, okay? They can talk to me anywhere now," Penny says.

Lost for words, I nod. She smiles and holds up a hand.

Chapter Forty-Seven

THE DAY AFTER CLASSES end, on the anniversary of Penny's death, Lottie meets her father. It took her a while to make contact with him. Fear that he might be as bad as Elora took hold. But Graham, in his text messages and calls to Lottie, doesn't appear to have the same spirit.

Murphy's Restaurant is an iconic part of Halifax's waterfront. It also happens to be Penny's favourite. Graham suggested it after Lottie finally called to schedule their meet up. Once more, I'm on an excursion to meet Lottie's family.

I sit at the back of Murphy's patio, staring out at the deep blue water of the harbour. Of all the restaurants I've been to in Halifax, I can see why Penny liked this one best. There's something truly magical at how far their enclosed patio stretches out into the water. The wooden beams and paneling inside make you feel as though you're on a fisherman's boat.

I scan the menu. It's mostly seafood, things both Lottie and I don't eat, but I see a few options for her, like salad, pasta, and roasted vegetables. My plan is to make sure everything's all good between the two of them, then skip out before dinner is served.

"You good?" I ask Lottie.

She nods. "Yeah, just a little nervous." She places her open menu on the table and smiles. "Thank you for this, by the way. I don't think I ever would have figured this out without you."

"You may have. Once Hale's DNA came in, you probably would have got there without me." I shrug off the accomplishment. There's no way Lottie would have ever given up on this.

Lottie opens her mouth to say something more, but freezes before getting a word out. I turn around and immediately see why. A man who bears a striking resemblance to Hale saunters into the restaurant and pauses at the hostess desk. His hair falls in the same unkempt curls, but instead of the darkness Hale got from his mother, Graham's hair is a light brown, almost red. Like Elora said, he has the same oval face shape and full lips as Lottie. The strong jawline and messy auburn beard are very decidedly all his own, though.

I reach across the table and squeeze Lottie's hand. The hostess nods and directs Graham toward us. He smiles genuinely at the hostess and holds up a hand. Lottie sits frozen, so I raise mine in a similar gesture. He registers me, but his eyes lock on Lottie.

"Um, hello," Graham says and rubs his hands on his jeans.

"Hi," I say and extend a hand. He takes it and shakes. "I'm Maryl. I'm Lottie's friend."

His lips upturn slightly, but his hesitation is palpable. It's a cute kind of nervousness I haven't seen in a grown man before.

"It's nice of you to come along," he says. His voice is gravelly, with a maritime twang.

"Sit, please!" I say.

I send a sidelong glance at Lottie. She lets out a stream of air and shakes her hair out. Graham takes a seat, pushing up the sleeves on his plaid shirt.

"Sorry," Lottie finally speaks. "I—I'm really nervous. I've spent a long time waiting for this to happen and when it finally does, it absolutely blows your mind and I'm here somewhere between wanting to cry and wanting to hug you, and I'm sorry, this comes on so strongly after such a huge tragedy and you know nothing about me so—"

"I know you're mine," Graham states. "That's all that matters."

Lottie stops mid-ramble and blinks away tears. "Thank you," she whispers.

"So should we get into this then?" he asks.

Lottie nods. I don't move, judging whether this is the time to leave. No warning bells ring in my head. No ghosts appear telling us to run. He seems safe.

"I wanted to say first off, that had I known you were mine, I never would have let you slip out of my life. I should have figured out when Penny was pregnant, but I was young and dumb and I'd just cheated on my wife. Which I assume you both know at this point. You can judge me for that. I deserve that. I wanted a way out and I thought that would be the best way. It was one I discarded once I found out Elora was also pregnant. I never cheated on her again once we had kids. I'm all in for my children."

"Wow," I say before realizing this maybe isn't my story to comment on. The eye contact between Lottie and her father breaks. "Sorry. I can go. This isn't part of my story, right?"

"You don't have to leave," Graham says.

"You can stay if you want," Lottie says.

I don't have to leave if I don't want to, but that doesn't mean I have to stay for my own need to know the story. From the five minutes I've spent with him, I think I get it. No one had an ideal situation back then, everyone felt isolated, and they did what they thought they had to do. I guess Elora thought she was doing the same. I push away from the table and excuse myself. Lottie smiles as I assure her I'm a text away.

I amble along the boardwalk, drawing my jean jacket around me and enjoying the breeze that sends my hair flying. I pass by the Maritime Museum of the Atlantic and watch kids climb on The Wave, something technically prohibited but everyone does anyway. It takes me a while to realize my body's on autopilot. I come across the bright orange hammocks lining a stretch of the boardwalk and know this is where I need to be.

I climb into a hammock and sit cross-legged in the centre. I close my eyes and breathe in the salty air.

"Aye, you look like a Haligonian," Sam says.

My eyes snap open as I jump. I purse my lips, but can't help the smile that breaks across my face. I scoot aside and hang my legs over the edge of the hammock as he settles in, with some leg-related difficulty, next to me.

"Following me?" I ask.

"Maybe," he says. "You seem to find trouble when you go off on your own. Plus, I was curious why you left Lottie."

"I didn't know you were here in the first place."

"I knew what was happening today," he says with a shrug. "Wanted to see what he looked like."

"He was very sincere and I got zero ghost warnings so I'd like to believe he's a good guy."

"I believe your ghost radar, then."

I sigh and close my eyes, letting myself drift away in the swaying of the hammock. Sam's arm comes around me and I nuzzle into his chest. The steady beat of his heart comforts me. It allows me to forget about life—how badly I've been sleeping, the displacement I feel about going back home soon, the vision of a gun pointed at me that still sometimes plays behind my eyelids, and of course, exams. Sam kisses my temple and breathes me in. I tilt my head upward and meet his gaze.

"I should be celebrating the end of semester right now," I mumble. "Or studying."

"We can celebrate if you want. We have other things to celebrate too, like solving a murder and not dying. I think those are both pretty cool things."

I laugh. "Who the hell goes to university and solves a twenty-year-old murder instead?"

"You, apparently." Sam shrugs as if this is normal and maybe, with me it is. "You solved a murder, Pokémon."

"I had help," I say pointedly.

"Barely. You were the ringleader. If you didn't have ghost superpowers, none of this would have happened. I wouldn't know you or my sister. I like my life better now with you guys in it."

I crane my neck and let him kiss me. We break apart and his hand finds my cheek. His thumb aimlessly traces lines on my skin.

"I like my life better with you guys in it too," I whisper. "Especially you. You have a way of calming down my ghost brain."

"Let me know if you see more. I'll help you solve their murders too. We could be like Mulder and Scully."

I laugh at the audacity of it, but he's kind of right. He can convince me to believe.

"All right, I'll let you know if I see a ghost."

A Ghostly Affair: The Playlist

1. illicit affairs | Taylor Swift
2. Spirits | The Strumbellas
3. Everywhere | Michelle Branch
4. Future Tripping | Hilary Duff
5. Surprise Surprise | Andrew Belle
6. The Killing Kind | Marianas Trench
7. Walking with a Ghost | Tegan and Sara
8. The Night We Met | Lord Huron
9. Where Is My Mind? | Pixies
10. Spring | Ed Sheeran

11. all my ghosts | Lizzy McAlpine

12. Any Dream Will Do | Donny Osmond

13. Love Like Ghosts | Lord Huron

14. us. | Gracie Abrams, Taylor Swift

15. Older | Lizzy McAlpine

16. Worlds Collide | Marianas Trench

17. I'm Not Calling You A Liar | Florence + The Machine

18. Life is Beautiful | Vega4

19. Run | Taylor Swift, Ed Sheeran

Acknowledgements

Wow. This book and these acknowledgements have been a long time coming. I first started writing this book in 2018, then promptly took three years to finish it. Over the years, it's had many titles, rewrites, and little momentary blips. I kept thinking it wasn't its time. Not yet. Not *yet*.

But now.

I'm so proud of this book and these characters. They occupy my brain far more than anyone will ever know. Except, since you're reading this, now you know.

So, let's get down to the many people who influenced this book along the way. My first thank you goes out to the man this book is dedicated to. Dad, I'm so glad you finally got to read the Halifax book. I've been talking about this book for years. *You've* been talking about this book for years. I remember being very early in drafting, on a train into Toronto, and having you hype this book to a friend we happened to run into. Thank you for always supporting me. And thank you for having the happenstance of growing up in Halifax. I would never have heard about this ghost story if we hadn't taken many trips out east.

To the ones I thank in every book: Mom, you are the best. Thank you for reading the initial draft of this book, then being game to go over my final rewrite last year. I'm endlessly thankful for you always being my first reader. We both agree this is the best version. Lisa, thank you for reading my frantic late o'clock texts about my blurbs. You always know how to make them better.

I also have to thank my author friends. When I started teasing this online, Emily Murray messaged me about her undergrad spent at Dalhousie. She helped me figure out some logistical things around campus. If I made any mistakes, it's not her fault because she's awesome. Thank you to the Beaver Tales crew who helped me with title woes and whether I should make a pen name. We figured it out. This book got me to Scotland and I will forever be thankful for that. Hey, Kelley and Melissa, I finally published it!

Shelly, thank you, once again, for taking on another of my weird ghost projects. I hope you enjoyed Maryl's adventures because you're going to be sick of her. Dana, this cover is beautiful. The ghost in the title!! You were so fun to work with. So quick, so seamless, so involved. I loved every minute and can't wait to see what we dream up for the next of Maryl's Mysteries. I'd also like to acknowledge the girl who let me into Shirreff Hall when I visited Dalhousie last October. I did not get your name and you did not have to do that for me, but thank you for that little piece of hands-on research.

And, finally, I'm so incredibly thankful to my friend Jessica, who, upon discovering I'd named my main character Maryl, didn't miss a beat and immediately responded, "Marill is a Pokemon." You started the most amazing inside joke in this book.

About the Author

MADELINE NIXON HAS BEEN a dog walker, a nanny, a baker, a shoe saleswoman, a chocolatier, and an editor, but the title she's most fond of is author. She writes books with swoony romance and spooky ghost stories. Sometimes, she publishes a combination of the two. She is also included in three romance anthologies. *A Ghostly Affair* is her first mystery. When she's not writing, you can find her hunting ghosts, planning elaborate theme parties, and baking new recipes. She lives in a suburb outside of Toronto.

Connect With Me!

www.madelinenixon.com

Facebook: www.facebook.com/MarkedWithAnM

Instagram: @MarkedWithAnM

Threads: @MarkedWithAnM

TikTok: @MarkedWithAnM

Bluesky: @MarkedWithAnM

Subscribe to my newsletter

www.madelinenixon.substack.com

Don't forget to leave a review on Amazon, Goodreads, or The StoryGraph!

www.ingramcontent.com/pod-product-compliance
Lightning Source LLC
LaVergne TN
LVHW050923080826
845145LV00001B/196

* 9 7 8 1 0 6 7 3 9 7 3 2 6 *